laced in lies
A SHELBY NICHOLS ADVENTURE

Colleen Helme

Dedication

To Dave Murphy and the Wasatch Music Coaching
Academy bands:
Creatures of Habit
Kenzie, Lexie, Alexis, Emilie, Gigi, Izzy, Layla
&
Sound Chase
Ella, Sarah, Callum, Miles, Cedar, Roman, Will, Amelia,
Nick
for bringing the song, *Devil Rider* to life! You guys rock!

And to the real Jodie McAllister ~ thanks for letting me
use your name!

ACKNOWLEDGMENTS

I would like to thank so many of my fans who let me know how much you love this series. All of you keep me writing! I'm grateful for my fantastic editor, Kristin Monson for finding my mistakes and making this a better book. I need to thank my daughter, Melissa Gamble for offering such great feedback and suggestions. Thanks to my whole family for your love, encouragement, and support. I couldn't do it without you!

To the kids at Wasatch Music Coaching Academy to whom I've dedicated this book, thanks for all of your hard work with your rendition of the song, *Devil Rider*, and for bringing it to life in your bands, Sound Chase & Creatures of Habit. I loved them both so much. You are amazing! Also, thanks to Barry Mork for doing such a great job on the music recording and production.

I'd also like to acknowledge the city of New York and the Algonquin Hotel where the New York scenes are based. I had such an amazing time there. And to the cast of *Aladdin* ~ thanks for such a great performance at the New Amsterdam Theatre. I loved it!

I'd also like to thank my audible producer, Wendy Tremont King. You are so talented and such an amazing voice for Shelby. It was so much fun to meet you in New York City and share some great times together! I will always remember them with fondness.

Last but not least, all my thanks and love to Tom for everything you do for me!

Shelby Nichols Adventures

Carrots
Fast Money
Lie or Die
Secrets that Kill
Trapped by Revenge
Deep in Death
Crossing Danger
Devious Minds
Hidden Deception
Laced in Lies
Deadly Escape
Marked for Murder
Ghostly Serenade

Devil in a Black Suit ~ A Ramos Story
A Midsummer Night's Murder ~ A Shelby Nichols
Novella

NEWSLETTER SIGNUP
Sign up for my newsletter for news and updates on new releases and special deals. To thank you for signing up you will receive a FREE book.
www.colleenhelme.com

Contents

Devil Rider

He came riding into town they say
Like thunder crashing on a cloudless day,
Demons chasing him from the past
Riding behind coming at him fast.
Bringing the storm, bringing the rain
Stirring the breeze, flowing with pain.
Chorus:
You love me, then leave me, you devil rider.
Hold me close, don't let go, you devil rider.
Break my heart, take my soul, you devil rider.
You broke my heart, you took my soul.

His lips full of promise, his eyes full of fire,
Offering me nothing but hot with desire,
His breath on my face, the touch of his hand,
Lights me on fire like a red-hot brand.
Nowhere to run, nowhere to hide,
Caught in his web, pulled to his side.
Chorus

Gone with the wind blowing hot and low,
Leaving me empty and oh, so cold.
Dying embers float away with pain,
Shattering my heart in an endless rain.
Breaking the bonds, breaking the chains,
Taking my soul, leaving the pain.
Chorus

Chapter 1

I stopped across the street from the shabby looking bar and turned off my car. The neon sign across the front read "Tiki Tabu," and it flickered on and off like a warning. In the silence, the heavy weight of impending disaster tightened my chest. What was I supposed to do now? None of my options looked good, but I'd promised my friend I'd find out what was going on with her husband. Too bad I didn't know how complicated that would be.

The man I'd been following had pulled into the parking lot behind the bar, and I watched him come around the building to enter through the front door. He looked nothing like Kyle, the handsome Pacific Islander I'd met a few days ago.

Instead of the usual expensive slacks and button-down shirt, he wore torn jeans and a worn leather jacket. With his rough, unshaven face, and strands of dark, wavy hair dancing over his eyes, he looked like a drug dealer, or some other kind of shady character.

So what was he doing here at four in the afternoon? This was such a break from his real life as a guidance counselor at a high school for troubled kids that I could totally understand why my friend had asked for my help. Only, how was I supposed to know if this was part of his job or something worse?

The only way to find out was inside that bar. But, for some reason, I had a hard time getting out of my car. I waited a good five minutes to bolster my courage. Then, with everything screaming at me to stay put, I took a deep breath and opened the door.

Luckily, I'd worn a grey t-shirt with my black jeans and black boots, so I reached into the back seat and grabbed my black leather motorcycle jacket and slipped it on. It was near the end of April, so not too warm to wear it. And from what I'd seen, it would help me blend in with the crowd.

Next, I slung my purse over my shoulder and felt for my trusty stun-flashlight. In my other hand, I kept a tight grip on the small canister of pepper spray attached to my car keys. Knowing I couldn't put it off any longer, I took a deep breath for courage and hurried across the street.

I hesitated at the door. Then, with my heart pounding, I swallowed my fear and stepped inside. The loud music assaulted my senses, and I squinted in the dark, needing a minute for my eyes to adjust before I could see well enough to find my way.

Taking it all in, my brows rose with surprise to find the place packed with people. At four in the afternoon. Didn't anyone work around here?

Spotting a couple of empty stools at the bar, I quickly took a seat, wanting to go unnoticed for as long as possible. With the bartender busy, I glanced around the place, hoping to spot my quarry before he spotted me. I couldn't see Kyle in any of the booths, but there were about four pool tables in the back. Maybe that's where he was?

"What can I get you?" the bartender asked. He was a big, brawny guy, and the white t-shirt he wore stretched tight across his chest and biceps. Along with his earrings and the tattoos all over his arms, his unfriendly scowl brought a spike of unease to my chest.

"Uh... could I get a Diet Coke with lemon?" His gaze narrowed at my non-alcoholic order, and he took in my fresh face and wondered what I was doing there. I didn't fit in with the usual clientele... at all. I smiled and continued, "Or lime... whatever one's easier will work, since I like them both."

His lips drew into a thin line before he shook his head and left to get my drink. From his thoughts, I picked up that he'd noticed me the moment I'd come in and correctly determined that I had no idea what I was doing there. I had to be meeting someone. But who was it, and what did I want with them?

He knew I wasn't a cop, since a cop would know better than to come in here alone. And even though I tried to pull off the bad-ass look with a motorcycle jacket and boots, I should have at least tried to cover my blond hair to fit in better. Then he hoped I didn't cause any trouble, because he had a feeling I was in way over my head.

With his instincts on high alert, he glanced over at Big Kahuna's booth, and his lips twisted with dismay. It was too late. Now I was in for it.

Alarmed, I followed his gaze to a huge man who straightened from a slouch in his booth across from the bar. He observed me with narrowed eyes like a wild tiger scenting its prey. I swallowed and noticed several more guys like him throughout the place, all of Polynesian descent. What had I stumbled into now?

Of course, not everyone looked that way, but it made me stand out more than I liked. So what was Kyle's connection to these guys? I knew he used to play football at the university, and these guys looked like football players.

Maybe he was just catching up with old friends? But if that was the case, why all the sneaking around?

In desperation, I glanced toward the back of the room, hoping to spot him. Just then, a man moved his head, leaving me with a clear view of Kyle in earnest conversation with someone in the far-corner booth.

With growing unease, I tried to block out the noise and listen to his thoughts so I could get out of there, but I had a hard time getting through. Then the bartender set my drink down in front of me, breaking my concentration.

"That'll be eight dollars," he said, asking for a higher price than the five he normally charged.

I glanced at the small glass. It was mostly ice and wasn't even filled to the top. Worse, it didn't include a lime or a lemon. I pursed my lips before catching his gaze. The mocking challenge in his eyes got my dander up, especially since he was thinking that I should take the hint that I wasn't welcome and leave before something bad happened to me.

In response, I took a five-dollar bill out of my purse and set it on the counter. His brows rose at my boldness, and he thought I might be tougher than I looked, but not quite tough enough for this crowd.

He was probably right, but it still hurt my feelings. Before I lost my nerve, I grabbed my drink and hurried toward Kyle's table. I knew this might be my only chance to find out what he was up to, even if it gave me away.

As I walked the length of the bar, everyone turned to stare at me, sending my blood pressure to a new high. It took a lot of self-control to keep focused and not react to the thoughts and stares following my every move.

I let out a relieved breath to reach Kyle's booth physically unscathed. But mentally I'd been through a gauntlet of assault-by-thoughts, and I might have sent a few well-deserved glares at some of the men along the way that probably didn't help me any.

Just then, Kyle glanced up. As he recognized me, his eyes widened with shock and distress. "Shelby!? What are you doing here?"

"Hi Kyle. Mind if I join you?" Before he could answer, I slipped into the bench beside him, making him move out of my way before I sat on him. He moved over at the last minute, still in disbelief that I was there. I took that opportunity to glance at the person sitting across from him and found a young man, probably close to sixteen or seventeen years of age, staring at me with dark eyes of distrust.

I smiled at him. "Hi. I'm a friend of Kyle's."

His suspicious gaze flew to Kyle, and he leaned over the table. "Did you bring her here? Is she a cop?"

"Hell no," Kyle answered, doing his best to keep his voice low. The boy began to slide out of the booth, but Kyle grabbed his arm. "Wait. She has nothing to do with this. Just give me a minute to figure it out." The boy slowed his movements but sat on the edge of his seat, ready to bolt.

"You owe me," Kyle hissed, clenching his jaw.

The boy let out a breath and slid back into the booth, willing to listen to what Kyle had to say. He did owe him. And so far, Kyle had held up his end of the bargain. Still, he had to play it cool so Kyle didn't suspect the truth or voice his concerns to Big Kahuna. That would ruin everything.

Kyle turned to me, swallowing the anger that caught in his throat. My presence here was destroying weeks of hard work that he could never get back. "I don't know what you're doing here, but you need to leave." When I didn't respond, he continued. "Did my wife put you up to this?"

At my nod, he let out a frustrated growl and swore a blue streak in his mind. Then he began cursing his wife, me, and all women in general. My eyes widened. Sheesh! Even though it was all in his mind, it still struck a nerve, and whatever sympathy I had for his situation flew right out the window.

Finally, under control, he spoke. "This is what you're going to do. You're going to stand up and walk straight out the door. Then you're going to tell my wife absolutely nothing. I don't care what she's paid you, she can't know about this. I'll even pay you more, but you have to leave now."

I couldn't believe he had the gall to order me around like that, especially since his wife and I had been friends since grade school. Then I picked up that his work to get back into the Polynesian gangs was shot if I didn't get the hell out of there.

Hearing that helped curb my anger, but my opinion of him fell off the lowest end of the charts. Even if he was a spy, or working undercover, talking to me that way wasn't going to earn him any points. Of course, I also picked up an underlying sense of anxiety that things could get dicey for both of us if I stayed any longer.

Hearing that was enough to cool my jets, and I swallowed my indignation. "Fine. I'll go. But I'm not through with you."

I thought it best not to tell him that I had every intention of telling his wife, mostly because of his unkind thoughts toward both of us. With a glare at him I stood, then glanced at the teenager, hoping to pick up something more about what he was hiding, but all I got was admiration for Kyle because he'd put me in my place.

Hot with anger at Kyle's terrible example, I shook my head and started down the aisle. At that moment, Big Kahuna moved out of his booth to stand in front of me. "Leaving so soon?"

Alarm tightened my stomach, and I stopped in my tracks. "Uh... yes."

Big Kahuna lumbered toward me, and I backed up until we both stood right next to Kyle's table. Stopping, Big Kahuna glanced at Kyle, then turned his attention to the kid, knowing he was more devoted. "Keola, you know this haole?"

"No," the kid said, thinking that he needed to sound completely loyal.

Big Kahuna turned his gaze to Kyle, who shook his head in disgust. "She's harmless," Kyle explained, shrugging with indifference. "My sister's friend. I think my sister dared her to come in here."

Big Kahuna turned his questioning gaze at me. "Is that right?"

It was easy to pick up Kyle's distressed thoughts that I'd better back him up or we were both in deep trouble.

"Uh... yeah," I agreed. Thinking fast, I blurted the first thing that came to my mind. "She said this was a happening place, so I just wanted to come inside and maybe play a game, but he wouldn't play with me." I motioned toward Kyle with narrowed eyes and a frown of disgust that I didn't need to fake.

Big Kahuna smiled, noticing my underlying nervousness and smelling the lie. "A game?"

"Yeah... you know... pool?" I motioned toward the tables. "Isn't that a thing here? I mean... I've never been here before... obviously, but I've heard about this place. It's pretty cool, except your bartender didn't put a lemon in my drink like I asked, but other than that, it's not bad."

Holy hell! What was I saying?

I caught that Kyle needed me gone before Big Kahuna got his hands on me and ruined everything. So he stood to loom over me with intimidation, deciding to take matters into his own hands. "You should go. You don't fit in here."

"Hey now," Big Kahuna said, pushing him back. "That's no way to talk. Let's show this haole some hospitality." He turned to me with a challenging smile. "You want to play? We'll play."

"Great." I glanced at the pool tables and let out a relieved breath to find them all in use. "Uh... it looks we'll have to take a raincheck. But I can come back later. How about tomorrow?"

He grinned widely, showing straight, white teeth, and knew he'd caught me in his snare. He asked one of the guys at the nearest table if he would let us play, and the guy gladly stepped away, willing to do whatever Big Kahuna asked.

"There," he said, turning back to me. "Problem solved." He arched a brow in challenge and waited for me to get my butt over to the table.

"Uh... great!" I started that way, hoping he didn't follow too closely, since he'd notice my trembling legs. On the other hand he'd already picked up that I was a bundle of nerves, and enjoyed calling my bluff. So, maybe if I got on his good side, I could leave in one piece.

One of the players handed me his cue stick while Big Kahuna racked up the balls. Once they were ready, he motioned toward the table. "Want to break?" he asked, thinking that if I didn't start playing, he'd take me in the back room for a little talk and find out the real reason for my visit. He already suspected that there was an ulterior motive for Kyle's recent return. Maybe I could shed some light on that.

"Sure. Uh... I need to put this somewhere." I pulled my purse from around my neck and ducked down to place it on the floor by my feet. While I was out of sight, I slipped my phone out of my purse and turned it on. Pushing the message icon, I quickly swiped in 'help' and sent it off.

"What are you doing down there?" Big Kahuna asked.

"Just getting my phone," I answered, standing and holding it up for him to see. "I'd like to get a picture of us playing together."

His eyes narrowed. "No pictures. Put it away." He was thinking that if I didn't do it right now, he'd be happy to take it and forget about the game.

"Fine." I shrugged and slipped it back into my purse, then glanced at the table, knowing I'd better start playing. "Okay... let's see." I grabbed the chalk and dusted the top of my cue stick before moving the cue ball into position.

It had been a while since I'd played, but we had a pool table at home in the basement, so at least I knew how. Still, I was terrible at breaking, and I hoped to get at least one ball into a pocket. I moved the cue stick back and forth between my fingers, knowing I needed to hit it pretty hard, but hesitated since I was a little shaky.

I swallowed to calm my nerves and picked up a lot of impatient thoughts from various minds that I was taking too long. There was also some loud cursing to go along with it. Discomfited, I took a deep breath and hit the ball as hard as I could. It popped up off the table before bouncing down, then barely moved, coming to rest right next to the headpin.

"I think it tapped it, so that counts, right?"

Big Kahuna's lips twisted, and he held back a laugh while his friends tittered behind my back. "Why don't I break?" Lumbering around the table, he came to my side for his turn, and I quickly moved out of his way.

He leaned over the table and moved the cue ball back behind the line, wondering if my ineptness was all an act. Of course, it didn't really matter, since he was pretty sure there was no way I'd come into his bar just to play pool with Kyle.

He lined up his cue stick and hit the ball with enough force and finesse to send two balls into the side and corner pockets. He glanced at me and smiled. "Looks like I'm stripes." Then he got to work and put a few more stripes into the pockets before deciding that maybe he should miss, just so he could check out my playing style and determine if I was sincere or trying to take advantage of him.

I swallowed my protest and glanced up, realizing that quite a crowd had gathered around us. My gaze slid to Kyle's booth, and my brows puckered with dismay to find both him and Keola gone. I sucked in a breath, disheartened that he'd take off and leave me to fend for myself.

Big Kahuna missed his next shot, just like he'd been planning, and sent me a nod. "Looks like you get another chance."

"Oh goody." I hoped that didn't sound too sarcastic, and I turned my attention back to the table. I looked for an open shot and picked up that he was thinking I should go for the blue ball, so I listened to how he thought I should accomplish that.

Hearing his thoughts of exactly what I needed to do made taking the shot a little easier. After lining the balls up, I let her rip and pocketed the ball. Wow, his strategy worked just how he'd imagined it.

Happy that I'd made the shot, I tried not to act surprised, since that might not go over so well. Then I studied the table and listened again for his recommendations. Moving into position, I took the next shot and hit the ball toward the pocket. I didn't hit it as hard as I should have, so I wasn't sure it would go in. As it teetered on the edge, I held my breath, and then let out a whoop as it fell into the pocket.

Smiling, I glanced up to find Big Kahuna staring at me with narrowed eyes. He wondered if I was playing him. There was nothing he hated more than being played, especially by a woman.

That wiped the smile off my face pretty quick. I studied the table for a moment, catching several different thoughts from those watching about the next shot I should take. I decided on the easiest one and sauntered with a confidence that I didn't feel to the other side of the table.

A few of the guys moved back to give me some space, but when I leaned over, their attention came to rest on my backside. Hearing their lustful thoughts rattled me so, without wasting any time to line up my shot, I hit the ball pretty hard. Naturally, the cue ball flew wide, missing the ball I'd wanted to hit. Then it ricocheted off the edge and into a ball with stripes, which then hit a yellow ball, causing it to roll into the corner pocket.

"Whoa!" I said, completely astonished. "Did you see that?"

Big Kahuna narrowed his eyes, thinking that I was either a pool shark or one lucky bitch. "Yeah. Nice shot." Then he wondered if I was silently laughing at him.

Oops. "Uh... thanks, but it was all luck." I swallowed, knowing I needed to miss my next shot before he got upset. But that shouldn't be too hard, since I wasn't any good at this. Still, I needed to make it look like I was trying to win.

I lined up my shot, picking the easiest ball to hit, and managed to hit it straight on without aiming at any of the pockets. The ball shot across the table and angled off the side to bounce back and hit another solid-colored ball, sending it into the far corner pocket. Crap.

Mortified, I kept my gaze on the table and caught thoughts of surprise from most everyone, along with a heavy dose of suspicion from Big Kahuna. Blocking their thoughts, I hurried around the table to the cue ball and went for an impossible shot. This time my true skill showed, and I totally missed it. With a sigh of relief, I straightened and glanced at Big Kahuna.

He'd caught my sigh of relief, and his lips twisted into a scowl. He was thinking that maybe it was time to take me in the back room and forget the game. Then he glanced at the crowd and tugged at his ear.

Not wanting to disappoint them, he decided that he might as well play through to the end. He could finish the game off pretty quick, so it wouldn't hurt to keep playing. Then he'd get to the bottom of my visit there.

Oh great! How was I ever going to get out of this?

He lined up his next shots pretty quick. One by one, they all hit their mark. Before I knew it, he was calling the eight ball into the corner pocket. He took the shot, and it went in. Just like that, the game was over, and my heart hammered in my chest. Now what?

I sent him a smile and leaned the cue stick against the pool table. Then grabbed my purse off the floor and slid it into place over my head and shoulder. "Uh... looks like you won. Thanks for the game. Let's do this again sometime." I took a couple of steps toward the door, but none of the guys would move out of my way.

"Before you go," Big Kahuna said. "Let me buy you a drink. One with a lemon in it." He was thinking that if I knew what was good for me, I'd go along with him. Otherwise, he'd have to get rough.

"Uh... okay."

"Hey Jet," he called to the bartender. "Get the lady another drink, and be sure to put a lemon in it this time."

"Sure boss."

"And bring it to my office." He glanced back at me before lifting his gaze to the two guys behind me. He nodded, giving them the silent command to physically move me if I refused to cooperate.

Now what? If I went into that office with him, who knew what would happen? My stun flashlight would only get one of the men standing behind me. As outnumbered as I was, I didn't think stunning one of them was a good idea. Maybe, once I was in his office, I could use it on Big Kahuna and slip out a window before anyone knew what was happening.

He turned toward the door that led to the restrooms and back office, expecting me to follow, but for some reason, I just couldn't get my legs to move. Behind me, one of the guys nudged my back, knocking me forward.

Furious, I caught my breath and turned around with my hands on my hips and a stubborn pout on my face. My bravado faltered just a bit when I saw how far up I had to look before coming to the guy's face, but I couldn't stop now.

"Hey," I said, channeling my inner tough-girl attitude. "Don't touch me. I don't like it."

His eyes widened with shock, and he sucked in a breath, thinking no one like me had ever talked to him with that cocky tone before. "Uh... whatever, lady. But you need to get moving."

"Exactly."

To his surprise, I shoved between him and the other guy to run in the opposite direction that led out the front door, but they were just too big. It was like trying to squeeze through the bars of a jail cell. Before I knew it, both of them had grabbed me under the arms, and they began dragging me backward toward Big Kahuna.

"That's enough! Let her go."

My breath caught. I glanced up to find Ramos standing in the middle of the room with a deadly scowl, and his eyes filled with fire. Even though he was surrounded by some big, scary dudes, not one of them made a move toward him. Whoa... he looked so bad-ass that my heart rate spiked, and I had to swallow before I drooled or something.

The men holding me stopped in their tracks, and the whole room went still. A few seconds passed, then they quickly let go of me and stepped away. Straightening my jacket, I took a few steps toward Ramos. Then Big Kahuna shoved between his men, not liking that I was getting away without an explanation.

"Hey, wait a minute," he said, reaching out to grab me.

Not about to get caught, I jerked out of his reach and scrambled toward Ramos, hearing frustration in Big Kahuna's mind that I was slipping through his fingers. Then I caught that he had a deal with Manetto to stay out of each other's business, so what was going on?

"Is she with you?" he asked Ramos. I thought it was a stupid question, but hey, what did I know?

"Yes," Ramos answered, keeping his frosty gaze on the big guy. "And she's no concern of yours. Unless you want to make something out of it."

Big Kahuna frowned and lowered his eyes. Going against "The Knife" was a death sentence, and their agreement hinged on keeping the boundaries drawn. But if I was with Ramos, what was I doing there in the first place? Was I spying for Manetto? Had he changed his mind and decided to take the business back. Was Kyle in on it? Was that why he'd come back to the gang?

Oh great! Now what had I done? I stopped in front of Ramos, picking up from him that he wasn't pleased that I was there either, and now I was making a mess of things for all of them.

Wanting to straighten everything out, I turned to face Big Kahuna.

"Uh... don't worry about a thing. I'll tell Uncle Joey it was all a misunderstanding. I'm sure he'll be happy to leave you alone. Unless you make trouble. Then he won't be so understanding. You know how he is. He might want to go back to the agreement you had before. You know... the one where you give him a hefty percentage of your profits? So... let's all just forget this ever happened. Sound good?"

I took a step back, bumping into Ramos' chest. The feel of his solid presence at my back uncoiled the leftover panic in my heart and helped bolster my courage.

Since Big Kahuna wasn't too happy with me, I decided to kill him with compliments and see if that softened him up. "Oh... and thanks for the game. It was great... fun. You're really good. Uh... see you around... well, probably not, but if I ever come back, let's play again. Okay?"

Big Kahuna relaxed his stance and shook his head. He couldn't help smiling at my spunk, and thought that Manetto certainly had his hands full with me, especially if I was his niece. He might have to send out a few inquiries of his own to make sure he knew what was going on, as well as have a long talk with Kyle. After so many years, showing his face in this bar had to mean he was up to something. If it involved Manetto, it'd be nice to know.

"Yeah, sure," he said. "Come back anytime."

I heaved a big sigh of relief, then smiled brightly, and gave him a nod. Ramos moved sideways to let me head to the door, then followed behind. Weak with relief, I pushed it open, grateful to get out of there in one piece.

Outside in the sunshine and fresh air, I threw my head back and took a couple of deep breaths, then turned to face Ramos. "Sorry about that, but thanks for coming. I wasn't sure if the tracker on my watch still worked."

He shook his head, catching my gaze with his dark eyes, astonished at the trouble I got into. How did I do it? "Come on. Let's go someplace where you can explain what the hell just happened." With his motorcycle parked right there in front of the bar, he moved toward it, swinging his leg over and starting it up in one smooth motion.

Not one to pass up an opportunity to go for a ride with him, even if it meant I might get chewed out, I obediently got on behind, noting that he must have been in a hurry, since he didn't have his helmet or his leather gloves.

I barely got my feet settled on the stands before he took off, and I had to grab him tightly or risk falling off. Not that I minded. With relief coursing through me, I gave into temptation and leaned my body close against his broad back, grateful to be safe.

Without a helmet, my hair flew around my face, but I didn't mind because it meant I could rest my cheek and forehead against his back and inhale his special scent.

This was a rare treat for me, since Ramos was off limits. Sitting behind him like this was about the only time I could indulge in the forbidden desire that I felt for him, so I held on and enjoyed it while it lasted.

The two of us had been through a lot in the last year that we'd known each other. As Uncle Joey's hit-man and bodyguard, he'd come to my rescue more times than I liked to admit, but since that was his job, I couldn't feel too guilty about it.

Uncle Joey was the main reason for most of my troubles. He was the local mob-boss, and I'd had to tell him that I could read minds in order to stay alive and keep my family safe. Now, after a year under his thumb, things had changed. In fact, we'd become like a real family, and I didn't see an end in sight, especially after the incident where he'd met my kids. I'd even introduced him to them as my *real* uncle.

My stomach clenched just thinking about it. Since meeting Uncle Joey, every aspect of my life had changed. My husband, Chris, was now a partner in his law firm, mostly because of Uncle Joey, who just happened to be his new main client. My kids thought we were related to him and had just met their 'cousin,' Miguel, who was Uncle Joey's eighteen-year-old son.

It was all a lie, and I hoped it didn't come back to haunt me.

Along with that, my kids didn't know that I could read minds, but I was afraid one day I'd have to tell them the truth. That scared me more than anything. Would they ever trust me again? They thought I had premonitions, like I told everyone else, and I hoped with all my heart that I could keep it that way.

Even when I wasn't helping Uncle Joey, our connection got me in and out of a lot of scrapes. Like today. Complicating my life even further, I'd started my own consulting agency, and I continued to help the police with cases needing my special touch to solve. I'd even helped a federal agent a couple of times.

But only a few people, like Uncle Joey and Ramos, along with Dimples (AKA Detective Harris), my husband, Chris, and Kate, Uncle Joey's erstwhile niece, knew the truth. Well, and Inspector Gabriel Dumont. But he lived in Paris, so I wasn't too worried about him spilling the beans.

Still, it was Uncle Joey who I always turned to when I was in trouble. I owed him a huge debt that probably spanned the rest of my life. It should worry me but, for some reason, I actually liked working for him. How crazy was that? Maybe I should see a shrink or something.

If that wasn't bad enough, reading minds created its own set of problems, and I had to keep everything I heard, spoken or not, straight. All the lies, half-truths, secrets, and hidden desires. I knew them all, and I had to remember which ones I could talk about, and which ones I wasn't supposed to know.

There were some days when I just wanted to run away. But sitting here behind Ramos... well, I guess it kind of made up for it. Plus, if I lost my mind-reading ability, I'd be devastated. It would be like losing a part of who I was. I'd hate it. So I probably shouldn't whine too much, even if there were times I could easily go insane.

Ramos pulled off the road into a park with stately trees, green lawn, and a little pond with a water fountain. He parked the bike and turned off the engine. I scrambled off, holding onto his shoulders for support, then walked the short distance to a picnic table under a tree and waited for him to slide into the bench across from me.

His deep, brown eyes warmed as he studied me, and he was thinking that even though it was a pain in the butt to come to my rescue all the time, taking me for a ride on the bike helped make up for it... mostly because he liked the feel of my arms around him, and my body pressed close against his back. Still, I'd better start explaining, and it had better be good.

"Okay, here's the thing," I began, trying to ignore the heat that flooded my face. "I went to lunch with my friends from high school the other day. I haven't done that since I got my mind-reading powers because I just wasn't sure I wanted to know what they were thinking... you know, about me and each other? Anyway, I kind of let it slip that I had my own consulting agency. At first they didn't believe me, so I told them about a few of my cases..."

His brows rose with alarm, so I quickly continued. "Nothing to do with Uncle Joey, just some of the smaller cases I've worked on... well, and the serial killer with the fire and all, since that was huge."

Ramos twisted his lips and shook his head, knowing exactly why I'd done that. "I'll bet that impressed them." Taking it one step further, he cocked his head and asked, "Did you tell them about me?"

Oh great! How did he know? "Um... yeah... I mean... you saved my life, so I sort of mentioned you and your, uh..." I wanted to say *total hotness*, but he was thinking that I'd probably gushed about him and he couldn't wait to hear what I'd said. "Uh... okay, so maybe I gushed a little."

He raised his brows in challenge, so I relented with a sigh. "Okay, I gushed a lot, but I didn't tell them your name or anything, so your identity's safe. Although, I have to admit, after I got through, they all wanted to get a good look at you because they honestly didn't believe me."

He chuckled, and I smiled, happy to give his ego a boost, even if he didn't need it. "So, anyway, one of my friends wanted me to check on her husband and see if he was cheating on her." I shrugged. "How could I say no to that? Especially after everything I'd told them, you know?"

He was thinking, *yeah, right... go on.*

"He's a counselor at a remedial school for troubled youth. Today I followed him after his school got out. He went home and changed into a completely different outfit, and then ended up at that bar. So... I had to follow him inside."

"Did he see you?"

"Yeah, and I found out what he was doing there. It looks like he's made friends with one of the boys, and he's trying to infiltrate the gang, but I don't know why. It sounded like he's been at it for a few weeks, so he wasn't happy to see me, but he left as soon as the game started."

"Game? What game?"

"Oh... the pool game." I shrugged and told him how Big Kahuna wouldn't let me leave until he knew what I was doing in his bar. "I couldn't exactly tell him the real reason, so I told him I was there to play pool. He knew I was lying, so he called my bluff, which turned out to be a good thing, since I had something to do while I waited for you to show up."

Ramos shook his head, a little upset with me that I got into these situations. "What if I hadn't made it in time? Or if you couldn't get to your phone to send me a message?"

"Oh, I had a backup plan. I figured once Big Kahuna had me in his office, I'd stun him with my flashlight and escape out the window or something."

He snorted. "A guy that big probably wouldn't go down with one stun."

"Well, yeah, I guess. But I have pepper spray, too. So between the two of them, I'd be fine."

He took a deep breath and slowly let it out, thinking how boring his life would be without me in it. But... sometimes I drove him nuts. "So this guy... the husband... what's his name?"

"Oh... it's Kyle Young, and the kid's name is Keola."

"You think he's working undercover for the cops?"

"I'm not sure. He didn't really think about that. But why else would he be trying to infiltrate the gang?"

"I have no idea," he said. "But... it's probably certain that you blew his cover, so you might want to have a chat with him and convince him that it's not a good idea to go back there."

"Uh... I don't think I blew his cover... but I did pick up that Big Kahuna doesn't trust him."

"So? Don't you think you should warn him?" I shrugged and his brows drew together. "Don't you like him or something?"

"Not really. He was thinking some pretty awful things about me... well... mostly women in general. Probably because I let it slip that I was working for his wife. Anyway... it doesn't make me want to help him much."

"Oh, I get that. Well... your call." He wasn't about to tell me what to do. Still, he'd hate for me to have Kyle's death weighing on my conscience.

My eyes widened. "You think they'd kill him?"

"They might," he said, shrugging. "It depends."

"Well, I guess for his wife's sake, I'd better warn him."

"Good." He was thinking that was the Shelby he knew and loved.

"What? You love me?"

He growled and shook his head. "Shelby... you know what I mean." It irked him that I'd heard that, and he didn't want me thinking that I could tease him and not face the consequences.

I smirked, then picked up just how he'd like to teach me that lesson. My eyes widened and my breath caught. Then my face heated up, and it seemed like the temperature rose at least fifty degrees. "You... stop that!"

He chuckled at my discomfort, but at the same time, he wanted to remind me that I shouldn't get too comfortable around him. He could only take so much, and I had to know that he didn't have much of a conscience, so I couldn't expect him to be all noble and everything. After all, he was used to getting what he wanted, and I needed to remember that.

I took a breath to tell him that I knew better, but he raised an eyebrow in challenge, and I shut my mouth. Whoa. He seemed a little testy. Was something wrong? "Are you okay?"

My insight surprised him. Before he shuttered his mind, I picked up that something from his past had reared its ugly head. He didn't need me worrying about him. "I'm fine. But we should get back. You need to warn your friend, and I've got work to do."

"O-kay. But... now you've got me worried."

"It's nothing... seriously."

"Fine. But if you need my help..."

"I won't."

That kind of hurt my feelings, so I shrugged and let out a sigh.

"Shelby... look... I'm fine. If I need your help, I'll ask for it. Okay?"

Our gazes met. His dark eyes hardened with resolve. He wasn't going to involve me in this... end of story. Still, a twinge of guilt that he'd hurt my feelings ran through his heart, but he pushed it aside. There were just some things in his life that he didn't want me to know.

"Okay... sure. But you know I'm here for you if you need me, right?"

His face relaxed into a smile. "Yes. I know."

"Good." I smiled back at him, and the tension left his shoulders.

"Uh... before we go," he said, his eyes gleaming with curiosity. "Jackie was talking about a barbeque tonight with you and your family. What's that all about?"

"Yeah." I sighed. "It's called a disaster." I quickly explained how my whole family had accidentally met Uncle Joey, Jackie, and Miguel at Miguel's last school performance a week ago. "I had to introduce them to my kids, and explain that we were related. I even told them that Uncle Joey was my real uncle, which meant Miguel was my cousin. That's when he invited us over for a family barbeque. How could I refuse? But I'm afraid that someday my kids are going to find out the truth. Not just about Uncle Joey, but that I can read minds. If that happens, I don't know if they'll ever trust me again. It would be horrible!"

"Hmm... well hopefully that won't happen. If it's any consolation, Jackie seemed pretty excited about your little get-together. She even left work early to get things set up."

"She did?" Hearing that sent a trickle of unease down my spine, and I hoped her expectations weren't set too high, because I didn't want to disappoint her.

"Hey... don't worry about it. You should look at it this way; at least you're not on Manetto's bad side. That would be a whole lot worse." He was also thinking that he and Uncle Joey had recently taken care of the Russians, so I needed to remember that I owed him.

"Yeah. There is that." I wanted to add that if Uncle Joey wasn't in my life, it wouldn't have been a problem in the first place, but that might sound inconsiderate.

He could tell I wasn't too happy about the whole thing, but there wasn't much anyone could do to change it. "Life is nuts, isn't it?" he asked, sending me a commiserating smile. "That bank robbery at the grocery store changed everything for you."

His thoughts turned to the moment the bank robber had pressed the gun to my head. He'd had to kill the bank robber to save my life. It was a close call, and he would have disappeared after that if Kate hadn't told Manetto about me. That was the day Manetto found out about my secret.

"It sure did," I agreed. "It's crazy how things that happen to you seem to take on a life of their own, and once the wheels start turning, you can never go back."

"Would you want to? Go back?"

I gazed into his dark eyes and knew the answer immediately. "No." I smiled and shook my head. "I guess not."

He smiled. "Good."

"What about you? What would you change?"

His smile faded a little as he thought about his life on the run and what had happened between him and his brother. After all that, he felt lucky that he wasn't rotting in prison somewhere. In his line of work, it could still happen; but all things considered, he had a great life with never a dull moment... especially with me sending him *"help"* texts.

I huffed out a breath and shook my head, but I couldn't stop the smile that widened my lips.

"Sure I have regrets," he said. "But who doesn't? Could my life have been different? Hell yeah. But there's always something on the horizon, so I'm good where I'm at." Then he thought, *mostly.*

An unbidden image of the text message he'd received popped into his head, but he quickly pushed it away, hoping I hadn't picked up on it. And if I had, he hoped I'd leave it alone, since it wasn't something he was going to talk about.

"We should go," he said, catching me with my mouth open to talk about it.

I snapped my jaw shut and sighed. "Are you sure I can't help?"

"Yes... I'm sure. Come on." He stood and waited for me to join him.

"Okay...." I sighed, hating that he wouldn't confide in me, but knowing there wasn't much I could do about it.

The ride back to my car went by in record time, and disappointment that it was over crashed in grumpy waves through my chest. After an extra-tight squeeze, mostly because it was hard to let go of him, I got off the bike and hurried to my car. A blush crept up my face since I'd also inhaled his scent one more time and, of course, he'd picked up on it.

His lips twisted, and I caught his gloating satisfaction that he was so irresistible. That choked a laugh out of me, and I shook my head before closing the car door. He waited while I started the engine, then followed me for a few blocks before turning back toward the city and Thrasher Development.

Watching him go brought another big sigh out of me. The temptation to ditch all of my responsibilities and ride off with him into the sunset sliced through my heart. Being with him would be fun for a while, but then my conscience would get the best of me, and I'd start to hate myself... then probably hate him.

Because deep inside, I knew I couldn't live with myself if I let my husband and kids down, and throwing that all away would kill me... so I swore I'd never think about it again... not for real anyway. But if it popped up in my dreams sometime, I wouldn't complain.

Chapter 2

I arrived home a little after five. Josh was outside shooting hoops with his friends, and I found Savannah in her room. She was already primping in front of her mirror and gave a guilty start that I'd caught her posing.

I blinked to catch her thoughts about our little get-together tonight. She'd barely turned thirteen on Friday, and here she was dreaming about Miguel. Even worse, she thought that tonight might be the start of something more.

Sure, he was a little old for her, but she'd just gotten her braces off and didn't look quite so young now. At least he'd talked to her after the play, which was better than most boys his age, even if he thought they were cousins. Although... the way I'd explained it to her, they really weren't. Maybe he didn't know, and she should tell him?

Yikes! Was she serious? That would ruin everything. I swallowed my response that she'd better keep her mouth shut and decided to talk to her like a *normal* mother would. "Uh, don't forget about our dinner with Uncle Joey tonight."

"Oh yeah, that's right," she said, acting like she'd forgotten all about it. "I'd better get ready."

"Yeah... hey, I might have to leave for a few minutes, but I'll be back in plenty of time for dinner. Okay?"

"Sure."

I closed her door and hurried downstairs before I told her what I really thought, knowing I'd have to be extra vigilant tonight so I could run interference if she tried to spill the beans.

With all of that going on, it took me a minute to remember what I was supposed to be doing. Oh yeah, my friend. I pushed her number on my phone and waited for her to pick up.

"Hi Shannon, it's Shelby. Hey... I know what's going on with Kyle, but I need to come and talk to you both. Is he there?"

"Uh... yes, he just got home a few minutes ago."

"Good. Make sure he stays there, and don't tell him I'm coming, or he might leave."

"Really? That was fast... uh... is it bad?" she asked. "I mean... can you give me a hint?"

"It's best if I tell you both at the same time. But don't worry, he's not cheating on you."

"Oh... that's a relief. Okay, I'll see you soon."

As I left, I reminded Josh about our dinner and told him I'd be back in half an hour. I picked up that he looked forward to going, mostly because he was curious about "Uncle Joey," and he hoped to find out exactly what was going on with that whole deal. It was enough to send my stomach into a queasy knot, but I managed to smile before getting into my car.

Shannon didn't live far, but at least the drive gave me a few minutes to calm down and figure out how to explain things to her and her husband without the information starting a fight between them.

After I rang the doorbell, she let me in, wearing a worried frown and thinking that Kyle was being a real grouch. She also worried that his finding out that she'd hired me to spy on him wasn't going to help his grouchy mood. But it was his fault... if he'd just tell her what was going on, she wouldn't have to resort to such drastic measures.

Since he'd basically told me to keep my mouth shut, a twinge of unease rushed down my spine. I didn't want to get in the middle of a family spat, but I wasn't about to leave Shannon in the dark, even if Kyle didn't like it. Still, why had I ever told my friends about my agency? At this point, wanting to impress them seemed pretty stupid. And now I had to worry about Kyle's treachery, and maybe even his life.

Just then, Kyle came into the living room and stopped dead in his tracks to see me standing there. His eyes widened, and his breath caught. He couldn't believe I had the guts to come to his house after what had happened.

Was I going to tell Shannon? He turned to her and didn't like what he found in her narrowed gaze. She was downright furious. With them staring angrily at each other, I decided it was up to me to break the ice.

"Kyle, I know you're not too happy that I'm here, so let me get to the point. Shannon knows you're hiding something from her, so she hired me to find out what it was. That's why I followed you to that bar today. So... what are you doing with the Polynesian gangs? Are you working for the cops?"

Shannon drew a surprised breath, and pinned him with a confused stare. "What is she talking about?"

His shoulders drooped, and he glanced at Shannon with guilt, knowing he had to tell her something, even if it wasn't the whole truth.

"It's time to come clean, Kyle," I said. "No half-truths. She needs to know what you've gotten yourself into. All of it."

He let out a frustrated growl and glared back at me. "Fine. You probably made them suspicious of me anyway." He turned to Shannon. "It's Lahni's son, Keola. He's gotten involved with the gang, and I swore I'd never let another member of my family go through that again. I thought if I helped him, he'd change his mind and leave before something bad happened."

Shannon knew he'd been involved with the gang before she met him. A couple of his best friends were still in jail because of it, and their arrests had forced him to take a long, hard look at his life. He'd been successful at making some positive changes and even had a college degree to help troubled kids. But he'd promised her that he'd never go back, and his disloyalty stung.

"How long has this been going on?" she asked.

"Just a few weeks."

"Look..." she began, shaking her head. "I know he's family, but... do you know the risk you're taking? If you cross them and they find out... they could kill you. You told me that yourself."

"They'd never kill me. Besides, I'm not getting in that deep. I know my limits... but Keola is family. I promised my sister I'd do something." He turned to me. "I was making some real progress with the kid... but I just need some more time with him. He doesn't trust me yet."

"He certainly liked the way you told me off," I said.

Kyle cringed. "I'm sorry about that. But I had to look tough so he'd listen to me."

He was telling the truth, but it wasn't the whole truth. A part of Kyle still had the mind-set of the gang, and he wouldn't hesitate to use it to protect his family. Getting back in with them brought it out, and he was walking a thin line.

"What was the bargain you made with Keola?" I asked.

He sucked in a breath. "I never said... how did you know about that? No one... I haven't told a soul."

"She has premonitions," Shannon explained. "That's why I hired her. She's really good. Now answer her question."

Kyle sighed, then ran his fingers through his hair. "I just told him that I wouldn't tell his mom about meeting him at the bar, since he's not allowed to be there."

"So... he thinks you've gone back to the gang for real?" Shannon asked.

"Yes. I thought if I was part of it too, I could look out for him."

Shannon shook her head in frustration. How could he do this now? She'd just found out this morning that she was pregnant. They'd been trying to have a baby for six long years, and now this? It sucked. This was the worst timing ever.

Oh crap! Kyle needed to know. But since I wasn't supposed to know, how could I tell her to tell him? She was thinking about giving him an ultimatum without telling him she was pregnant, like it was the ultimate test or something. So it was either her or the gang, and I knew that wouldn't go over very well. Not with his nephew in trouble. He'd never go for it, and she wasn't thinking clearly.

Before she opened her mouth, I spoke up. "Kyle... Shannon has something really important to tell you." They both glanced at me like I was nuts, but I ignored it and forged on.

"Shannon, you need to tell him what you found out this morning, and then you can both decide what to do. I've found that it's best to give people all the facts before issuing ultimatums... they respond much better, and you don't have all that angst to deal with."

Her jaw dropped. "What? How did... you... oh my gosh! You know?"

I nodded. "Yes... uh... my premonitions, remember? Look, I'm going to go now, but... you should tell him." I turned to Kyle. "Um... I'd like to help you out with Keola. I picked up that he's into something with his friends that he doesn't want you, or Big Kahuna, to know about. It could be dangerous, but I might be able to find out what it is if I can talk to him again."

His brows rose with bewilderment, so I quickly continued. "Uh... you know... using my premonitions. It will help me figure out what's going on. So, if you can set it up someplace safe, I'll meet with both of you, and get to the bottom of it. Sound good?"

He glanced at Shannon, wondering if she believed I could help. Was I for real? And what the hell did she need to tell him?

Shannon nodded her agreement, her eyes wide with wonder. "You should trust her. I have no doubt that she can help you figure out what's going on with Keola."

"Okay," he said, glancing back at me. "I'll set it up and call you."

We said our goodbyes and I left, wondering what I'd gotten myself into this time, but what choice did I have? Especially with a baby on the way? Still, I hoped Keola wasn't involved in something too bad. Ha! Who was I kidding? Considering all the trouble a gang person could get into, I should probably expect the worst.

With that troubling thought, I pulled into my garage and noticed that Chris' car wasn't there. My watch read six-twenty, and panic gripped my chest. Where was he? We needed to leave within the next ten minutes. I grabbed my cell phone and sent him a quick text, then hurried inside to change my clothes.

Since this was a backyard barbeque, I figured it was all right to wear jeans along with a nice top, and maybe a sweater to ward off the chill. Chris sent a text back that he was on his way, and I sighed with relief. We might be a few minutes late, but still close enough, and I was grateful that Jackie had refused my offer to bring a salad since I didn't have time to make one.

A few minutes later, Chris got home and hurried into our room to change into something more comfortable. I called to Savannah and Josh that it was time to go. Josh came into the kitchen wearing the same clothes he'd had on for school. He'd also been playing basketball and was a little sweaty. I got close and sniffed.

"Uh... Josh, why don't you put on a clean shirt while we wait for Dad?" I wrinkled my nose, and he let out a big sigh before heading to his room. "And wash your face while you're at it."

I glanced at Savannah, grateful I didn't have to tell her what to wear. She looked real cute in her outfit of jeans and a sky-blue crew-neck top. In fact, she looked a little older than normal, probably from all the makeup she was wearing. "You look good."

"Thanks. Uh... Miguel's going to be there, right?"

"Yes," I answered, picking up that she was both excited and nervous to see him again. "Uh... Savannah... Miguel thinks we are real cousins, and it means something to him that he has family here. He grew up in Mexico with just his mom and no one else, so we're like the only extended family that he's ever known. Try to remember that, okay?"

"Oh... sure." She hadn't thought of it that way, but she could see what I meant.

"Good," I said, relieved to get something through her crush-addled mind.

Both Josh and Chris came into the kitchen at the same time. "Is everyone ready?" Chris asked, looking us over. At our nods, he continued, "Okay. Let's go."

On the way to Uncle Joey's mansion, I thought it best to prepare my kids that he was filthy rich, so it didn't come as a complete shock. "Uh... just so you know, Uncle Joey has a lot of money and influential friends. He lives in a mansion, and he's your Dad's biggest client, so try not to get on his bad side, all right? And be on your best behavior."

Chris raised his brows, wondering what I was doing warning the kids like that. "Uh... don't worry guys, he's..." Chris almost said *a good guy*, but couldn't quite make the words come out of his mouth. "He's... uh... it should be fun."

"Does he have a swimming pool?" Savannah asked.

"I honestly don't know, but probably," I answered.

"So he's Dad's client as well as your uncle?" Josh asked. "Have you worked for him too?" He thought it was strange that I'd been hiding him from the family. Why was that?

"Uh... yeah. I've helped him out a few times," I hedged. "He's... uh... kind of an influential person. Anyway, this little get-together should be fun. I'm sure Miguel will be happy to see you both. Like I was telling Savannah, he's never had a lot of family around so, in a way, we're his family, you know?"

Josh nodded, thinking that Miguel was cool, so at least that would save an otherwise boring night, and if he could glean more info on Uncle Joey, he was all ears.

Savannah took a deep breath to help contain her eagerness and could hardly wait to see Miguel again. Then she thought about how cool it was that he was rich, and she bounced in her seat with excitement to see where he lived.

Plus, if he thought they were cousins... well, maybe he'd be more open and friendly. That could work in her favor.

Before I could shake my head in despair, we pulled into the long driveway that led past a neatly manicured yard to the front of the house. I sighed with relief that an armed guard wasn't standing by the big, front door, and hoped Uncle Joey had sent them all home for the night.

Catching sight of the mansion brought an explosion of surprise from my kids. Even though I'd told them he was filthy rich, they'd never realized exactly how rich that was. Josh was even more curious about Uncle Joey now. He had to be worth millions, so what did he do for a living?

Savannah's thoughts turned toward the romantic, and I caught that she thought Miguel's story was like a rags to riches sort of thing. And now he was like a prince in a castle. Yum.

Oh hell. This was going to be pure torture. Maybe I should just put up my shields and be a normal person for the night. It might be the only way to keep my sanity around my kids. But then I wouldn't know what everyone else was thinking, so I nixed that idea. I'd just have to work hard on my poker face and do my best to keep my expression serene and pleasant.

Chris parked the car at the end of the circular driveway, and we all marched up to the beautiful front door with etched glass panels on either side. Savannah impatiently pushed the bell, and we waited only a few seconds before Miguel answered the door. His handsome face lit up with a happy smile. "Hey guys. Come on in. We're out in the backyard. Dad's cooking up a storm."

The mental image of Uncle Joey wearing an apron and armed with a spatula and hot pads sent a wave of hilarity through me, but I managed to hold it in. Miguel led us through the house and into the kitchen, where he opened the French doors which led outside onto the beautifully covered stone patio.

My breath hitched to find an amazing outdoor kitchen built off the side of the house. It held state-of-the-art appliances, including a grill to die for. Beautiful rock work surrounded the appliances and ran the length of the kitchen, then circled around into a tall pillar with a wide-arched opening into another pillar on the other side of the patio. This side held an outdoor table and chairs, along with some nice outdoor couches and easy-chairs.

But the sight that took my breath away was the pool. Between the two pillars, stairs led directly into the dark, turquoise-blue water. At the other end, the pool curved around a beautiful, natural-looking rock waterfall. Along the side of the waterfall, I caught sight of a slide that curled into the pool. It looked just like something out of a trend-setter magazine, and my jaw dropped open in wonder.

"Shelby, Chris, nice to see you," Uncle Joey said, leaving the grill to greet us. "Hello kids."

I snapped my mouth shut and managed to smile. "Hey Uncle Joey, thanks for inviting us."

"Hope you're hungry," he answered. Then he turned back to the grill and the sizzling aroma of top sirloin. "How do you like your steak?"

We all hurried to respond, each of us feeling the instinctive need to please him. Then Jackie joined us, asking me for help in setting the table. The relief of doing something normal broke the tension, and Miguel took Josh and Savannah on a tour of the pool and pool house, while Chris and Uncle Joey began a conversation about sports.

It hit me that Uncle Joey didn't look one bit out of place, even while cooking our steaks. Of course, he didn't wear an apron or anything, but he still ruled that grill, just like he ruled about everything else.

Soon everything was ready, and we sat down to eat. The only awkward moment came when Savannah made Josh trade her places so she could sit next to Miguel.

I picked up that Miguel knew she had a crush on him, but he had the grace to hide his smile, not wanting to embarrass her. He thought it was cute. And even though they were cousins, he thoroughly enjoyed the attention. Glancing around the table, his heart swelled with happiness to be surrounded by family.

Guilt flared, sending a pain to my chest since it was all a lie. In fact, this whole charade was laced in lies. My stomach clenched, and I cringed. What were we doing to our kids? We were supposed to teach them to be good, honest people. Not lie and deceive them. What kind of an example was that?

Ready to begin, Uncle Joey called for everyone's attention. He thanked us for coming, saying it was good to be with family. Then he bowed his head and said a prayer over the food. Luckily, he didn't catch the shock on my face, but what the heck? A mob-boss... praying? After that, I figured nothing else he did would ever surprise me again.

We began passing the food around, and everyone dug in. As we ate, Uncle Joey asked my kids questions about their favorite subjects in school and other things they liked to do. They answered all of his inquiries with deference and respect, mostly because the authority he exuded would make anyone afraid not to. Then he cautioned them about not wasting too much time in front of the television and encouraged them to do their best in everything they tried.

"Hard work is important in this family," he continued. "It's the key to success, so you need to make sure you get good grades and go to college."

Sitting at the head of the table, his fatherly advice came across like a scene right out of *The Godfather*, and shock hit me like a punch in the stomach. Not so much that he offered his advice, but that he meant every word.

With a jolt, I realized that he actually cared about my kids. And here I didn't think anything else could surprise me. I must have been staring at him, because he caught my gaze and raised one eyebrow, thinking *what are you looking at?*

I blinked and quickly turned my attention to my plate. Luckily, Savannah chose that moment to tell him all about our Aikido classes, and how we'd both advanced to fourth kyu. I glanced up to find Uncle Joey smiling at me with approval.

"I'm happy to hear that," he said to her. "You should keep at it. Someday, it might come in handy." He was thinking that it had already helped me a time or two, and he was glad I had the foresight to see that Savannah got some training too.

Well damn! While I tried to form a coherent response, the conversation turned to Miguel and his plans after he graduated from high school. I sighed with relief to be off Uncle Joey's radar and managed to swallow the food in my mouth.

"I'm planning on working for Dad this summer," he said. "I've been accepted to the university, so I'll probably start there in the fall."

"But what about your musical career?" I asked. "Did the talent scouts get back to you?" Miguel had an amazing voice and was the lead in the high school musical of *Joseph and the Amazing Technicolor Dreamcoat*. In fact, talent scouts from New York had come just to hear him perform.

He shrugged. "Yeah. But I'm not sure what I want to do, and it's too late to apply to the music programs at the university level." He was thinking that the scouts had wanted him to audition for a part in a musical on Broadway, but he hadn't told Uncle Joey about it yet. He wasn't sure how his dad would take it, mostly because it meant he couldn't work for him this summer. Plus, he'd have to put off college for a while.

Holy cow! A chance to audition for a Broadway musical? And he hadn't told Uncle Joey? That was huge. Somebody needed to spill the beans. So naturally, I took it upon myself to get it out in the open. "Wait, so what did they want when they called you?"

His brows drew together in alarm, and he caught my gaze. "What do you mean?"

"You just said they got back to you, but you weren't sure what you wanted to do... so I was asking what they said."

Miguel licked his lips, unsure how to answer that question without giving himself away.

"I thought they were talking with Chris, not you," Uncle Joey said, picking up the underlying friction of deceit. "Did they call you personally?"

Miguel would have to talk now, and I had to hand it to Uncle Joey that he was so perceptive.

"Uh... yeah." Miguel let out his breath and decided to come clean. "They wanted me to audition for a musical on Broadway."

"What?" Jackie blurted. "A Broadway musical? Which one?"

"*Aladdin*," he said. "I guess the lead's contract is up, and he's moving on. The scouts actually thought I might have a good chance to get the part. Not that I'd get it for sure or anything... they made that clear. It's just an audition."

"That's so cool!" Savannah said, bouncing in her seat. She thought with his long, dark hair and good looks, he'd totally rock the part.

"It's a good thing you didn't cut your hair," I said, mentally agreeing with Savannah.

"When's the audition?" Uncle Joey asked. "You haven't missed it, have you?"

"No."

Before Miguel could explain further, Uncle Joey turned to Chris, barking orders to get the scouts on the phone, and find out all the pertinent details. While Chris took out his phone and stepped away from the table, Uncle Joey glanced at Miguel, disgruntled that he'd been left in the dark. What else hadn't Miguel told him?

He glanced my way with a nod, wanting me to listen in and get to the bottom of it. Instead, I turned to Miguel and placed a hand on his shoulder. "I think you should do the audition. Like you said, auditioning doesn't mean you'll get the part, but it would be a great experience, right Uncle Joey?"

"Of course," Uncle Joey said, clearing his throat. "If that's what you want."

Miguel hated to disappoint his father, but just thinking about auditioning sent a thrill of excitement through him. He'd tried to ignore that hunger and be more practical, but now it might actually happen, and he couldn't deny it any longer. He'd even practiced all the songs. And his teacher had given him some special vocal coaching on how to sing them.

He glanced at his father with enthusiasm shining in his eyes. "I'd like that. If you're okay with it."

Uncle Joey nodded, then sighed, wondering why Miguel didn't just talk to him about these things. Didn't Miguel know that he wasn't some tyrant? "Sure. Let's get it set up." He was thinking that it wasn't likely that Miguel would get the part, but who knew? It could happen.

Chris came back from his phone call, telling us that the agent would put Miguel on the list and call Chris tomorrow with the details. That's when it struck me how quickly Chris had jumped to do Uncle Joey's bidding, and a trickle of unease ran down my spine. When had Uncle Joey so totally taken over our lives? How would this affect our kids?

As if he'd heard me, Chris sat down in his chair beside me, sending a tight smile my way and squeezing my hand under the table. I picked up a flicker of worry from him, and my breath hitched in response. What had we gotten into now?

Somehow, I managed to calm down and finish eating. After that, we all pitched in to clear the table. Miguel asked Josh and Savannah if they'd like to go swimming, telling them that there were all sizes of swimming suits in the pool house, and the water was plenty warm. Josh jumped at the chance, but Savannah wasn't sure she wanted to ruin her hair and makeup.

"You should totally go for it," I said to her. "I mean... look at that slide."

"Okay." She smiled and followed the boys to the pool house. Soon, they were in the pool having a great time, like they'd known each other their whole lives. It was kind of like they were part of one big happy family, just like Uncle Joey kept insinuating. My stomach clenched. He'd told me I was family, and now I was beginning to realize just what that meant.

"Shelby," Uncle Joey said. "Help me take these inside." He motioned toward a couple of trays, along with the salt and pepper and the other accessories needed for grilling. I hurried over and took one of the trays and followed him into the kitchen. "Just set them on the counter."

"Okay. I can wash them up if you want."

"There's no need for that," he said, thinking the housekeeper would do it in the morning. Then he glanced out at the patio, making sure we wouldn't be interrupted.

"I'm worried about Ramos. There's something going on, and I'd like you to find out what it is."

At my raised brows, he continued. "I wouldn't ask if it wasn't for his own good. So here's what I'm going to do. I'll send you on an errand with Ramos tomorrow. I have a delivery that Ramos usually does on his own, but I'll tell him that you need to go so you can learn if anything suspicious is going on. Should be simple. While you're out, maybe you can pick up what's bothering him. Sound good?"

I didn't have the courage to tell him that Ramos had come to my rescue earlier today, so I asked Uncle Joey a question instead. "But what if he doesn't want me to know?"

"Just try and figure it out. Ask a few questions. He might be willing to tell you, and then you can tell me."

"Okay, I'll see what I can do, but he knows how to block his thoughts pretty well."

"Yeah, but you'll probably pick up something. Any kind of a clue might be enough to confront him with it, and he'll open up."

"Uh... how about I tell you the clues and you confront him?" I asked.

He snickered. "Afraid he might be mad at you?"

"Well... yes. He's kind of scary when he gets mad."

Uncle Joey shook his head. "Fine." But he was thinking Ramos had a soft spot for me, so I shouldn't worry so much. "Another thing," he continued. "What do you think about going to New York with Miguel? If you went, you'd know what they thought of him, and I'd really like to know if he has a shot at making this a career. If not, I'd rather he didn't waste his time."

"Uh... I see what you mean, but don't you think it might be weird if I went? I mean... he's eighteen. He can certainly take care of this himself, right? So having me along... I don't think that would go over very well."

Uncle Joey sighed. "I suppose you're right, but I don't think he'd object. In fact, he might like having you along. Better than going alone, don't you think? It would just be for the day, or maybe overnight depending on when it was, and you could go in my private jet."

"Hmm... well, okay," I agreed. He sure knew how to sweeten the deal. I mean... how could I pass up a trip to New York in a private jet? "But you should talk to Miguel about it first and make sure he's okay with it."

"Sure." He nodded, thinking Miguel would be fine with it, since he usually went along with most everything Uncle Joey wanted. Plus, we could stay at his hotel, and he was sure Syd would take good care of us, so there was nothing to worry about.

Uncle Joey owned a hotel in New York? Sheesh! Before I could ask about that, and who Syd was, he'd walked back out onto the patio, and I'd missed my chance. I followed him out, finding that Chris and Jackie were sitting in lounge chairs arranged in a comfy spot by the side of the pool.

A diet soda and glass of ice sat on the round, glass table for me, so I thanked Jackie and took a seat beside Chris. Uncle Joey sat beside Jackie with a cold beer, and we began chatting about mundane things while watching the kids enjoy themselves in the water. Just like regular people.

Half an hour later it was fully dark, and the air took on a sudden chill. Not wanting to overstay our welcome, I called to my kids that it was time to get out. They begged me to let them swim a little longer, and I couldn't blame them.

Heck... I wished I could have gone swimming too. With the waterfall and rocks bathed in spotlights, along with the pool lights reflecting in the water, the whole yard took on an enchanting and magical tone. But since it was a school night, I stuck to my guns, mostly because I knew that Uncle Joey had some phone calls he needed to make.

It wasn't long before we had gathered to leave. We stood on the front porch, saying our goodbyes and thanking them for the fun evening.

"Don't forget to come by the office in the morning," Uncle Joey said to me.

"I won't. I'll be there around nine."

"Good." Then he turned to Chris. "Call me after you talk to that talent scout. I want to know what's going on so I can make arrangements."

"I will," Chris answered. "Goodnight."

We crowded into the car and drove home with only the radio for company, since all of us were lost in our thoughts. Both Savannah and Josh were a little star struck about the whole filthy-rich-mansion and coolest-pool-ever part. Along with Miguel's awesomeness, it made them both a little pensive about who they were and what they had, comparatively speaking.

Chris and I both felt a bit overwhelmed about our burgeoning relationship with a mob-boss and his family, mostly the "family" part of that association. Did that mean he'd want to get to know our kids better and be involved in their lives? My throat began to ache, feeling like how I imagined a noose pulling tight around my neck and sucking all the life out of me would feel.

Much later, after everyone had gone to bed, Chris let out a sigh and climbed under the covers. I moved to his side and snuggled against him.

"I hate to admit it," he began, "but I'm a little shell-shocked. Did you notice how Manetto talked to our kids? I mean... it's one thing to have dinner together as friends, but it's another for him to zero in on them with his advice."

"I know," I agreed. "And he used the "f" word a lot."

"What?"

"You know... family? He kept saying stuff like 'in our family we do this,' and 'college is important in this family.' It made me wonder what he's thinking."

Chris let out a chuckle. "I can't believe you just said that."

I huffed out a breath. "You'd think I'd know what his intentions are toward them, right? But I couldn't pick up anything besides interest. Still, that could mean a lot of things. I guess I'll have to make sure he doesn't step across the line."

Chris' brows rose with surprise. "You mean like... offering them a place in his organization someday?"

"Sure, why not? It could happen."

Chris frowned and shook his head. "He wouldn't do that, and if he tried, we'd just tell him it wasn't going to happen. You still have a lot of leverage, honey. You can use that to keep him in his place. If he wants your services, then there's no interfering with our kids."

"Huh. I hadn't thought of it like that, but you're right. That could work. Hey, thanks... I feel lots better now."

"Yeah, me too." He let out a sigh, hoping it never came to that. "So how was your day? Did you make progress with your friend's husband?"

"Uh... yes. I think that case is coming along nicely. I need to meet with him another time, but I think he's going to cooperate. After that, I'll be done." It wasn't exactly the whole story, but hopefully Chris would never find out any more than that. "What about you? How was your day?"

"Busy. There's a lot going on right now. But it's all good." He sighed deeply and closed his eyes with fatigue. Almost at once, his head drooped forward. The movement startled him enough to wake him, but he was so tired that his eyes drooped shut a second time.

I glanced at the clock to find it was nearly eleven-thirty. Chris had been up since five-thirty that morning, which was a typical day for him, but I could understand why he was so tired. He never got enough sleep.

"Hey, you're falling asleep. Why don't you turn off the light?"

"Hmm... yeah. Sorry, but I'm exhausted."

"It's okay. We can talk some more tomorrow."

He nodded, then turned out the light and settled deeper into bed, pulling me into his arms. After a moment, his breathing evened out and he was asleep. With a sigh, I moved out of his embrace and turned over, wishing I could get to sleep so quickly.

Chapter 3

The next morning, I drove to Thrasher Development wearing my leather motorcycle jacket and boots. I smiled, looking forward to going on another ride with Ramos. It was a perfect, sunny, spring day, with the temperature in the sixties, and hopefully climbing into the lower seventies by mid-day.

That was the good part, since getting Ramos to tell me what was going on could be a problem. I'd probably have to get him thinking about it, since I was pretty sure he wouldn't actually tell me. I sighed, knowing he'd be mad once I got it out of him, but if I told him it was all Uncle Joey's fault, he couldn't be too upset, right?

I got out of my car and hurried to the elevator, sneaking a quick peek around the corner to make sure Ramos' motorcycle was there. Yup! There it was, all black, sleek, and shiny. I smiled, and my heart filled with joyful anticipation.

In the elevator, I sent a smile and wave at the camera, just in case Ramos was watching the feed. It didn't hurt to start out on his good side, right? Then it hit me that Uncle Joey knew me pretty well, because it had hardly bothered me to spy on Ramos for him. What kind of a friend did that make me? Was it because a motorcycle ride was involved? I had to admit that had something to do with it, but since Uncle Joey was also worried about him, it was for his own good.

Ha! Who was I kidding? Ramos would probably hate it and think I was meddling. Not much I could do about that now. Hopefully, it wouldn't ruin our friendship. With that disturbing thought, I exited on the twenty-sixth floor and hurried into Thrasher Development. Jackie glanced up from her desk and greeted me with a smile.

"Hi Jackie. Hey, thanks again for a wonderful dinner last night. We sure had a great time."

"Yeah," she agreed. "It was fun, and the kids got along really well. Let's get together again soon." She was thinking that Savannah obviously had a crush on Miguel, but then... what teenage girl didn't? "Joe and Ramos are in Joe's office. Why don't you go on back."

"Okay, thanks." I made it to the door, hoping for the best, and knocked, then put on my friendliest smile, and pushed the door open.

"Shelby," Uncle Joey said. "Come on in."

Ramos stood beside Uncle Joey's desk and straightened at my approach. He was dressed in full hit-man-enforcer mode, wearing a tight, black t-shirt, and sporting a leather holster holding a gun around his shoulders. He caught my gaze and frowned, wondering what I was doing there.

"I want Shelby to go with you," Uncle Joey said. "Just to make sure they're not skimming off the top and cheating me out of my money."

Ramos let out a breath, not too pleased about having me along. He picked up his leather jacket but didn't put it on. "All right," he said, stone-faced.

It didn't take a mind-reader to know he wasn't happy about this arrangement, and my stomach clenched.

"You're headed to my club," Uncle Joey explained to me. "Ramos is picking up some money from the guy who runs it for me. All you have to do is make sure he gives Ramos everything he owes me."

"Okay, I can do that."

"Good." He smiled but was thinking: *and find out what's going on with Ramos.*

I nodded, hoping that Ramos wasn't picking up anything suspicious between us. Just in case, I glanced his way and smiled, hoping I didn't look as guilty as I felt.

After we left Uncle Joey's office, I turned to Ramos. "So how's it going?"

"Fine."

"Uh... that's good." I waved at Jackie and followed Ramos to the elevator, a little nervous about how upset he seemed to be with me.

Once the doors closed, he caught my gaze and raised his brow. "So, what's the real reason you're going with me?"

"What?" Alarm spiked through my chest, and my eyes widened.

"Come on, Shelby. I know something's going on."

"I'm not sure what you mean," I hedged.

Ramos pursed his lips, thinking I was giving him the run-around. We made it all the way to the parking level without speaking another word to each other, and Ramos stalked out. I quickly followed, worried that he might just leave without me. Would he really do that?

He popped the trunk on his car and grabbed the spare helmet he kept there for me, placing it on the back of his car along with his leather jacket. Then he turned, crossed his arms, and waited for the truth, not about to hand me the helmet until I spilled my guts.

Ramos had that whole intimidation thing going for him, but I'd never felt the full effect until this very moment. Of course, I'd never felt guilty about spying on him before either. The unforgiving scowl on his face probably had something to do with it. Even his guarded thoughts didn't tell me much.

My stomach clenched, and I met his gaze, ready to apologize, but for some reason, nothing came out of my mouth. Probably because the way he leaned against his car with his arms crossed, and showing off his bulging muscles, had a different sort of effect on me. Add to that his dark, brooding gaze, and I couldn't seem to form a coherent thought.

"Shelby?"

I jerked my gaze away with a guilty flush and took a deep breath to break the spell. "Uh... well, first of all, you have to know this wasn't my idea. I'm just following Uncle Joey's orders, so if you're going to be angry, you should be angry with him, not me." I dared to glance his way and noticed that his eyes had narrowed, but I also picked up that he held back a smile. That was a good sign, right?

"So what is it?"

"I'm not sure I'm allowed to tell you that." He lost the smile, so I continued, "How about I tell you when we get back?"

He huffed out a breath and shook his head, thinking I exasperated the hell out of him. "Fine. Here."

Relieved, I took the helmet from him and slipped it on while he shrugged into his jacket. A minute later, we were ready to go, and I let out a thankful sigh to be on the back of his bike.

The Comet Club wasn't too far from Thrasher Development, so that took some of the fun out of the ride. Ramos pulled around back and parked. I got off and glanced at the empty parking space not far from us, remembering how I'd been locked in the trunk of a car right in that very spot.

A crazy judge had taken me hostage to get back at Uncle Joey. He'd planned to kill me in the basement of this club, and he'd almost succeeded. A sudden twinge ran down my arm, and I automatically rubbed the place where I'd been shot.

Taking a calming breath, I pushed the memory away and followed Ramos to the back entrance, hoping nothing like that ever happened to me again.

Next to the door, a delivery truck had backed into the supply dock, and several people hauled boxes inside. One of them spotted Ramos and yelled for us to go inside.

Ramos pushed the door open and led the way down a hallway to the last office on the left. The door was ajar, and Ramos entered the office with me following behind. A man in his forties, with his long, dark hair pulled back into a ponytail, and in casual clothes, glanced up from his work at the desk.

His face broke into a smile, and he stood. "Ramos," he said, extending his hand. "Nice to see you." He turned his attention to me and frowned, thinking there had better be a good reason I was there. "Who's this?"

"Hi," I said, smiling. "I'm Uncle Joey's niece, Shelby." How easily that lie fell from my lips surprised me, but I felt safer saying it. Still, how far to the dark side had I gone?

The manager remembered hearing about me, but he couldn't place the particulars. "I think I've heard your name before. Do you play poker?"

"Uh... yeah."

"I remember you now. You're the one who beat everyone. Even Manetto." He thought normally that wasn't a good thing, but being Manetto's niece explained how I got away with it.

"Is everything ready?" Ramos asked, still in a bad mood.

"Sure. I've got the money right here." The manager turned to a large, standing safe in the corner and twisted the lock, hitting the combination until it clicked. Then he pulled the lever and opened the safe. "Here's the ledger. Manetto's copy is on top." He pulled out a binder and handed it over to Ramos, then proceeded to empty the stacks of cash into a black, leather, messenger-type bag.

Ramos glanced through the papers, thinking that the manager had been doing this for over ten years and would never think about cheating Uncle Joey. That's how Ramos knew sending me with him was a bunch of baloney.

After checking the ledger, Ramos took his copy. Folding it in half, he slipped it into the inside pocket of his jacket and handed the ledger back to the manager, who exchanged it for the bag of money. Ramos slipped the bag over his shoulder.

"Thanks," he said. "See you next week."

"Sure. Oh, hey, before you go, there was someone here last night asking about you." The manager shuffled through some papers on his desk before finding a business card. "He left this and asked if you'd be here tonight. It sounded like he wanted to meet up. I didn't tell him anything one way or the other, but he said you were old friends. Said his name was Dusty, and that you went way back."

Ramos took the card with barely concealed anger, then he turned it over and his breath caught. His jaw tightened before he slipped the card into his back jeans pocket. "Thanks. I'll take care of it."

Ramos stomped out of the office, so I smiled at the manager. "Uh... nice to meet you."

"You too."

I followed Ramos out of the building and scrambled to keep up with him. I picked up his fury that Dusty had come to the club. It was bad enough that Dusty had made contact with someone who'd given him Ramos' phone number, but this was going too far. What game was he playing now?

Dragging Ramos into it was bad enough, but Jodie's name on the back of the card was Dusty's ace in the hole. Dusty knew Ramos would meet him if Jodie was involved. *But what the hell? Hasn't she learned anything in all this time?*

Ramos slipped his helmet on and straddled the bike, then glanced at me, realizing I'd just heard every single thought. He closed his eyes and swore in his mind, then let out a resigned breath. "Get on."

I finished snapping on my helmet and got on the bike, a little nervous about how upset he was. To my relief, he calmed down pretty fast. Riding his bike had that effect on him. He also took the long way back to get it out of his system.

I tried to enjoy the ride, even though that little devil of guilt rode high on my shoulder. Ramos' past was none of my business, especially since he didn't want me to know, and guilt that I'd invaded his privacy turned my stomach.

Then the name he'd been thinking about so hard clicked. Jodie McAllister. I knew that name. She was the multiple-Grammy-award-winning country singer. She'd had a ton of hits in the last several years. So Ramos knew her? Wait a minute. I knew Ramos had a special affinity for country music. Was that why? So, who was she to him? And who was this Dusty person?

Ramos' thoughts were shut up tight, so that didn't help, but I knew they were related. The card said Dustin McAllister on it, with Jodie McAllister on the back. So maybe he was her husband?

Yikes! That could be bad, because judging from Ramos' reaction, it seemed like he still cared for her. So what was going on?

Then another realization struck me. Jodie McAllister had an upcoming concert scheduled. I'd just seen it in the paper this morning. In fact, it was this week. I'd read that the first concert on Thursday had sold out, so she'd decided to do another one on Friday, which had also sold out.

Holy cow! This was huge. Maybe she wanted to meet up with Ramos and sent Dusty to set it up. But if Dusty was her husband, why would she do that? It had to be something else. Maybe Dusty wanted to settle a score? It had to be something unsavory, or it wouldn't bother Ramos so much. So what had happened between them?

I needed to find out before all this speculation drove me crazy.

We pulled into the parking garage, and I picked up that Ramos wished he could have ridden the bike a little longer, but with all that money riding in the bag, he couldn't risk it. Whoa! In the excitement, I'd forgotten all about the money.

He parked in his usual place. We got off the bike and, without saying a word, he took my helmet from me and stored it with his in the trunk of his car. It didn't seem like he was going to open his mouth, or his thoughts, so it was up to me to get him talking.

"So... Jodie McAllister, huh? Is that the disaster you didn't want to tell me about, or is it something else?"

He huffed out a breath. "That has something to do with it."

"Can you tell me about it?"

He shook his head. "I'd rather not... but I guess it's kind of late for that."

"You bet your sweet... cakes it is." I smiled at his surprise, and the moment lightened a bit.

"Fine," he said, giving in. "But first tell me why Manetto sent you with me on that little errand."

"Oh... he wanted to know what was bothering you. Kind of like I did."

"What? You told him about that?"

"No! I didn't say a word to him, I promise. He picked it up all on his own... from the way you were acting. You know... because you've been kind of upset lately? I may have even encouraged him to leave it alone, but I certainly didn't tell him about it first."

Ramos sighed, realizing he'd jumped to the wrong conclusion because he'd let his emotions get in the way. He needed to lock them up tight so he could deal with this.

"Hey... you should be flattered that we both care."

"Yeah... right."

That sounded a little sarcastic, and I couldn't help twisting my lips and raising my brow at his grumpy attitude. It was the look I'd mastered with my kids to tell them to straighten up.

Ramos shook his head in exasperation. "Hey, I know I've been a little preoccupied with this, but Dusty's not a good person, and I'd rather not get involved with him."

"Is he married to Jodie?"

"No," he said, thinking that was disgusting. "He's her brother. In the text I got from him, he just said he wanted to meet up for old time's sake, but that's not how he works. There's always a reason, and it's never good. If he's found a connection to me at the club... he's going to keep pestering me until I agree to meet with him."

"I can see why that's got you upset. So... do you really know Jodie McAllister? I mean... *the* Jodie McAllister?"

"Yeah."

"Whoa. That's... nuts. How did you meet?"

He sighed, thinking I wasn't going to let it go, but maybe he could put it off a little longer. "We need to go in." He didn't like standing there with all that money, and there was also a chance anyone around here could eavesdrop on our conversation.

"Oh yeah, right. Sure. Then you'll tell me?"

A deep growl came out of him, and I wasn't sure if that was a "yes" or a "no." Deciding to be positive, I took it for a "yes," and hurried to point out the advantages before he changed his mind. "Good. I'm sure I can be helpful. If he's as dangerous as you think, he'll probably lie... a lot, but with me around you won't have to worry what's on his mind."

We got onto the elevator, and I pushed the button for the twenty-sixth floor. I held my breath for his response, hoping he'd take it the right way and maybe laugh it off. By the tenth floor, Ramos hadn't said, or thought, a word, but a simmering energy emanated from him that started to worry me.

As we passed the twentieth floor, it was still going strong, so I cast a quick glance his way. He leaned back against the elevator with his eyes closed tight, like he was in pain. Guilt that maybe it was my fault tightened my chest.

I took a breath to ask if he was okay, but the bell chimed and the elevator stopped. The doors slid open and his gaze caught mine. He was thinking that if I knew what was good for me, I'd just stay on the elevator and go home where I belonged.

My breath caught. Of all the nerve! That was totally uncalled for. He started to pass me, but I stepped in front of him to exit first. Unfortunately, he hadn't expected that and bumped into me, knocking me right out of the elevator. I tried to take a step, but my legs got tangled, and I started to fall.

Ramos grabbed my arm, but my forward momentum took him off balance. To avoid stepping on my tangled legs, he lurched sideways but couldn't get his feet under him before gravity pulled us both down.

In the split second before we hit the ground, Ramos caught me around the waist. He pulled me against him and twisted to his shoulder and back, taking the brunt of the fall. He continued to roll until I ended up underneath him, but managed to stop rolling just before his weight completely smothered me.

Panting for breath, our gazes met and desire darkened his eyes. His face was so close to mine that I could feel his warm breath on my cheek. I swallowed, realizing I was pinned under him and totally at his mercy. A wicked smile twisted his lips, and my breath caught. He leaned forward, intending to ravish my mouth and there was nothing I could do to stop it.

"Are you done rolling around out here?"

Ramos froze, wanting to kiss me in the worst way. He closed his eyes and let out a breath, then nimbly rolled off me and stood. With a sardonic smile, he held out his hand to help me up, thinking that, once again, I'd been saved by the bell... or Jackie, in this case.

"What's going on?" she asked.

I scrambled to my feet and let go of Ramos' hand like it was on fire. With guilt surging through me, I took a breath to explain. "Uh... I tripped coming out of the elevator and Ramos caught me. But then he lost his balance and we both fell."

"Uh-huh." She caught that, but thought there was a lot more to it. Was Ramos putting the moves on me? She shook her head, thinking she needed to have a talk with him. He should know better... and so should I. Chris was a wonderful man, and she didn't want me to screw that up. And what about my kids?

Drowning in guilt, I opened my mouth to tell her it would never happen again, but Ramos spoke first. "I need to get this money in the safe." He turned on his heel and left me to face Jackie alone.

"Uh... I need to report to Uncle Joey," I said, turning to follow Ramos.

"Wait." Jackie grabbed my arm. She glanced at the door to make sure Ramos was gone before continuing. "What's going on with you two?"

My shoulders sagged, and I let out a breath. "Nothing. I swear." She didn't believe me, and I knew I had some explaining to do before she thought the worst. "Look... there's something going on with Ramos and he won't talk about it. We sort of got into an argument over it, and now he's mad at me."

"Huh." She thought that kind of made sense, but it wasn't like him to let his emotions get the best of him. She thought it more likely that I was the one giving him fits, since we had that whole physical-attraction vibe going on between us.

"Uh... just think about how he's been acting lately," I said, knowing I had to convince her it had nothing to do with me, even if it might. "Uncle Joey noticed that something was bothering Ramos. He's the one who asked me to find out what it was. That's why he sent me with Ramos in the first place."

"Oh." Jackie nodded, more convinced since it came from Uncle Joey. "Now it makes sense. I wonder what it could be. Did you pick up anything?"

"Not much. Just that someone from his past has come back into his life and he's pretty upset about it. But that's it.

Please don't say anything to him. I don't want him to know I told you. He's mad enough as it is."

"Sure, sure. I won't say a thing." What in the world could ruffle Ramos – the King of Cool? She was thinking that she may not say anything to Ramos, but that didn't mean she couldn't ask Uncle Joey.

"Uh... I've got to get going." She stepped onto the elevator, lost in her thoughts about Ramos and his past, convinced it had to be a woman... probably someone he cared about....

The door slid shut on that thought, and I sighed with relief. She was right about the woman part, and it made me more curious than ever to find out what had happened between him and Jodie McAllister.

I hurried inside just as Ramos came down the hall from Uncle Joey's office. He caught the wary look in my eyes and pursed his lips together, thinking that he should probably apologize. My mouth dropped open in surprise, and he shook his head. "Not for wanting to kiss you, but for thinking you should go home where you belonged."

"Oh... right. Well, I might forgive you, as long as you tell me what's going on."

Exasperated, he shook his head, but his breath came out in a sigh of defeat. "Want a diet soda?"

"Yes."

I followed him to the end of the hall, and he opened the door into the apartment where he spent most of his time. I knew he had a home somewhere, but for his job, this was more convenient. Inside, the stark contrast from the offices seemed a little jarring.

White plush carpet and a kitchen off to the side, with white cabinets and black granite counter tops, along with stainless steel appliances, made the place extremely stylish. In combination with the white leather furniture in the living room with splashes of colored pillows, and bright, abstract paintings, I would have thought this place came right out of a penthouse apartment building.

Ramos opened the fridge and pulled out a can of diet soda, then filled a glass with ice and brought them to me. While I poured my drink, he grabbed a dark bottle of finely crafted beer and popped the lid, then took a long swig, thinking this was one time he needed a drink.

"Come and sit down," he said. "This might take a while."

I moved into the living room and sat on the couch, taking a moment to gaze out the huge window at the amazing view of the city. Ramos sat opposite me on the recliner and took another pull from the bottle. It helped settle him down. And since I wouldn't let it go, he was ready to tell me, just to get it over with.

I picked up that he hadn't told another soul about this, mostly because it made it easier to forget. Too bad Dusty had come back into his life and ruined it. He finished the bottle and set it down, then glanced my way and took a deep breath, ready to talk.

"After I ran from that mess in Orlando, I drifted for a while without any purpose or direction. All I knew was that my life was over, and I could never go back. Not that I wanted to, especially since I thought my brother was dead.

"I don't remember how much time passed, but after a few months, I ended up in Nashville, where I managed to land a job at one of the live music bars as part of their security team. I worked there for about eight months, and I enjoyed it for the most part.

"I didn't like country music at the beginning, but things changed once Jodie started playing there. She was different from most of the singers I'd heard... more on the soulful side, like she'd been through some hard times of her own. Definitely something I could relate to. Anyway, we started seeing each other. It was good for a while, until her brother showed up."

Ramos shook his head and sighed. "That kid knew how to use people, and he had Jodie wrapped around his little finger. She was always trying to help him out of the stupid things he did, even bailing him out of jail when she didn't have enough money for herself. It drove me crazy.

"One night I'd had enough, and I told him he was nothing but a loser who mooched off his sister. We got into a fight. Jodie came between us and stopped me from kicking the... crap out of him. Then she took my side, begging him to get a job and make something of himself. He refused to talk to her after that, and she blamed me for pushing him away. She said I'd gone too far."

Ramos shrugged. "Maybe I did, I don't know. Things changed after that. It was like he drove a wedge between us even when he wasn't around. Then, a week later, Dusty came back, acting like nothing had happened. I warned Jodie not to let him take advantage of her, but she was so glad to see him, she wouldn't listen. So I cornered him one night and told him I didn't care if he ruined his life, but he'd better damn well not ruin his sister's life too. It seemed to do the trick, and he straightened up after that.

"I thought things were getting better, but I found out the hard way that Dusty wasn't about to change. One night he came in with some friends, high on something. Jodie was right in the middle of her set, and there were some bigwig producers who were interested in offering her a contract. It was a huge deal.

"He started making a nuisance of himself, clapping and whistling, then saying that Jodie was his sister, and how awesome she was. He was ruining everything, so I did my job and asked him to leave. He started yelling and threw a punch at me, knocking over the table.

"I grabbed him and carted him out, with him kicking and screaming the whole way. I got him outside to the parking lot before I realized his friends had followed us. One of them tackled me from behind. Pretty soon, all of them had ganged up on me.

"I was holding my own just fine, until one of them pulled a gun. He pointed it my way, so I shoved his friend into him." Ramos shook his head and sighed before continuing. "Somehow the gun went off and shot the kid right in the chest. He died pretty quick. Then Dusty started yelling that it was my fault, and I'd killed his friend. He picked up the gun to shoot me but, by then, another security guard was there and knocked the gun out of his hands.

"The police showed up. After giving them my statement, I knew I had to get out of there. So I left. I never saw or spoke to Jodie again."

"Wow. That's so sad. Did Dusty go to jail?"

"Not that I ever heard."

"What about Jodie? Did she get the contract?"

"Not then. She missed her chance with those guys. But about a year and a half later, she came out with her first album. It went platinum, and I'm pretty sure she made it big because of me." He caught my gaze, and his lips tilted up in a sexy smile.

"Oh yeah? How's that?"

"Her breakout album is called "Letting Go," and it's all about me." At my raised brows, he continued. "Even if you don't know the album, I'm sure you know the song *Devil Rider*."

"Well, sure. Everyone knows that song." It was one of the few cross-over country songs that got played everywhere. And it was Jodie's biggest hit. The words to the chorus came to my mind, and my eyes widened. "The devil rides a motorcycle in that song."

He just smiled and nodded.

"Damn." The whole song made sense now that I knew it was about Ramos. *His lips full of promise... his eyes full of fire... offering me nothing... but hot with desire. His breath on my face, the touch of his hand, lights me on fire like a red hot brand.*

Then the chorus, *You love me, then leave me, you Devil Rider... Hold me close, don't let go, you Devil Rider... Break my heart, take my soul, you Devil Rider. You broke my heart, You took my soul...*

I took a deep breath and shook my head. This was not what I expected. If that album was all about him, he totally broke her heart. "No wonder you're so full of yourself."

A sensual smile played over his lips. "What can I say?"

I smiled and shook my head, knowing that behind his macho attitude, his heart had been broken a little as well. "So what do you want to do about Dusty?"

"I'll meet him at the club tonight and see what he wants."

"Okay. I can probably be there someplace where he won't see me."

"No." Ramos shook his head. "You're not coming." He was thinking that he didn't need me there to figure this out. Talking about it had settled something inside him. He was back in control, and it felt good.

"Okay," I said, deciding to agree for now, since he wouldn't accept my help without a fight. "I'm sure you're right. I mean... maybe he's changed, and he just wants to apologize or something."

Ramos shrugged, but he didn't think that's what Dusty had in mind. It was probably something illegal; otherwise, why meet up with people who knew Ramos? But it didn't matter. He could take care of it.

"All right, then." I took a deep breath and let it out. "Thanks for the soda. I need to talk to Uncle Joey before I leave." I stood, still a little worried that he wanted to do this by himself, and that nothing I said would change his mind.

On the other hand, he was Ramos. He didn't get where he was by doing anything crazy or stupid.

"What are you going to tell Manetto?"

I took my glass into the kitchen, then turned to catch his gaze before replying. "Um... how about that it's someone from your past, but you're taking care of it, and if you need anything, you'll let him know."

He nodded. "That should work. Thanks Shelby." Thinking that also went for listening to his story and being a good friend.

"Sure." I patted him on the arm in my most motherly fashion. "Just promise me you won't kill him."

He laughed, startled that I'd said that. But since the thought had crossed his mind, he couldn't blame me. "Of course not."

Was that a lie? I sighed and shook my head. "Okay. See ya."

I hurried out the door and down the hall to Uncle Joey's office, knowing that most of Ramos' story was another secret that I'd have to keep to myself. Although I was pretty sure I could tell my best friend, Holly, all about the song *Devil Rider*, and that it had been written about Ramos. She'd totally flip over that.

I knocked on Uncle Joey's door and peeked inside. He was on his phone but motioned for me to come in. A second later, he hung up and indicated the chair in front of his desk. "So what's going on with Ramos?"

"Someone from his past showed up at the club last night asking for him. Apparently they go way back, before Ramos even met you. This person, Dusty McAllister, wants to meet with him, and Ramos is suspicious about what he wants. It brought back a lot of old memories that Ramos wanted to forget, but I think he's doing better now. Ramos is planning on meeting Dusty at your club tonight. I offered to go so I could listen to Dusty's thoughts, but Ramos refused my help."

Uncle Joey shook his head, muttering, "Damn pride," under his breath. "Maybe you should go anyway. What kind of a threat is this guy to my organization?"

My eyes widened. Uncle Joey was giving me a reason to be there whether Ramos liked it or not. "Uh... there's a possibility that he wants something from Ramos that could probably include you and the business. So he might be a threat. I picked up from Ramos that Dusty's not a good person, and definitely not someone you could trust. Ramos even thought he had a hidden agenda."

Uncle Joey smiled and nodded with approval. "Then it looks like I need you there, for the sake of my organization and business dealings."

"I think that's a good idea, only I don't know the specific time it's taking place."

"But it's at my club, right?"

"Yes."

"I'll find out and let you know."

I swallowed and nodded. "Okay, sure."

"Good. It will probably be late, but I'll have Ricky take you and bring you home. You'll be fine." He was thinking Ramos wouldn't like it, but this wasn't his call to make. He felt better sending me because Ramos didn't normally get upset by anything. In fact, he'd never seen Ramos this way, so there must be a woman involved.

Since he just thought that instead of saying it, I decided I didn't need to answer. But it was kind of getting on my nerves that everyone blamed "a woman" for their problems. Although, in this case, it was mostly true. I mean, Ramos wouldn't have been so upset if Jodie hadn't been involved.

He had strong feelings of nostalgia when he thought about her. It kind of made me want to buy her first album, since it was all about him. I also had a sudden desire to go to her concert, or at least find out about her life now. Was she married? A mother? Still pining for Ramos? Did I really want to know? Maybe not. Did he have tickets to the performance? I should have asked him about that. Maybe he did and that was part of his whole "bad mood" thing. Walking down memory lane could sometimes do that to a person.

"Is that right?" Uncle Joey asked.

"Uh... what did you say?"

"Is there a woman involved?"

"Oh... um... yeah." Uncle Joey wanted to know the whole story, but I wasn't sure Ramos would like that. Then he narrowed his eyes, thinking that I'd better start talking, so I forgot all about my qualms and spilled the story.

"He met her in Nashville after what happened in Orlando. In fact, it's Jodie McAllister, the singer. Dusty is her brother, and Ramos had to leave in a hurry because one of Dusty's friends got killed after a fight. Ramos hasn't seen her or Dusty since, but she's coming to town for a concert, and now Dusty wants to talk."

"Hmm... he wants something from Ramos. It's a good thing you'll be there tonight."

I nodded, even though I was sure Ramos would hate it. "Yeah."

"Good. I'm glad that's settled. And the timing is perfect because I just got off the phone with your husband. The agent scheduled Miguel's audition for tomorrow afternoon. So you'll be leaving for New York in the morning. It's sooner than we thought, but it will all work out. The audition is set for four o'clock."

"Okay. That should work." Wow, it seemed like things were moving awfully fast around here.

"There's one more thing." Uncle Joey leaned forward in his chair. "You could probably come straight back, but the agent offered to give you and Miguel tickets for the show tomorrow night. Do you want to stay?"

"You mean tickets to *Aladdin*? On Broadway?"

Uncle Joey smiled, thinking he'd just made me an offer too good to refuse. It always made his day when that happened.

"Ha-ha." I smiled. "But you know what? You're totally right. I'd love to stay."

"Good, I'll let Chris know and have Jackie make the arrangements."

"How about I tell him? It's almost time for lunch, and I could run over there right now."

"Sure. But if he gives you any trouble, tell him he has to answer to me."

I laughed good-naturedly, even if it was only a little bit funny.

"Now that you're going, there's something you should be aware of. But don't worry, it won't be a problem." He was thinking that since I was staying the night at his hotel, it was probably important that I know.

"Know what?" My stomach clenched, and I almost asked if the hotel was haunted. That could be bad. But since he didn't know that I could sometimes hear ghosts, I kept my mouth shut.

"Let's see. Where to start? I guess at the beginning. You see, my grandfather began the business in New York after he arrived from Italy. He had two sons and several daughters who all worked together to make the business what it is today."

Uncle Joey took a breath and shrugged. "Needless to say, the two sons, one of which was my father, had a falling out. With my grandfather's blessing, and his half of the inheritance, my father left New York and ended up here. He continued the family business and thrived with several of his friends who came with him. You know the Barardinis, and the Falzones, and a few others that I won't name, but you get the picture.

"With only two living children, me and my sister, my father passed the business over to me. My sister... well, let's just say she wasn't suited for it. In fact, she became a nun, and I haven't seen her for years. Anyway, my cousins in New York got into some trouble.

"Over the years, several ended up in prison and others ended up dead. A few years ago, my cousin, Frank, contacted me. Our two families hadn't spoken for years, so it was a surprise to hear from him. He told me the family was basically destitute. The last thing they owned was up for auction, and he asked me if I'd consider buying it. So we worked out a deal."

Uncle Joey sat back in his chair. "Before my father passed, he warned me about getting involved with them, but what could I say? They're family. So I bought the hotel. My cousin, and what's left of the New York Manettos, is running it for me."

"Wow." I had no idea what else to say. With all the revelations coming at me, first from Ramos, and now Uncle Joey, it was turning into a crazy day.

"So I thought you should know, since you're going as my niece and all."

"What about Miguel? Does he know about this?"

"Yes." Uncle Joey leaned forward and met my gaze. "I filled him in last night, but I'd rather not tell them he's my son. If you know what I mean."

"Oh... yeah." I swallowed. "I take it you don't trust them?"

"One can never be too careful around mob families."

I nodded and just barely managed not to burst into hysterical laughter.

He caught my mirth and smiled. "You mistake my meaning. I only say that about mob families who are related by blood, not like what we have here. Blood relations tend to have a sense of entitlement, which ruins everything. See the difference?"

"Yeah, that makes perfect sense." I didn't want to point out that it hadn't stopped Kate from trying to take over the business a year ago. Although, since she thought she was Uncle Joey's niece, maybe he had it right. "So... what's the story about me? Am I still going as your niece?"

"Yes. Since Miguel thinks you're his cousin, we have to keep that up. So this is the story. I told Miguel that before my sister became a nun, she gave birth to a beautiful baby girl. She gave you up for adoption, and we found out about you a year ago. That explains how we just recently brought you and the kids into the family."

"What?" I felt the blood drain from my head and thought I might just pass out. "That's nuts!"

"No it isn't," he said, scrunching his brows together. "It works out great."

"But I told my kids that you were my aunt's first husband, and I knew you when I was a child before you were divorced, so I keep calling you my uncle, even though you're not anymore." Holy hell! Could this get any worse?

Uncle Joey's eyes narrowed. Then he nodded his head. "That's okay. I doubt the kids will ever talk to each other about it. But I guess we should have gotten our stories straight." He shrugged. "Oh well, nothing we can do about it now."

He caught my gaze, so I nodded my agreement, even though I was still in a state of shock.

"Anyway... an old friend of the family, Syd, is working there as the hotel manager. My cousin, Frank, doesn't know that Syd's been reporting to me, but if you need anything at all, he's the one you can trust. I don't expect any trouble from Frank, especially when it's just one night, but it pays to be prepared."

"Wait a minute. If they think I'm your niece, how does Miguel fit in?" If he thought I looked old enough to say I was his mother, I might just scream.

"It would never work to say you're his mother, you look too young for that, so I'm open to suggestions."

I let out my breath, relieved at least one thing was going my way. "Well, can't we still be cousins? I mean... if I'm adopted, I could still have cousins from my adoptive family, right?"

"Yes... I like that. And it's always a good idea to stick as close to the truth as possible, so you don't get mixed up."

"Right." Did he realize what he'd just said? The truth? No part of this was even close to the truth. Then I picked up that it was the truth as far as Miguel was concerned, so I guess that's what he meant, but still...

"I think that just about covers everything. I'll have Jackie call Frank and get it all arranged for your stay."

"Maybe we shouldn't stay the night..."

"I'm sure you'll be fine," he said. "But it's up to you." He was thinking Miguel would certainly be disappointed and, with my superpower, there really wasn't anything that could go wrong. Then he hoped he hadn't just told me his life story for nothing.

"Uh... you're right. We'll be fine if we stay. I'll go tell Chris right now."

"Good. When I find out what time Ramos is meeting this Dusty person, I'll let you know. But it will probably be late."

"Okay."

I left the office in a bit of a daze, wondering how my life got so complicated so fast. Tonight, I'd agreed to spy on Ramos, even though he would hate it, and tomorrow I was on my way to New York and meeting the rest of the Manetto family.

It seemed a bit overwhelming, so I took a deep breath and decided to take it one step at a time so I wouldn't freak out. First, I concentrated on my mission at the club tonight and how that might work out.

All at once, my stomach got a little queasy. Would Ramos forgive me if I showed up? Would it ruin our friendship? Would he ever trust me with his secrets again?

By the time I got to the car, guilt had punched a painful hole in my chest. Even though I could always blame Uncle Joey, there had to be something else I could do. Then it hit me. I still had my black wig. I could just wear that, and hang out in a corner somewhere. Ramos would never know I was there.

Relieved, I massaged my chest, and let out my breath.

Chapter 4

I stepped off the elevator and waved at the receptionist, then walked around the corner toward Chris' office. Since I hadn't called or sent a text to let him know I was coming, I hoped I wouldn't be interrupting anything.

At least I knew he was there, since he'd just talked to Uncle Joey. And with any luck I hoped we could go out to lunch together, since I'd mostly missed breakfast. Plus, with everything else that had happened so far, I needed some time to unwind.

Chris' executive assistant, Elisa, sat at her desk outside his office, looking gorgeous as usual. She glanced up and smiled with surprise to see me.

"Hey Shelby. I didn't know you were coming in today." She glanced over my clothes, thinking I'd dressed up like I was in a motorcycle gang or something. All I needed was a helmet in my hand and she might believe it. But on second thought, that was just silly. I was a housewife, I didn't ride motorcycles.

I clenched my jaw to keep from blurting that she was wrong, and somehow managed to smile without showing my teeth. "Hi Elisa. Is Chris in his office?"

"Yes. Go on in."

"Thanks."

I pushed the door open and stepped inside. After this morning's revelations, it did my heart good to set my eyes on the man I loved. Chris glanced up from his paperwork, surprised to see me. "Hey gorgeous," he said, leaning back in his chair and smiling broadly. "I didn't expect to see you here."

I smiled back, drinking in the warmth in his eyes, and shrugged. "I was over at Uncle Joey's office when you finished talking to him. He was going to call you back about tomorrow, so I told him I'd just come over and tell you instead."

"Yeah, about that..." Chris began, pursing his lips in frustration. "You didn't tell me you'd agreed to go to New York with Miguel."

"I didn't?" I paused in front of his desk, knowing Chris wasn't up to giving me a hug and a kiss right now. "Oh crap! I'm sorry."

"Yeah, Manetto just told me over the phone a few minutes ago. I had to pretend like I knew all about it."

"Uh... that's too bad. I guess I forgot." With a sigh, I sat down in the chair in front of his desk, hoping he wouldn't be mad at me for too long.

He was thinking that I conveniently forgot, since that meant I got to go gallivanting off to the Big Apple. Of course, it was hard to refuse those kinds of offers from Uncle Joey, so he couldn't really blame me. "So... did you tell him you wanted to stay and see the play?"

"Uh... yeah. He kind of made me an offer I couldn't refuse."

"You might as well," he said, surprising me with his candor. As much as he didn't like it, he knew I didn't have much of a choice when it came to Manetto. "I mean, if you're going all that way, you might as well see the play while you're at it." He knew going to New York and seeing a Broadway play was something I'd always wanted to do. He just wished he was the one taking me.

I brightened. "Maybe you could come too."

Chris shook his head. "No, I can't. I've got a deposition in the morning that I can't miss. But why exactly does Manetto want you to go? Miguel's old enough to go on his own, isn't he? Or at least with Jackie... or his own mother."

"Yeah, but Uncle Joey wants me to listen to their thoughts so he'll know if Miguel really has a chance at making a career out of his singing."

"Oh... yeah... of course. I didn't think about that." He sighed. "Well, I guess I'd better call the agent back and let him know you're coming and you want the tickets."

"Yeah," I agreed. "And we'll be staying the night at Uncle Joey's hotel. Did you know he owned a hotel in New York?"

"No, I didn't, but it doesn't surprise me. He seems to have connections everywhere."

"That's true. Anyway, he told me this crazy story about the hotel. Apparently he has cousins there, and they run the hotel for him."

"Are you serious?"

"Yeah." I nodded. "He calls them the New York Manettos. So it should be interesting."

"Wait... what does this mean about you? Is he keeping to the story that you're related?"

"Yes, but with a few twists." I explained the whole story, that I was now adopted, and my real mother was Uncle Joey's sister. Chris got a kick out of that, especially the part about his sister being a nun.

"Hey, that part's not made up."

Chris snorted with laughter and shook his head. "What about Miguel? Do they know about him?"

"Uh... he didn't want them to know about Miguel yet, so he's going to be my cousin, like he is now only.... you know... from my adopted side of the family."

Chris sat up straight, and his brows drew together with concern. "Why doesn't he just tell them?"

"I don't think he trusts them with that information, and I don't blame him." I shrugged. "So... it should be interesting."

Chris was thinking that if Uncle Joey was concerned about Miguel, then what about me? If they thought I was his niece, couldn't that be bad as well? Why hadn't Manetto thought about that?

"He's got an inside man there who will be watching out for us. I think his name's Syd. We'll be fine. You don't need to worry. Plus, it's only overnight. As long as the hotel's not haunted, we'll be fine."

"Oh... yeah. I guess you have to worry about that too. An old hotel... that could be bad, especially if it's been in a mob family for a lot of years. Who knows how many people could have died there?" He shook his head. "How do you get into these things?"

My lips twisted into a frown, and I scowled at him. If he wanted me to feel bad, he was doing a great job of it.

"Shelby," Chris said, holding out his hand. "Come here."

I let out my breath, then stood and took his hand. He promptly pulled me onto his lap. Grateful his chair was extra roomy, I snuggled against him and laid my head on his shoulder. His warmth and love seeped into my skin, and I finally relaxed in his arms.

He was thinking that he hated sending me off, but this wasn't anything like the last time. I'd be fine, especially with Manetto looking out for me. Manetto would never let anything happen, so he shouldn't worry... and it was just overnight.

"I hate to admit it," I said. "But now I'm a little nervous about going."

"Hey, it'll be fun to go to New York," he said, wanting to reassure me. "This is nothing like Paris. You're not meeting with spies or anything crazy. You'll be fine. Just... try not to get into trouble, okay?"

I pulled back to meet his gaze. "Hey... I never try to get into trouble."

"I know, I know. But if you hear something you're not supposed to know, just keep it to yourself and tell Manetto when you get back. Don't try to fix it."

I huffed out a breath. "Geeze honey, you make me sound like a moron." I struggled to get off his lap, but he wouldn't let me up.

"I didn't mean it that way Shelby... I love you. I just want you to come back in one piece."

I stopped struggling and caught his gaze. "I will, I promise."

His brows rose, and he thought *you'd better*. So I kissed him to seal the deal. After a thoroughly hot kissing session, I pulled away. We were both a bit breathless, and neither of us was thinking about my departure in the morning.

A loud knock sounded at the door. With a groan, Chris helped me stand before clearing his throat, and called for the interloper to enter. Ethan opened the door, knowing he had interrupted us, but since people could see into the office, he thought it was a good idea, especially since it was giving Elisa fits.

"Hey, Mrs. Nichols. How are you?"

"Good, thanks. And call me Shelby."

"Uh... sure," he agreed, but knew that would never happen. I was his boss' wife. Calling me by my first name was just wrong. "I don't mean to interrupt, but I've got those files you wanted to go over before your client gets here in fifteen minutes."

"Sure," Chris said. "Bring them in, and I'll walk Shelby out."

"I guess this means we can't have lunch together?" I asked.

"Afraid not." As we walked to the elevator, Chris pulled me close. "I'm glad you came, though."

"Yeah, me too." Whispering, I asked, "Have you figured out what's going on with Ethan yet?" A week ago, I'd picked up that Ethan had ties to the district attorney's offices and was interested in Chris because he represented Uncle Joey.

"Not yet. You might have to help me with that."

"Okay, maybe when I get back. In the meantime, be careful. You can't trust him, remember that."

"I know. I'll be careful." He thought it ironic that I was telling him to be careful for a change. But he liked it. The elevator doors slid open. "I'll see you tonight."

"Uh, yeah... see you later." I hadn't told him about my visit to the club, but there wasn't time now. I only hoped he'd take it as well as my trip to New York. He gave me a quick kiss, and I stepped onto the elevator.

As the doors slid shut, I blurted, "Don't forget to call the agent." I caught his nod before he disappeared.

In the parking lot, I got in my car and checked my phone, finding I'd missed a couple of calls. The first was from Kyle, so I called him back.

"I talked to my sister," he began. "She thought we could come to her house after school today and talk to Keola. Will that work for you?"

"Sure. What time?"

"Three o'clock."

"Okay. Text me her address and I'll meet you there."

The second message was from Dimples, wanting to know if I could stop by the precinct. With everything on my plate, I really didn't want to go over there, but I could always call first and see how important it was, right? With a sigh, I pushed his number.

"Hey Shelby, thanks for getting back to me," he said. "Are you busy?"

"Actually, yes. I'm pretty busy for the next couple of days. What's going on? Can it wait?"

"Uh... not really. This is a big deal, and I need your help. I've got a kid here who won't talk, and I thought maybe you could sit in on the questioning. It shouldn't take long. His parents are here with him, but I think I can get them to wait for a few more minutes if you say you'll come. Okay? Please?"

I checked my watch. It was just a few minutes past one o'clock, so that gave me plenty of time. I was kind of starving to death, but when he asked me like that, how could I turn him down? "Sure. I'm not far from there, so I'll be right over."

"Great. Thanks so much. See you soon."

We disconnected and I let out a sigh, then scrounged around in my purse for a granola bar. All I came up with was an empty wrapper. Didn't they usually have donuts sitting around in police stations? Maybe today would be my lucky day and I could get one with sprinkles.

After parking, I got my special ID badge out of the glove box and slipped the lanyard over my head. Inside the precinct, I took my time getting to Dimples' desk, hoping to spy a box of donuts on someone's work station. My stomach gurgled with anticipation, but I couldn't even see a box in the garbage. What was wrong with these cops?

In the detective's offices, Dimples waved me over. As I approached, he shoved the last of something into his mouth and started chewing.

"Was that a donut?" I asked.

"Um... yeah. The family's waiting in the office, so let me tell you what's going on."

My stomach growled, and I sighed. "Fine, but I want one after."

He smiled, and his dimples started doing that crazy dance that always made me smile, so I couldn't be mad at him for too long.

"Sure," he agreed. "First of all, we think the kid might know who sold some drugs to a couple of junior high school students. One of them died, and the other one's in a coma."

"Oh no. That's terrible. What school was it?" My heart rate jumped at the thought of it happening at Savannah's junior high school. These could be kids I knew.

"Jefferson Junior," he said.

"Oh." My breath came out in a relieved whoosh. Not hers after all. Still, that was awful news. "How did you know to question this kid?"

"He's best friends with the other two, so we were hoping he'd know something, but so far, he's not offering anything. This drug is deadly, and we'd like to stop anyone else from taking it."

"What do his parents say?"

"Well, as you can imagine they're pretty defensive and worried about us questioning him, but I'm sure there's more that you could pick up... you know?" He was thinking because I was so special like that.

I smiled. "I'll do my best."

He led the way into the room where the parents sat on the couch, and the boy sat in a chair next to them. His eyes were shut and he leaned forward, resting his elbows on his knees and holding his face in his hands.

His hair was shaved on the sides, but long and hanging over his eyes in the front. His jeans and a ragged hoodie covered his thin frame. He looked about fifteen, and I picked up that he was scared out of his mind.

"Hello," Dimples began. "Thanks for waiting. This is Shelby Nichols, a special consultant with the police. We just have a few questions for Owen, and then you can go."

The parents nodded, and I picked up panic from them both. They worried that this could be Owen's fault, but if he confessed, what would happen to him? It had to be an innocent mistake. They couldn't let him go to jail. He was just a kid.

I took a seat on the chair across from them and picked up that while they'd waited for us, the father had told Owen not to say anything that might incriminate him. He'd basically told Owen to keep his mouth shut until they got a lawyer, and I knew it was a good thing I'd come.

Dimples grabbed a folding chair and pulled it closer to Owen, then sat down facing him. "You know that Wyatt died, right?"

At Owen's quick nod, Dimples continued. "Well, Cole's in a coma, and they're not sure he's going to make it. I need to know what drug they took, and where they got it. We don't want anyone else to die. Do you know where the drug came from?"

"I told you, I don't know anything." He was panicking and wondering how this could have happened. Wyatt must have taken them from his backpack and given some to Cole. The stupid idiot. Now he was dead? It couldn't be true.

"Who gave you the drug?" I asked.

He shot a quick glance my way before lowering his gaze, not about to breathe a word about Tory. He knew her old man put her up to it, and she couldn't say no to her dad without suffering the consequences. Besides, they looked like normal pain pills. They weren't illegal. That was the only reason he'd agreed to tell some of the kids at his school. But it had all gone wrong. Wyatt couldn't be dead. It was all a lie.

"Did they look like regular pain pills?" I asked. His eyes widened, and he sucked in a breath, then nodded his head in surprise. "That's good to know. Thank you." I glanced at Dimples, giving him a slight nod.

Dimples sighed and stood before speaking. "I guess that's all for now, but if you remember anything that might help us, please give me a call." He took out his card and handed it to the father, then turned to Owen and placed a hand on his shoulder. "Remember, we don't want anyone else to die."

Owen shuddered and gave a quick nod. He swore in his mind that he'd never be caught dead with anything like that again. Then he thought that if Wyatt hadn't taken the packet of pills, he might have tried one himself, and he'd be dead. On that frightening thought, he stood, eager to get out of there.

After they left, Dimples sat down next to me. "So what did you get?"

"A girl named Tory from his school gave them to him, but he was thinking her old man put her up to it, like she didn't have much of a choice in the matter. I also picked up that Owen didn't actually give the drugs to his friends. He was thinking that they must have taken them out of his backpack after he'd told them about it."

"Okay. That's a great lead. Thanks Shelby." He was thinking he'd find out who Tory was from the school, and then see if her father had a record. If he did, they could always bring him in for questioning without putting Tory in danger, although they might need me for that too.

"Sure," I agreed. "As long as it gets this drug off the street."

We wandered back to Dimples' desk where I noticed the napkin and crumbs from his donut. "So where's the donuts?"

"Uh... there's a box here somewhere." He glanced around the room, then pointed to a pink box on the breakroom shelf next to the coffee and mugs. "There should be two boxes. If that's the box with one donut left, don't eat it."

I hurried over and pulled back the lid to find one plain, glazed donut. I turned to ask Dimples why he'd told me not to eat it, but he was talking to one of the other detectives.

Had someone else called for it? It didn't look the best, which was probably why it was still there, but I was starving. I grabbed a napkin and picked it up, then took a bite. It might be a little stale, but not too bad. I caught Detective Bates staring at me. He wondered if that was the last donut and I'd just taken a bite.

I smiled at him and kept chewing. If he'd called for it, I didn't feel too bad about beating him to it, since he was the one detective in the whole precinct who didn't like me much. Then I picked up that no one had eaten that donut because they all thought a suspect may have spit on it.

Gah! I froze, then gagged a little and quickly spit it out into my hand. All the noise I made caught Dimples' attention, and he rushed over and pounded me on the back.

"Are you okay?" He checked the box, then swore in his mind. "I told you not to eat that." He grabbed a paper cup and filled it with water. "Here. Drink this."

Instead of drinking it, I swished the water around in my mouth and spit it out into the sink. After doing that a couple of times, I leaned over the sink to catch my breath, and tried not to think about what I'd just done. In that moment, I knew I could never eat another glazed donut again in my life.

"Hey... look what I found," Bates said, coming to my side with a similar box. "It was in the garbage." He opened it, and there was a glazed donut sitting in the corner. Droplets of moisture had soaked into the box in a spraying pattern around it.

"Eww. You mean... that's the one? Not the one I was eating?"

"Yeah. Yours was fine," he said.

I slumped against the counter in relief, picking up that Bates was impressed. Now he had to believe that my premonitions really worked, or I wouldn't have had such a violent reaction to the donut. Somehow, I'd picked up that a donut had been spit on. Too bad it wasn't until after I'd taken a bite, but at least it had been highly entertaining to watch.

"Uh... thanks for showing me that," I said.

"Sure." He smiled and threw the box into the garbage, then went back to his desk.

Dimples handed me another napkin, and I wiped my mouth. "Are you all right now?" he asked.

"Better, thanks. But that was disgusting."

"Sorry about that." His brows drew down with concern, but he pressed his lips together real hard to hold back his laughter. The look on my face when I'd spit out the donut...

"Go ahead and laugh," I said. "I guess it's funny now."

He chuckled and shook his head, thinking *only Shelby*.

"Uh... I'm going now. Good luck with those kids. Let me know if you need me again. Uh... I'm not available tomorrow, but maybe the next day."

"Oh yeah? What are you doing?"

"I'm headed to New York." That sort of came out automatically. Then I realized who I was talking to and knew I couldn't tell him the truth.

"Wow, that's cool. What are you doing there?"

"Uh," I said, panicking a little. "Just a little sight-seeing, and then we're going to a Broadway play. Something I've always wanted to do. It's a real quick trip, but it should be fun."

Dimples thought by 'we' I meant me and Chris. I wasn't about to say a word to correct his thinking, since that meant I wasn't lying to him... exactly. So why did a pang of guilt hit me between the eyes?

"Nice. Well, have fun."

"We will. Thanks!" I hurried out of there, hoping I wouldn't get struck by lightning for lying, even if it was by omission. Still, could this day get any crazier?

I made it home and grabbed a cookie, then stuck a piece of bread in the toaster. While it cooked, I searched my closet for my black wig and found it in a box on the bottom shelf. It was mostly intact, but some of the bangs were poking up, so I tried to fix it.

Of course, without a head to put it on, I didn't have much luck. So I pulled my hair back into a bun, and put the wig on. Then I had to wet the bangs down and use the hair dryer and a round brush to get it to look right.

By the time I got it fixed and straight on my head, I figured it would do the job. But would it fool Ramos? He certainly wouldn't be expecting to see me there, so maybe. Plus, it had been about a year since I last wore the wig, so he wouldn't put it together even if he saw me from the back, right?

My stomach growled, and I hurried to the kitchen to find my toast dry and hard. I added some butter and ate it anyway. That's when I realized that I needed to pack for

New York. Since I'd never been to a Broadway play, I had no idea what to wear. Did people dress up?

I shuffled through my closet and pulled out the short, black, lace dress I'd gotten on a winter clearance sale. It still had on the tags since I'd never worn it, but it might be just the perfect thing to wear to the play. Sophisticated, but sassy and cute at the same time.

Since it was just overnight, I grabbed my smallest carry-on bag and opened it up. Besides an extra shirt along with the dress and shoes, all I needed was my make-up and a pair of pajamas. That left plenty of room for a souvenir or two, so I hoped I got a chance to do some shopping.

On the drive over to Keola's house, it hit me that things were moving along at a breakneck speed, and I sure hoped I could keep up. At least talking to Keola should put an end to helping Shannon and Kyle, so I wouldn't have that on my plate anymore.

I parked on the street behind Kyle's car, grateful he was already there. He answered the door and ushered me inside, then introduced his sister, Lahni.

"Nice to meet you," she said. "Keola's not here yet, but I expect him any minute. Please sit down." She ushered me to the couch, thinking that her son was the cause of all this trouble and she hoped I could tell him something to straighten him up. She'd done all she could, but it hadn't helped much and just made her look like a bad mother. She didn't like that one bit.

Kyle was hoping I could perform some kind of miracle as well, because he wasn't too happy about going back to the bar or the gang after finding out Shannon was pregnant. He thought Keola was acting like an idiot, and he hoped it would stop before the kid made any stupid mistakes.

Lahni sighed, thinking Keola was late and she hoped he hadn't seen me or Kyle outside and taken off. He was usually home by now, so where was he? Shaking her head, she picked up her phone. "I'll give him a call and see where he is."

I worried that he wouldn't answer, but was pleasantly surprised to hear Lahni talking to him. From her mind, I picked up that he was at a friend's house. Lahni told him he needed to come home right this minute, but he argued with her and disconnected before agreeing to anything.

"I don't think he's coming home for a while," Lahni said, discouraged. "Can we set it up for another time?"

"Sure," I agreed. "Hey, does he go to Jefferson Jr. High?"

"No. He's in high school. Why?"

"Oh yeah that's right. But you should know that there were a couple of kids at Jefferson who took some kind of pills. One of them is dead, and the other is in a coma. You should ask him if he's heard about anyone selling pills, and tell him that they're lethal. If he knows anything, it might be helpful to call the police."

Lahni sucked in a shocked breath. "That's terrible. You think he might be involved?"

"No, not at all. I'd just hate for anyone else to, you know... die."

"Yes," she agreed. "Of course. I'll be sure and talk to him about it."

"Good. I'd still like to talk to him myself, but I'm busy tomorrow. Maybe the next day?"

"Yeah, sure. I'll set it up and call you and Kyle."

"Sounds good. Here's my card." I stood, offering her my business card.

"Thanks." She took the card, thinking that this was more serious than she realized, and Keola better not be involved with drugs or he was grounded forever.

Kyle followed me out, wondering if I'd had a premonition that Keola was involved with the pills and that's why I'd brought it up. How else did I know about it? But that was just freaky. He wanted to ask, but he couldn't bring himself to admit I could be psychic or something.

I got to my car and turned toward him. "Was there something you wanted to ask me?"

"Uh... yeah," he stammered. "Do your premonitions tell you Keola's involved with these pills?"

I shrugged. "I don't know for sure, but he's involved in something, so it doesn't hurt to ask him about it, right?"

"Absolutely," he said. "Thanks. I think I'll stick around a little longer and see if I can talk to him."

"That's a good idea. Call me when you have something set up so I can talk to him, too."

"I will. Uh... thanks Shelby." Kyle didn't want to admit that he was sorry we got off on the wrong foot, so thanking me was the best he could do.

"Sure." I nodded and got in my car.

I got home at a little after four. Savannah and Josh were already there, so I sat them down and asked if they'd heard about anyone selling pills. Lucky for me, all I got were blank stares and blank thoughts. I explained about the two boys at the junior high school, and that I was helping with the police investigation.

"If you hear anyone talking about it at school, please let me know, okay?"

They both assured me that they would. After talking for a few more minutes about school and their homework, I told them I was headed to New York with Miguel in the morning.

"What?" Savannah asked. "How come you're going?"

"Uncle Joey wanted me to go," I explained. "He's uh... hoping I can pick up something with my premonitions about how well Miguel does in his audition."

"Oh... I get it," Josh said, thinking that was the connection. I worked for Uncle Joey because of my premonitions. Now it all made sense. So what exactly did he do? "Do you help him out a lot?" He was thinking that if he could get me to tell him what sorts of jobs I did, it would help him know more about Uncle Joey's business dealings.

"Now and then," I hedged. "Anyway, Miguel's audition is in the afternoon, but we're staying to see *Aladdin*, and then we'll be home early the next day."

"You're seeing the play?" Savannah cried, a surge of jealousy rushing over her. She could hardly believe that I was going with Miguel, like he was my kid or something. Sharing me with Miguel hardly seemed right. What about his own mother? So what if I had premonitions, that didn't mean I should go with him.

Yikes! I certainly hadn't expected that. "Hey, I'm sure if Miguel gets the part, we'll all go to the play in New York to see him. That's lots better than seeing whoever they have now, right?"

"I guess," she answered. "Do you think he will?"

"I think he has a good chance."

"She'll know tomorrow," Josh answered, catching my gaze. "Right, Mom?"

"I think I'll have a good idea."

He nodded, then glanced at Savannah. "Don't worry, Savvy, you'll know soon enough if you get to go to New York. Besides, it's nice that Mom can help Miguel out, right?"

Wow, when did he get so grown up? But what was that underlying glint in his eyes for?

"Yeah. Sure." She caught my gaze, thinking I had it pretty good, but she was also glad someone in the family would be with Miguel. "So what are you going to wear to the play?"

"Let me show you," I said, taking the opportunity to get out from under Josh's all too correct scrutiny. "And you can tell me what you think." She followed me upstairs, and we shared some girl time as I showed her the dress.

"That's perfect," she agreed. "You'll look great. Hey... maybe while you're there you can pick up something for me?"

My eyes widened with surprise. Wow, she had great manipulation skills to capitalize on my guilt like that. "I suppose I could. There might be a cute stuffed animal you'd like."

"Mom! I'm too old for that."

I grinned to let her know I was teasing... sort of. "I'll see what I can do."

"Yeah, and... maybe Miguel could help you?"

"Okay," I said. "I'll ask him." How could I say no after hearing her thoughts that I was putting Miguel above her? Another pang of guilt ran through me. Dang, why did she have to think that?

It wasn't until I was fixing dinner that something she'd thought hit me between the eyes. Savannah had been thinking that I was going with Miguel because we were family. It wasn't just a job. This time, it was family, and I knew that no matter what happened next, we'd just passed the point of no return. The Manettos were now considered family. Unease slid down my spine. What had I gotten my kids into?

Chapter 5

I got a text from Uncle Joey around eight, telling me Ricky would be there at ten to pick me up. He apologized that it was so late, but it couldn't be helped. I sighed. On the good side, at least my kids would be in bed, so they wouldn't need to know, but what should I tell Chris?

I didn't want to tell him Ramos' story, especially since no one was supposed to know... and, you know, it was Ramos. Chris didn't like to hear me talk about Ramos. So it was probably best to leave him out and tell Chris that Uncle Joey just needed me to eavesdrop on someone at the club. No big deal.

Still, I waited until the last minute to bring it up, probably because I hated confrontation, and I was a big fat chicken. At nine forty-five, I slipped on my black jeans, boots, and my red, eyelet-laced top. Then I pulled my hair back and pinned it down. Next, I fixed the wig over my head and tugged it into place. I darkened my eyebrows to match and put on my red lipstick.

Hmm... I studied my reflection in the mirror, adding a bit of dark eyeshadow. I nodded with relief at the results. I hardly looked like me anymore. This could actually work. I slipped on my leather motorcycle jacket and found Chris in the kitchen.

He glanced at me, and his brows rose up to his hairline. "What the hell?"

Oops. That wasn't exactly the response I'd expected. "Uh... what do you think? Do I look like me?"

He shook his head. "What's going on?"

"I have to go to Uncle Joey's club. He wants me to eavesdrop on someone, so I'm going incognito." At his widened eyes, I continued, "I don't even have to sit anywhere near them, so they won't know I'm there, but I thought, why take a chance I'd be recognized, you know?"

When he still didn't respond, I kept talking. "I thought this might be better after the Russians mistook me for the blond who double-crossed them. I mean who's going to know it's me with the wig, right?"

Chris rubbed his face and sighed. "Okay. So when are you going?"

My phone buzzed with a text. It was Ricky saying he was waiting in my driveway. "Uh... it looks like Ricky's here to pick me up."

"Right now?"

"Uh-huh. But there's nothing to worry about, and it shouldn't take long. I'll be back before you know it! Love you." I waved and hurried out the door, eager to put a little distance between us since he wasn't too happy with me. Plus, I felt guilty enough without hearing all of his frustration, even if I deserved it.

I picked up Ricky's shock that I looked totally different after I sat down in the front seat. He snapped his mouth shut without saying a word and backed out of the driveway. But that didn't stop him from wondering why I was wearing the wig.

"Uh... Ramos didn't want me to come tonight, so I thought if I wore the wig he wouldn't know I was there."

"Oh, sure," he said. He could understand not wanting to get on Ramos' bad side. So why was I going?

"Uncle Joey asked me to go," I explained. "Uh... what could I say?" He nodded, surprised that I'd answered his thoughts, so I continued, "You don't say no to the big boss, right?"

"Yeah. That's true."

Since it seemed like I was just digging a deep, dark hole from which I could never escape, I kept my mouth shut after that. Ricky wasn't one to talk much anyway, and I finally relaxed for the rest of the drive. Ricky pulled into the back and parked in Uncle Joey's reserved stall. He turned off the ignition and checked his watch, then turned to me.

"Mr. Manetto told me that Ramos' friend would be showing up any time now. There's a corner booth reserved for us where we can sit and observe most of the room. You ready?"

"Yeah."

"Okay, let's go."

We entered through the same back entrance that I'd come through just that morning. This time, we took a different hallway to a door that led into the club. I followed Ricky's lead, slipping through the door as quietly as possible.

On the other side, we came to the left side of the stage with a curtain shielding it. A band was playing live music, and it was loud and dark, so I could hardly see or hear a thing.

Ricky pushed the curtain aside and we stepped out onto the crowded dance floor. Ricky took the lead, and I followed him toward the bar and a small corner booth with a reserved sign on the table. The cushioned seat went around the circular table, making it a great place from which to observe both the crowd and the bar.

Before I sat down, I glanced at the bar and surrounding tables hoping to spot Ramos before he spotted me. Not finding him anywhere, I let out my breath and slid toward the back corner, hoping my luck held and he never found out I was there.

To my surprise, Ricky didn't sit with me. He just nodded and moved toward the bar. I picked up that he was letting security know I was there, so they could keep an eye on me like Uncle Joey had instructed. A nice, warm feeling came over me. Uncle Joey really did care. Just then, a waitress stopped by with a drink and scooped up the reserved sign.

"Diet Coke with lime," she said with a smile, disappearing almost as quickly as she'd come. Whoa, was I a V.I.P. or what? Getting the royal treatment certainly helped my queasy stomach, since I was basically here to spy on Ramos. Now if I could manage to stay out of his sight for the next little bit, I'd be home free.

For something to do, I took the paper off the straw and took a swig. Trying to act casual, I glanced at the bar and nearly choked. Ramos leaned casually on one elbow, staring straight at me, his gaze hard and unforgiving. His lips thinned, and one of his brows rose. Caught like a deer in the headlights, I couldn't take my gaze off him.

Dressed all in black, with his motorcycle jacket hanging open, he exuded danger from every tantalizing muscle. I couldn't pick up a thing from his thoughts. Unless... wait... who was I fooling? That wave of frustration and anger could only be coming from him. My eyes widened and I swallowed. But as long as he stayed where he was, I should be okay, right?

He straightened to his full six-foot-four-inch height, then grabbed his drink and stalked over to my booth. I stiffened with alarm. My heart raced with that fight or flight instinct, but before I could move a muscle, Ramos slid into the booth right next to me, pretty much blocking my only way out.

"Babe," he said, his voice a low growl. His gaze swept over my face, pausing for a moment on my red lips before shifting to catch my gaze. "What are you doing here?"

"Uh..." I swallowed, then shrugged. "Would it help if I said I was looking out for a friend?"

"No."

"Uh... okay, well then, how about if I said Uncle Joey made me do it? Because he totally did, and you can't say no to a mob-boss."

Ramos shook his head. "Then why are you wearing the wig?" This time I picked up a wave of mirth under his act of outrage. Then I caught that he was thinking that the bangs were poking out a little on the side. I automatically smoothed the bangs down and caught a grin that he tried to hide.

I huffed with indignation. "How did you know it was me so fast? I think I look totally different."

He shook his head, wondering how in the hell I thought I could fool him.

"Hey... maybe in the dark... and from a distance it could work."

"There's not a disguise in the world that would keep me from knowing you, Shelby. You're one of a kind. But I'll give you points for trying."

I wasn't sure if that was a compliment or not. "So are you still mad at me?"

He snorted with derision. "Hell yes. But since you're here..." He shrugged, then glanced toward the bar and froze. His jaw clenched at the sight of Dusty. Then he glanced at me thinking *play along*. He slid his arm around my shoulders and pulled me against his side, leaving plenty of room on the other side of the table.

The bartender pointed Dusty our way, and a smile broke out on his face. It surprised me that, behind the smile, Dusty was genuinely happy to see Ramos, and some of my worry disappeared.

"Ace!" he said, using Ramos' nickname and rushing to our table. "It's so good to see you, man. It's been... forever. How are you?" He held out his hand for Ramos to shake. Ramos hesitated for an uncomfortable moment before finally reciprocating.

Ramos motioned for Dusty to sit down in the booth with us and introduced me. "This is Shelby."

"Good to meet you. I'm Dusty McAllister. Ramos and I go way back." He glanced at Ramos, thinking he hadn't changed a bit. Still the cold-hearted bastard he knew from before. "How long has it been anyway?"

"About ten years," Ramos answered.

"Almost eleven," Dusty countered. "Still, it's hard to believe how much time has passed since those days. I hear you've made quite a name for yourself." He was thinking that Ramos' name was legendary as a hit-man with ties to organized crime, and a tingle of unease ran down his spine.

He was thinking that if he knew what was good for him, he wouldn't mess with a man like Ramos. He was taking a huge risk to come here, but if everything went according to his plans, it was a chance he was willing to take. Now he just had to convince Ramos to play his part, and hope he never found out the real reason until after it was all over.

As the silence between them increased, Dusty grew uncomfortable. Ramos wasn't asking about Jodie, and he wondered how he could bring her up without sounding abrupt. She was the only angle he could use that might allow him to pull this off. "Did you hear Jodie's coming to town?" he finally said.

"Yeah," Ramos answered. He wanted to ask about her but wouldn't give Dusty the satisfaction since it was obvious that was exactly what he was after.

"You've probably heard that she's done well for herself," Dusty said, as if Ramos had asked about her. "She's won a few Grammy Awards. Her first album even went platinum." Ramos didn't respond, so Dusty swallowed and continued. "Anyway... she's the reason I'm here. She heard you lived in the city and wanted to say hello. That's why I've been trying to meet with you. I've got a couple of tickets to her show on Friday with a backstage pass. I thought maybe you'd like to come. You can bring Shelby." He glanced at me. "Would you like to go?"

"Sure," I said. "That would be amazing." I caught Ramos' gaze. "We should go." Dusty was lying. Jodie had no idea Ramos was here, so what was Dusty up to?

Sighing with relief, Dusty pulled an envelope from his pocket and handed it to Ramos, grateful that I was a witness to the transaction, and hoping the person following him was watching.

Alarmed, I snatched it out of his hand before Ramos could take it. "Sweet! Let me see." I tore the top open and pulled out the tickets, then held them up with a wave. "This is great! Tickets to the concert! Thanks so much!"

Ramos sat back, wondering what was going on. Dusty's eyes bulged a little, then he glanced at the envelope, grateful the packet hadn't fallen out. But that was close. What the hell was he going to do if I noticed it? It would ruin everything.

Smiling, I slipped the tickets back inside the envelope, and felt the bottom corner with my fingertips. Yup. Something else was in there, but I couldn't tell what it was.

So what was Dusty up to? Was he trying to frame Ramos? Get him in trouble? Who was the guy following him? Was he close by and watching?

"What's the real reason you're here?" Ramos asked, raising an eyebrow. "And don't give me any of that crap about Jodie wanting to see me. That's the last thing she'd want, and we both know it."

"That's not true," Dusty said. But he knew it sounded hollow, and Ramos wasn't buying it. He swallowed, and then nodded. "Fine. You're right. She doesn't know you're here, but I know she'd like a chance to see you, even if it's only to tell you off. You broke her heart, and she never got over it."

"She got married, didn't she?" Ramos shot back.

Dusty snorted. "Yeah, but it didn't last. You know that." When Ramos didn't respond, Dusty went in for the kill. "Did you know she has a ten-year-old daughter?" He held Ramos' gaze, clearly implying this was something Ramos needed to know.

Ramos didn't move a muscle, but his heart sped up, and he swore a blue streak in his mind. He hadn't known anything about that. Then he narrowed his eyes and cocked his head to one side. "Are you implying that she's mine?"

Dusty leaned back on the bench. "I don't think Jodie knows for sure. But she could be yours. Don't you want to know?" He took a photo from his wallet and set it on the table. "Maybe it's time you found out." He pushed the photo of a sweet, smiling, dark-haired girl toward Ramos. "Her name's Lacie."

Ramos held Dusty's gaze, not wanting to look at the photo and get taken in by the conniving weasel. But the temptation was too great, and his gaze slid to the picture, drinking in her dark hair, happy smile, and large brown eyes. He swallowed. She was a beautiful kid. Did she look like him?

He let out his breath, trying to remember the photo he'd seen of Jodie and the man she'd been married to. He knew they hooked up right after Ramos left. That guy had even looked Latino like him, but he couldn't picture his face, so that didn't help. Dusty was probably up to something, and this was just part of the ruse to get Ramos to take the bait.

"Just come to the concert," Dusty said. "You can talk to Jodie and settle things between you."

Ramos shook his head, not trusting Dusty for a minute, but his heart said something different. He wanted to see Jodie, if only to tell her he was sorry about the way he'd left all those years ago. And if the girl in the picture was his... no, he couldn't think like that. It was too much. She would have told him... except... he'd disappeared without a trace.

Concerned that his reasons weren't working, Dusty made one last pitch. "Lacie's on tour with us. Jodie might want you to meet her."

Dusty was hiding something, so I jumped into the conversation and asked the first thing that came to mind. "What about her education? Shouldn't she be in school?"

He glanced at me with annoyance. "She has a tutor who travels with us. Jody wouldn't neglect her own daughter like that." I picked up that Dusty had a lot of conflicted feelings about the tutor. There was some anger and even a little hate... along with love, affection and downright misery. Yikes. It sounded to me like he was in love with a crazy person, and I felt a little sorry for him.

"Besides, Jodie's got a boyfriend now," he said to Ramos. "So you don't have to worry that she'd want to get back together with you... which is a good thing in my opinion."

Ramos sent him a piercing glare before giving in. "Fine. I'll come." Then he leaned forward and grabbed the front of

Dusty's jacket, pulling him close and letting him see the menace in his eyes. "And between now and then, I promise you that I'll find out what this is really all about, and when I do, you're going to answer for it."

"Hey." Dusty pulled back but couldn't get out of Ramos' grip until he let him go. Dusty sent Ramos a glare and straightened his collar. "Geeze man, there's nothing going on. I'm just looking out for my sister."

While tugging at his sleeves, Dusty glanced at the bar, then at the surrounding people, before his gaze came back to our booth. He hoped the idiot following him had missed that. But even if he hadn't, it wouldn't matter in the long run. Things would work out just fine. They had to.

He pulled a special V.I.P. pass from his pocket and handed it to me. "Make sure you bring this when you come. It will get you backstage for a few minutes alone with Jodie."

I took it from him with a nod, feeling the desperation coming off him in waves. Dusty glanced at Ramos, thinking how much he'd like to tell him off, but nodding instead. "See you Friday."

"Unless I change my mind," Ramos answered, still not sure whether he wanted to go or not.

Dusty grimaced and shook his head, then turned on his heel, eager to get out of there before he said something he'd regret. As he exited the club, I watched carefully to see if anyone followed him out.

There were several people that exited after him, but they were mostly couples. From Dusty's thoughts, I knew it was a man, and he was alone, but I couldn't see anyone like that... or pick up any thoughts that would help me. To top it off, several people gathered around the bar and totally blocked my view.

"Uh... Shelby?"

"Huh?" I jerked my attention back to him. "Did you say something?"

"Yeah. Who are you looking for?"

"I was just trying to see if someone followed him out, but I couldn't tell. There were too many people in the way."

"Why?" he asked.

"Because he was thinking that someone was here, watching him meet with you."

Ramos shook his head and swore in his mind. "What else?"

I sat back in my seat and took a swig of soda. "Well, he seemed sincere about wanting you to meet with Jodie to settle things between you."

Ramos fingered the photo of the little girl Dusty had left and glanced at me. "Is she mine?"

"I don't know. Dusty wasn't thinking that she was or wasn't. Maybe he was telling the truth that Jodie doesn't know. It's hard to say."

Ramos sighed and shook his head. "Go on."

"Um... from what I could pick up, you're right that there's more to it. He has plans that he needs you for. I wish I knew what they were, but he never thought about that." Ramos clenched his jaw, thinking that wasn't much help, so I quickly continued. "But there's something in the envelope besides the tickets."

With narrowed eyes, he picked up the envelope and peered inside. His breath caught at what appeared to be a tiny zip-lock bag with a couple of encapsulated pills inside. "What exactly was he thinking about this?"

"Are those pills?" I asked. "Dimples told me just this afternoon about some pills that a couple of junior high school kids had taken. One of them died. Do you think they're the same pills?"

Ramos shrugged. "I don't know but, if they are, I'd be interested to know why he'd give them to me. Can you tell me what Dusty was thinking about them?"

"Yeah. He was pretty worried that I'd see them. Then he worried that the packet would fall out and ruin all his plans. He was also hoping the man following him had seen the exchange. That's actually why I grabbed it first. In case he was framing you with what he'd hidden inside and the guy was a cop. Dusty didn't think about it being drugs though, so I didn't know what it was."

Ramos thought he needed to take them to someone who could determine exactly what was in them. They could just be regular old pain pills, since there was a market for them. But since Dusty had gone to all the trouble, there had to be more to it. So, why would Dusty give him the packet and not say anything about it? What was his endgame?

He glanced at me, knowing I'd picked up his thoughts, and tried to tamp down his annoyance. "Anything else?"

"Yeah, he knows all about your bad... uh... bad-ass... reputation, but despite that, he thought coming to you was worth the risk, whatever that means. I think he's in some kind of trouble."

Ramos' brows rose, and he thought that was pretty obvious, but he didn't want to say it and hurt my feelings. Although... he'd just done that, hadn't he?

"Oh... it's okay. You didn't hurt my feelings. I just wish I had more information to give you."

"I do too," Ramos said, grateful I wasn't one to get easily offended.

"So what are we going to do now?"

His gaze caught mine with that no-nonsense glare that raised my ire. He was thinking that there was no 'we' about it, and I'd done enough. He'd take care of the rest, especially since I was in cahoots with the police.

"Hey... I'm not about to give you up to the police." That kind of hurt my feelings, and here he thought I wasn't easily offended. "At least let me come to the concert with you."

He shook his head. "Who says I'm going to the concert?"

Now it was my turn to raise my brows at him. "You are. I know you want to go. You can't hide that from me. Maybe it's a good thing. I mean..." I took a breath and glanced down at the photo. "If she's your daughter..."

"No. You've got it all wrong. If she's my daughter, then she's better off without me in her life." He meant it, but I also caught the yearning in his heart to claim her as his own. He was all mixed up about it and not sure of anything. It raised all kinds of questions and brought out an emotional side of him that he didn't like. "She's probably not mine anyway."

"Maybe not," I quickly agreed. "Maybe Dusty was just trying to get to you the only way he knew he could, first through Jodie, and if that wasn't enough, then through her daughter."

Ramos nodded his agreement, relieved that I'd pulled things into perspective for him. "You're right. Now I need to figure out why." He was thinking it was time to call in a few favors and... his gaze caught mine. "Uh... thanks Shelby, I'll take it from here."

I tried not be offended and took in a deep breath, then slowly let it out, knowing this was as far as he wanted my help. "Okay. Sure. Um... let me know what you decide to do about the concert, okay? I'd still like to go. And if you want to know about her..." I glanced at the photo. "I'm sure it wouldn't be too hard for me to pick it up."

He twisted his lips and nodded, then signaled to Ricky to come and get me. In a way, I couldn't believe he was just dismissing me like that. But I also knew getting involved with the kind of illegal plans he wanted to make was probably not a good idea, especially in light of my work with the police.

Still, I wasn't quite ready to leave. I'd wanted to talk to him about my visit to New York in the morning and ask him what he knew about the New York Manettos. It would have been nice to hear his take on them, but he was already lost in a million thoughts about how to figure out what Dusty was up to.

Ricky appeared by my side, so I scooted out of the booth and stood. As I turned to say goodbye to Ramos, he was already standing right next to me. Catching me off-guard, he leaned in and kissed my cheek. I inhaled with surprise, and he glanced down at me with that sexy half-smile of his. "Thanks Babe. I owe you one."

Standing this close, I felt the heat of his body radiate over me and picked up the faint scent of his aftershave. I fought the urge to close my eyes and breathe in his scent, since I didn't want him to see how much his close proximity unsettled me.

"I'll talk to you soon," he promised, then stepped away, and I could finally breathe again.

I nodded and then turned to follow Ricky with a shake of my head to break the spell. I picked up satisfaction that Ramos had totally rattled me. He also thought that putting on the wig to fool him was pretty funny... uh... cute. But as much as I rocked the black wig, he liked my blond hair much better.

I shook my head again, tempted to glance over my shoulder at him, but his thoughts about me had ended. Without looking, I knew he'd disappeared somewhere behind a door, leaving a noticeable emptiness in his wake.

Ricky pulled back the curtain behind the stage, and I followed him down the hall and out of the building. I breathed in the cool evening air, grateful that had gone so well and that Ramos wasn't mad at me anymore for being there.

As Ricky drove me home, I had a moment to decide what I was going to tell Chris. I'd told him this whole meeting was about Uncle Joey before I left, but that wasn't true, and a pang of guilt curdled my stomach.

In the past, I'd decided there were things it was best that he didn't know, but that hadn't always worked out so well. Still, it was hard to talk to him about Ramos. But did I even have a choice? Ramos was part of my life. If I wanted Chris to trust me, then I needed to tell him what was going on. He deserved the truth, even if he didn't like it.

Ricky pulled into my driveway. I thanked him and climbed out of the car. He watched while I unlocked the door, so I waved and closed it behind me.

Only the lamps in the living room gave off light, so I flipped the switch, plunging the room into darkness. I hurried up the stairs to my bedroom, eager to take off the wig and wash my face. The light coming from the bedside lamp lit up the hall, showing me the way.

I paused in the doorway. Chris slept sitting up with a book resting against his chest. He'd been waiting up for me but lost the battle. A wave of warmth washed over me, and I crept to his side, easing the book from his chest, and setting it on the nightstand.

"What time is it?" Chris asked. His eyes squinted open, then he closed them and rubbed a hand over his face.

"Uh... close to eleven-thirty." It was closer to midnight, but if he kept his eyes shut, he'd never know, and eleven-thirty sounded lots better.

"Hmm... so how did it go?"

"Good. It went really well. Hey, I'm going to wash my face and take this wig off. Then I'll be right back. Is that all right?"

"Sure," he said, sliding down under the sheets and getting comfortable. "But if I'm asleep, wake me up. I want to know what's going on."

"Okay." I hurried into the bathroom and pulled off the wig. Then I pulled out the pins and ran my fingers through my hair, grateful to massage my scalp. After washing my face and brushing my teeth, I changed into my pajamas.

Chris' breath came deep and even, and I hated to wake him up, but I knew he'd be mad if I didn't try. So I slipped into bed, then reached across him and turned out the light. As his arms closed around me, I snuggled against him and breathed in his scent.

"So what happened?" he asked, barely awake enough to talk.

Deciding to tell him the important parts, I began with Uncle Joey's request that I go to the club and listen in while Ramos chatted with someone from his past. I explained the connection to Jodie McAllister and her brother, then ended with Dusty having a hidden agenda that included plans for Ramos.

"I don't know what they are," I concluded. "But at least that's a start, and Ramos can take it from there." Chris didn't answer for a long time, and I thought he'd fallen back asleep and missed everything. I didn't know if that was good or bad.

"Mmm... good," Chris finally mumbled, pulling me close against him. "I'm glad you're back."

"Me too," I said.

He nuzzled his face into my neck and trailed kisses along my collarbone. "You're not going to be here... tomorrow night... are you?"

"Uh... no," I answered, breathlessly.

"Hmm... all of this gallivanting around... I'm not sure I like it."

I gasped as his lips found that ticklish spot behind my ear. "I guess... I'll have to... make it up to you."

"Hmm... I like the sound of that." He kissed me deeply, only pulling away long enough to growl some of my favorite words. "Oh baby, oh baby."

Chapter 6

The next morning, Chris pushed the snooze button until the last possible moment, then we both had to rush to get ready for the day. While he showered, I made sure the kids were up and set cereal on the table for their breakfast. At least it was better than Pop Tarts, right?

Uncle Joey sent me a text to say the limo would pick me up at nine a.m. sharp, so that gave me enough time to get everyone out the door before I needed to get ready. As Chris left, he gave me a quick kiss. "Call me when you get there, okay?"

"You bet," I agreed.

"And... I'm not sure I got everything you said last night, especially that thing about going to a Jodie McAllister concert with Ramos. What was that all about?" He didn't like that part, and he thought he must have heard me wrong.

I let out my breath in exasperation. "You missed it? It's kind of the main part of the whole story. Now I'll have to explain the whole thing again." I let out a breath. "Don't worry, you'll understand it better then, but there's not enough time to go into it now."

"Wait, so you're really going to the concert with him?" He hadn't heard much of anything else, since that had kind of stuck in his craw. How could I go to a concert with another man?

Surprise and a little guilt tightened my stomach, so I backtracked to make it easier. "Not necessarily... but I need to be there when he talks to Jodie about her daughter." His blank stare told me all I needed to know. "... because she might be his."

His eyes widened in astonishment. "Oh... wow. I must have missed more than I thought." Mollified, he continued, "Okay... we'll talk later. I want to hear it all again."

"Sure. I'll call you." I gave him a smile, trying not to let my annoyance show, and he rushed out the door.

As the kids left, Josh told me to have fun in New York, even though he was a little concerned that I was going off in a private jet that belonged to someone with a questionable reputation. He'd had a chance to google Joe E. Manetto, and what he'd found troubled him.

I made a mental note to google Uncle Joey myself, just so I'd know what Josh had picked up. Would it really say that he was a crime boss? Or had ties to organized crime? Yikes.

Savannah reminded me to pick up a souvenir for her. "And wish Miguel luck for me!"

"I will. Love you! See you tomorrow."

I closed the door and let out a sigh. When did my life get so complicated? Oh yeah... when I went to the grocery store to buy some lousy carrots. Who would have thought? Now if Josh found out about Uncle Joey... how was I ever going to explain that? My stomach clenched, making me grateful I hadn't eaten breakfast.

I showered and dressed in my comfy jeans and a tee with a grey hoodie for traveling, then I finished packing my overnight bag. Along with my pajamas and make-up essentials, I packed my lacy black dress with my black pumps and jewelry to match.

I could probably wear the same clothes home, but I decided to add an extra shirt. Then I threw in my black jeans to go with the shirt. After that, I didn't want to leave my black, leather motorcycle jacket at home, so I stuffed that in as well.

Then I remembered that I didn't have to pass through security to get on a private jet. I could take as much luggage as I wanted. So I switched out my small overnight bag for my carry-on bag with rollers, throwing in my hair dryer and some lotion, as well as shampoo and conditioner.

Since there was still plenty of room, I threw in my black boots and zipped it up, leaving just enough space for a few souvenirs. It seemed like a lot of stuff for just one night. But hey, it was one night in New York.

I had just enough time for a bowl of cereal before the limo arrived. As I walked out to the car, I noticed my neighbor looking out her window. I waved as the curtain fell into place, grateful I couldn't hear her suspicious thoughts about me getting picked up by limos at all times of the day, although I could certainly imagine them.

Miguel slipped out and held the door open for me with a smile. "Hey Shelby. Glad you could come."

"Holy cow! Look at you!" He'd gotten his hair cut, and it totally reminded me of Aladdin in the movie. "It looks really good."

He shrugged. "My agent thought it would be a good idea." He had to admit that he really liked the shorter cut. It gave him a boost of confidence, and that was always a good thing.

Ricky was our driver, and he came to my side to take my luggage and put it in the trunk. Miguel waited while I slipped inside the limo, and then he followed inside. I kind of expected to see Uncle Joey, but it was just me and Miguel. No Ramos either.

"My dad couldn't come see us off because of a meeting, so it's just you and me." Miguel worried that Uncle Joey had coerced me into going with him. He certainly could have done this by himself, although he didn't mind having my company. "I hope you're okay with coming."

"Of course. I'm excited to be here. Are you ready for your audition?"

"I guess." He sighed. "I'm a little nervous though."

"Don't worry. You'll be great."

"Thanks."

We spoke about New York City, and Miguel confessed that he'd never been there before. Since I'd only driven through once when I was a kid, I didn't have much to add except that it was a big place. All I remembered were the buildings that went on for miles and miles with no end in sight.

It didn't take long before we were both inside the plane and ready for take-off. I marveled again at how rich Uncle Joey had to be to fly the two of us in his jet to New York for an appointment that would probably take less than an hour.

Miguel was thinking close to the same thing. He hadn't forgotten those hard years in Mexico with his mother, and he was grateful to his father for every opportunity that came his way. He had mixed feelings about this whole thing. The opportunity to be a star in a Broadway production... well, how could he say no to that? But he also wanted to please his father. Could he do both? He didn't know.

We landed a few hours later and exited the plane at a small airport I'd never heard of. Lucky for us, a car was waiting, and a stocky, older man close to Uncle Joey's age greeted us with a crooked smile.

"I'm Syd," he said. "You must be Shelby and Miguel."

"Hi. Nice to meet you."

He nodded, wondering what Uncle Joey had on me, since he knew I wasn't his 'real' niece. That whole bit with being Maggie's daughter was pretty hilarious. Then he studied Miguel for similarities to the Manettos. Even though Miguel was obviously Hispanic, it was easy to see the strong forehead and jawline that was a Manetto trait, so it had to be true.

"Come on. The car's this way."

We followed him to the curb where a nice, black, four-door sedan awaited us. I picked up from Miguel that it was a new Cadillac, and I nodded in appreciation. The interior was roomy and nice with jet-black leather upholstery and red accents. It had that new-car smell too, and I inhaled deeply with appreciation.

Hmm... this was just another confirmation of Uncle Joey's success, and it was hard not to be even more impressed.

"It'll take about forty-five minutes to get to the hotel," Syd said from the front seat. "So make yourselves comfortable, but be sure to buckle-up."

In a car like this, with about the smoothest ride I could imagine, I didn't mind how long it took. Then Syd turned on some classical music and the sound system about blew me away. Sheesh! This car was amazing.

As we drove, I kept my gaze glued out the window, taking in all the sights. Then I remembered what Syd had thought about Uncle Joey's sister. I didn't know her name was Maggie, and Syd had obviously known her. At least he knew the truth about me and Miguel, and I didn't have to worry about lying to him. I just hoped the rest of the family was as nice as him.

With all the traffic, I had no idea where we were, but we soon pulled into a parking garage under a tall building that was just one of many to me. Syd parked in a reserved spot and grabbed our luggage from the trunk.

We followed him to an elevator entrance with "Hotel Perona Times Square" in rectangular, bold letters on a gold panel above the elevator doors. We stepped inside, and he pushed the button for the lobby.

I picked up that he was a little worried about the reception I would get from Frank and Sylvie... well, mostly Sylvie, since she didn't like long-lost relatives showing up at her doorstep, especially from Joseph's side of the family. So it was bound to be interesting. Good thing we were only staying one night.

Hearing that rattled my nerves, but I was grateful to know what to expect. Sylvie may not like me, but what could happen in one night? Miguel and I would both be gone by this time tomorrow, so no big deal, right?

The elevator doors swished open into a stunning lobby with rich, dark wood paneling and crystal lights that bathed the room in a warm glow. A beautiful Italian piece played over the speakers, adding to the ambiance. I took a deep breath and my eyes widened. Besides looking so elegant, the whole place smelled really good, and I kept sniffing just to keep smelling the lovely fragrance. Wow. This was amazing.

Syd led us to the desk where he was greeted respectfully by the girl manning the hotel registrations. She smiled at me, but her gaze locked onto Miguel with instant admiration, or was it more like adoration?

Her mind flew in a million directions of what his relationship to me could be. But when she found that we had two separate rooms, her interest grew exponentially. "Welcome to Hotel Perona," she said catching Miguel's gaze. "It looks like you have two of our best rooms on the twelfth floor. Here are your key-cards. Enjoy your stay. If you need anything at all, please don't hesitate to let me know. I'll be happy to help."

Syd cleared his throat, thinking she was going a little overboard, but easily picked up her interest in a handsome face. He smiled, thinking that if she knew Miguel was the hotel owner's son, she'd probably start to drool.

"Is Frank in his office?" Syd asked the clerk.

"Yes."

Syd turned to us and smiled. "Frank wanted to meet you. His office is right back here." We followed him behind the desk to an office door. He knocked and turned the knob, then escorted us inside. The small office held photos of famous people taken in different places in the hotel.

An older version of Uncle Joey sat behind an exquisite cherry-wood desk. The uncanny resemblance sent my blood pressure to a new high. His gaze took in our little group, and recognition brought a smile to his face.

"You must be Shelby," he said, coming around the desk to greet me. "It's a pleasure to meet a long-lost relative." He shook my hand, then turned to Miguel and shook his hand as well. "And this must be Miguel. I've been looking forward to meeting you both."

This close, I could see the differences between Frank and Uncle Joey. Frank wasn't as tall, and he carried more weight around the middle. His hair was just as white, but much shorter, and his face had deeper worry lines, so I guessed he was a little older as well. But he had the same assessing gaze that didn't miss a thing.

"Nice to meet you too," I said. "I have to admit that I had no idea Uncle Joey had relatives here in New York."

His brows rose slightly, but he smiled at my mistake. "It sounds like we're your relatives too. Isn't that right?"

"Oh yes, of course." I smiled brightly. "I meant that, too."

He let it go, and turned to Miguel. "And this is the talented young man I've heard so much about. Your cousin, is that right?"

"From my adoptive family," I said, needing to clarify our relationship.

"You must be pretty good to get an audition for a Broadway show, so I'm sure you'll do great. I should let you go freshen up and prepare. What time is your audition?"

"Four o'clock," Miguel answered.

Frank checked his watch. "It's two-thirty now, so that should give you plenty of time to warm-up. Are you hungry? I can have some sandwiches sent up to your room."

"That would be great," I agreed.

"Good. Before you leave, I have a question. I was hoping you'd join me and Sylvie for dinner before the show."

"Oh... sure." I glanced at Miguel. "We'd be happy to."

"Good." He smiled, looking just like Uncle Joey did when something went his way. I listened real hard to his thoughts but couldn't pick up anything concrete, just satisfaction to have me under his care. "See you later. Good luck young man."

"Thanks," Miguel said.

Frank nodded at Syd, silently commanding him to take good care of us. Then he thought that since Syd was Uncle Joey's man, he probably didn't need to be concerned. He nodded at us once more before we left his office.

Hmm... it didn't look like Frank had missed a thing and knew all about Syd being Uncle Joey's inside man. So much for that secret.

"I'll take you to your rooms," Syd said, dragging our luggage behind him. In the elevator, he gave us a history lesson. "This hotel was built in nineteen-oh-two and was actually designated as a New York City Landmark in nineteen-eighty-seven.

"The Manettos acquired it in the late seventies and poured millions into renovations during the eighties. When your... uh... Uncle Joey took possession a few years ago Frank had just spent another eighteen million in new renovations.

"He replaced the plumbing, electrical, and environmental systems in the whole building. Every room and suite were renovated and refurbished, with all the carpets and wall decorations redone as well. He also added a new business center, fitness center, and guest hospitality area."

"Wow, no wonder it's so nice," I said.

"Yes. But with all the changes, Frank got in over his head and couldn't make the payments. If Joe hadn't stepped in, Frank would have lost the hotel." He glanced at me, then Miguel. "I'm telling you this so you know how much Frank loves this place. He'd never do anything to jeopardize it, but it was hard for him and his family to turn it over to Joe."

"That makes sense," I agreed. "I mean, we knew Uncle Joey bought it to help out the family."

"Right, and the hotel belongs to your uncle now, no matter how Frank may feel about it." He shrugged, like it was no big deal, but he was thinking that when Uncle Joey died, Miguel would take the reins, and he didn't want another war between the families.

Now his explanation made sense, but I couldn't see Uncle Joey wanting Miguel to rush in and take over the hotel. It seemed to me that he was more than happy to keep Frank's family in charge. Plus, it wasn't a forgone conclusion that Miguel would want to take over either.

The elevator came to a stop, and we stepped onto the top floor. Because of his spiel, I certainly had a new appreciation for the hotel, and I admired how well-designed and stylish it was.

"You have a suite with a connecting room. I'll let you fight over who gets what room, but I'll show you around." We turned down the hall, and I inhaled through my nose enjoying how good it smelled, even up here, which kind of blew me away. He opened the door to a beautiful sitting room with chairs, a couch, a coffee table, and a flat-screen TV mounted on the wall.

He led the way to the large bedroom with a king-size bed, and another flat-screen TV over a chest of drawers, and an easy-chair in the corner. A window overlooked the street, with an amazing view. The bathroom held a big stand-in glass shower, hair-dryer, and other amenities.

"The other connecting bedroom is through here." He led us back through the sitting room to the other side, where a door opened to another king-sized bedroom suite with a flat-screen TV and bathroom comparable to the first.

"This is the suite the original owners let out to many of their celebrity guests. From what I understand, they had quite a gathering back then."

"I'll take this room," Miguel said, not wanting to get stuck hearing about the olden days. He slipped through the door and set his bag on the bed.

"I guess it's settled then," Syd said, turning toward me. "Take a moment to relax. Your food should be here soon. I'll be back around three-thirty to take you to the audition at the theatre. It's within walking distance, so it's not far. If you want to do anything before that, like some sight-seeing or something, just call the front desk and they'll let me know. But I'd prefer it if you didn't go anywhere without me."

He was thinking that Uncle Joey had told him to keep us in sight the whole time we were here, mostly because of me... since he'd claimed that I always managed to get into trouble without even trying.

Again, Syd wondered exactly what part I played in Uncle Joey's organization. From what he could tell, I looked pretty normal, with nothing extraordinary about me, although he had to admit that I was a babe.

I felt my cheeks flush and hurried to answer him before he thought something I really didn't want to hear. "Okay. That's great. Thanks so much."

As soon as Syd closed the door, I inhaled the wonderful fragrance again, then grabbed my bag and dragged it into my room. I unpacked my clothes and toiletries, and wandered back into the sitting room just in time to get the door, and let in the server with the tray of food. Miguel came back in, and we both grabbed a sandwich.

"This is so good," I said, after a few bites. Taking a drink of soda, I asked, "So what do you need to do between now and the audition?"

Miguel shrugged, but I noticed that he'd only eaten half the sandwich before putting the rest down, and I could tell that his nerves were getting to him. "I brought a change of clothes for the audition and I need to warm up. So I think I'll go take a shower and get ready."

"Sounds good."

After he left, I finished my sandwich and took my diet soda into my room, then pulled out a change of clothes. I slipped on my black jeans and boots, along with a turquoise-blue shirt, and topped it with my leather jacket.

It sure seemed like I wore this outfit a lot. Like every time I went out. At least the shirt was different. But I had to admit, I kind of liked the look. It was sassy and spunky, and certainly kept me from looking old enough to be Miguel's mom.

Next, I put a call through to Chris. He was glad to hear from me, but too busy to chat, so I told him I'd call later tonight, and we disconnected. I sent Uncle Joey a text, letting him know we'd arrived safely and that I loved the hotel. I also mentioned that Syd was nice, and that we were going to dinner with Frank and Sylvie tonight before the show.

With that done, I wandered back into the sitting room and looked out the window. A little thrill went through me that I was in The Big Apple, and I looked forward to doing a little sight-seeing as well as going to a Broadway play tonight.

Sounds of Miguel's beautiful voice floated from his room, and I smiled. He really was amazing, and I looked forward to his audition and finding out what the people in charge thought about him. He certainly wasn't as experienced as they probably wanted, so that could go against him. But he had the chops, the looks, and was the perfect age to be a great Aladdin.

A knock sounded at the door. I checked my watch, surprised that it was already time to go. As I moved to the door, Miguel opened his door and stepped into the sitting room looking splendid in jeans, a white dress shirt, and a blue blazer.

"Looking good," I said to him.

I opened the door to Syd, and he ushered us to the elevator. "It's about a ten minute walk to the theatre where you're auditioning, so we'll get there in plenty of time." He was thinking that the kid looked a little nervous, but if he was a Manetto, he'd be fine. He was also looking forward to hearing Miguel sing.

"Are you staying for the audition?" I asked, surprised.

"I thought I would," he said, his brows drawn together in a frown. *Was something wrong with that?*

"No, that's great. It's nice to have the support." I smiled, realizing I'd just answered his thoughts. I hoped he didn't think too hard about it.

He glanced my way, not too sure what was going on. Luckily the elevator doors opened, and we stepped into the lobby. Once again the elegance of the place washed over me, and I smiled with enthusiasm to take to the streets of New York City.

Outside, we began our walk to the theatre. The crowded streets and the sounds of sirens and honking cars filled me with delight. This city contained a pulse of activity that never seemed to stop.

"I'm looking forward to seeing the play tonight," I said to Syd. "Do you think the audition will be on the same stage?"

"I don't know," Syd answered. "But I guess we'll find out. Someone should be there to tell us where to go."

Since I hadn't heard anything about that part, I hoped he was right. We took a couple of turns, and soon we walked beneath several huge marquees and flashing banners. Then the big theatre marquee featuring Aladdin in gold lettering with a purple background and bright golden lights flashing all around it came into view.

My heart sped up with excitement to see it. I felt the same nervous excitement from Miguel. We both stopped in our tracks and stood there for a moment, taking it all in. Syd stopped as well, then nudged us on and we walked in a daze to stand beneath the marquee.

The agent we'd met at Miguel's school waited in front of the doors for us, and I let out my breath to find a familiar face. We followed him inside and up a wide corridor which led through another set of doors into the lobby. One side held a gift shop, and the other had all sorts of posters and paraphernalia about the play.

From here, he took us through the main doors that opened into the actual theatre. We turned left and followed him down a side aisle toward the front of the stage. The lights were turned down low, and a young man sang on the stage. He was good, but I thought Miguel was better.

Several people sat a few rows back from the front of the stage with notebooks, and the agent had us sit down on the left side while he got the attention of a woman sitting behind the main director. She glanced back at us and nodded, thinking that the kid nobody'd heard of was here, and she hoped he was as good as the agent made him sound.

The singer finished his song, and one of the men asked him to sing another. Once he was through with that one, the director told him thanks and said they'd let him know. I picked up that this guy was one of the three understudies for Aladdin in the cast, so he knew the play inside and out, which was to his advantage. He also had a great voice, and he hoped he had it in the bag.

Then it was Miguel's turn, and my chest tightened. From what I'd picked up so far, it didn't look like Miguel's chances were very good. Not without an impressive resume like most everyone else who'd auditioned. Miguel may have been the lead in his high school play, but he hadn't gone to a musical college like most everyone else.

Miguel followed the agent's instructions to enter the stage. The director asked him to give his name, and to tell them a little about himself. From what I could pick up, they wanted to know how his speaking voice sounded and how he presented himself.

Miguel had prepared for this, so he did a good job and didn't fumble at all. That's when it hit me that he didn't have an accent. After growing up in Mexico, how had that happened? Then I realized there was a lot about his life that I didn't know.

Not having many acting gigs under his belt didn't stop him from looking confident. Then they asked him to sing *Proud of Your Boy*, which was the exact song he'd warmed up on at the hotel. The pianist did the intro, and Miguel came in strong and clear.

He put a lot of expression into the song and brought the words to life, making it seem so effortless. As I listened to the words, it amazed me how much this song probably matched how Miguel felt about his own life, and how he wanted to make his mother... and now his father... proud.

Caught up in his performance, I forgot to listen to the director's thoughts, so I quickly tuned in and heard some of the same things coming from everyone there. He was really good... looked the part... wow... he might be the one... how did he look without a shirt? How old was he again? Maybe he could start out as an understudy?

Miguel finished, and the director stood, which took the others by surprise. I picked up that he didn't do that very often. "Miguel, would you mind putting on a bit of the costume for us?" The director asked for a stage manager to find a vest for Miguel, then he glanced into the back of the auditorium and asked if Rachel was there.

I picked up that she was the female lead, and he wanted her to sing with Miguel, just to hear how they sounded together. The small figure of a young woman with beautiful long, dark hair stood from the shadows on the other side of the auditorium.

As she came down the aisle, she was thinking that Miguel's voice was pretty amazing. But he seemed awfully young for the part, even if he looked great. She didn't like breaking in novices, and what if he was a jerk? What about his experience? He had nothing, and it didn't seem fair to everyone else in the cast.

She got up on stage at about the same time that Miguel came back out wearing only the vest along with his jeans and shoes. My lips widened into a smile at the intake of breath that came from most of the people in the room. Even Rachel did a double take. He was a lot taller than the former Aladdin, which seemed pretty awesome to everyone, including Rachel.

The director asked them to sing *A Whole New World* together. Miguel knew from the agent that Aladdin and Jasmine sang this while they rode the magic carpet. He didn't hesitate to sing the song to Rachel like she was the real Jasmine and he the real Aladdin. From her response, she seemed just as caught up in it as he was. A spark of chemistry flowed between them and caught the director's attention. He grinned, liking what he saw.

At the end of the song, the director stood again. "Really great, Miguel. There's one more thing. Can you dance?"

Miguel smiled and nodded, thinking that all of those lessons learning the Jarabe Tapatío and other traditional Mexican dances would finally pay off. He began moving through his steps and got faster and faster, then ended with a big finish.

"Wow. Great. Thanks Miguel. Uh... go ahead and change. We'll be in touch through your agent." He was thinking that he might have to have him come back in the morning and get another opinion from the rest of the creative team. The others who had auditioned were more experienced, and he wasn't sure he could go with someone so young and unknown, especially without a bigger resume.

But Miguel was simply amazing. As much as he liked the others, his gut was telling him that Miguel was made for this show. And that kid could certainly dance. Whoa! He was everything in one awesome package.

Still, it would be taking a big chance on an unknown, and not something he'd ever done before. The resume counted for a lot in this business, and offering him the job would make a lot of people unhappy. But he couldn't shake the feeling that Miguel was special, and if he didn't sign him now, he might lose him. Curiosity about the new lead could bring people back who'd already seen the show, and there would always be new fans who would love him, too. It could be a huge draw.

The agent chose that moment to ask the director what he thought, and he got enough of a positive reaction that he knew he needed to sign Miguel with his agency before someone else snatched him up. That meant calling Chris and working out the details.

Wow. I took a deep breath and let it out. Things had happened so fast, and now it looked like Miguel had a chance at the part. How was Uncle Joey going to take that? What about Miguel? Even as an understudy, he'd have to move here. This would be a big change for everyone.

Miguel stepped from behind the stage and came toward me with a big smile on his face. He knew he'd done a great job, especially after the stage manager told him that he hadn't seen the director so excited after an audition before.

"Good job," I said, patting his arm.

"Thanks."

The agent hurried over and told us that he'd walk us out. He spoke to Miguel about signing with his agency in case he got an offer for a spot in the play. Miguel readily agreed, with the stipulation that the agent talk to Chris first.

"Great," the agent said. "I'll give him a call and have the papers drawn up."

"So is this happening soon?" I asked him. "You think he's got a part?"

"It looks promising, but I don't know anything for sure. I told them you were going back home tomorrow, so we should hear something either tonight or in the morning." He turned to Miguel. "They might want you to come back in the morning. When does your flight leave?"

"It's not set in stone, so we could probably leave a little later if we need to, right Shelby?"

"Yeah... if they want you to come back tomorrow, that shouldn't be a problem."

"Good." The agent was thinking that this was moving faster than he thought, but he had a standard contract ready to go. He could work on any changes Chris might want, although he didn't see a problem unless Mr. Manetto changed his mind. If that happened, he didn't think Miguel would ever get another chance in this business.

The agent pulled the door open and ushered us out. "Thanks everyone. Oh... here are your tickets for tonight. I hope you enjoy the show."

"Awesome. Thanks," I said, taking them from him.

"I'll call you as soon as I know anything." He disappeared back inside the building, and I glanced at Syd, realizing he'd been awfully quiet this whole time.

"What do you think?"

Syd glanced at me, then at Miguel and shook his head. "I think it will be a surprise if he doesn't get on the show in some capacity. You were amazing, kid. Your dad... well, I hope he's ready for this."

Miguel nodded his thanks, then sighed, unsure how his dad would take it. "I hope he'll be good with it."

"He will," I said. "You'll see." I smiled broadly, hoping it was true.

"Thanks Shelby."

We followed Syd down the street, and I was grateful that he knew where he was going, since I had no idea. "Oh wait! I promised Savannah I'd get her a souvenir. Is there someplace we can find something?"

Syd glanced back at me with a smirk, thinking *are you kidding me?* "Of course, follow me."

I took in the sights and smells of the street, marveling that I was in the heart of New York City. Syd motioned us to cross the street and led us into the center of a plaza. He stopped and smiled. "Here we are."

"What do you mean?" I asked.

"Times Square. This is it."

My breath caught, and I turned in a circle, seeing the huge, brightly adorned billboards and advertisements with constantly changing lights. I finally recognized my surroundings from seeing it so often on TV and in the movies.

"Wow. It looks different standing right here in this spot. This place is huge."

Around me, bright signs advertising all kinds of things lit up the entire area going halfway up the buildings. The square itself was bigger than I thought. In fact, there was so much going on, that it was hard to know where to look.

"Let's take a picture," Miguel said. He held out his phone and pulled me against him. Then I took out my phone and snapped some more. We laughed and smiled, drinking it all in.

"This is crazy," I said. "We're standing right here in this famous spot!"

"Yeah... I know what you mean," Miguel agreed.

"Hey look! There's the Disney store. Should we look for something in there for Savannah?"

"Sure," Miguel said, thinking she might like something from Aladdin.

"That's a great..." Oops. I glanced away and tried to come up with something that made sense. "Uh... a great spot for the store."

"Yeah," he nodded, his brows dipping together, not sure he really wanted to go in there. Then he shrugged and glanced at Syd. "Come on Syd."

Syd took a deep breath, thinking he'd never been inside the Disney store, and he didn't want to start now. With a shake of his head, he followed us in. We managed to stick together, mostly because we were all looking for the Aladdin section, but it was hard not to get sucked into some of the amazing displays. Still, once we found Aladdin, the lack of items was a little disappointing.

Jasmine was on everything, and there were a couple of Aladdin and Jasmine dolls, but that was it. Plus, pretty much everything here was for little kids. Miguel was thinking that maybe this wasn't such a good idea after all. Savannah was too old for this stuff, and this place was starting to get to him. All the toys... all the kids. What was he doing in here?

"You know... maybe we should look somewhere else," I said.

"That's a great idea," Miguel answered, grateful to get out of there.

Syd let out a relieved breath. "There's a real souvenir shop not far from here."

We made it out of the store and crossed the street, dodging lots of people to find the shop. Inside, Miguel picked up a cute little stuffed bear that had "I Love New York" written on it. "Do you think she'd like this?"

I laughed. "I think she'd love it."

We found a couple of other things that I had to buy, one of which was an "I Love New York" t-shirt for me. I got Josh an "I Love New York" baseball to go with the theme, and I got Chris a New York license plate that said, "fuhgedaboudit," which I knew would crack him up.

Then of course, I bought me a pair of silver earrings that had nothing to do with New York except that they would always remind me of this trip.

I took everything to the register and glanced up to find both Syd and Miguel with pained expressions about the whole shopping thing on their faces. "Hey... why don't you guys wait for me outside while I pay for this?"

I didn't have to tell them twice. By the time I got through the long line, and paid a bazillion dollars, I was ready to get out of there myself.

I came outside and glanced in both directions, but with the huge crowds of people, I couldn't find either of them anywhere. I pushed my panic down and took a couple of deep breaths, then held still and looked harder. They couldn't be too far. I mean, they wouldn't just leave me, would they?

"Shelby!"

I turned toward Miguel's voice and found him waving at me. With a relieved sigh, I hurried to his side. He handed me a soft pretzel dipped in sugar and cinnamon. "We saw these and had to get some."

"Oh nice. This looks amazing. Thanks." Enjoying every bite, I gladly followed Syd and Miguel back through the crowds to the hotel.

Syd stopped in the lobby, checking his watch. "Frank wanted to have dinner with you before the show, so you'll need to come back here at about six-thirty. The show starts at eight, right?"

I pulled out our tickets to make sure of the time. "Yes, that's right."

"Okay. The restaurant seating is right over there." He pointed to the back section of the lobby, where several people sat at tables covered with linen tablecloths, crystal goblets, and candles. "I'll come find you after dinner, at about seven-twenty, and walk with you to the show."

"Okay. Thanks, Syd."

He nodded and left. Miguel and I took the elevator to our rooms. Miguel used his key-card to unlock the door, and we hurried inside. I pulled the stuffed teddy bear out of the bag and propped it on the table. It was just so cute that I knew Savannah would love it, especially if she knew Miguel had picked it out.

Miguel's phone rang. He retrieved it from his pocket and glanced at me with surprise. "It's your husband."

As they talked, I picked up that Chris had just gotten off the phone with the agent and wanted to let Miguel know that he was going over the sample contract the agent had sent him. He told Miguel he would talk to Uncle Joey about the terms and didn't want him to sign anything before that.

"Okay. I won't," Miguel said. Chris finished up, then asked Miguel if he could talk to me. "Sure. Here she is."

"Hi honey," I said. "How's it going?"

"Good. Sounds like Miguel did great."

"Yes he did."

"I want to hear all about it. Will you call me after the show tonight?" I told him I would, and we chatted for another minute before disconnecting.

"I told my dad I'd call him after the audition," Miguel said, taking his phone from me. "Wish me luck."

I did, and Miguel took a deep breath. His mind was full of apprehension, but with a lot of hope mixed in. He hurried into his room and shut the door. I shook my head and went into my room as well, knowing that Uncle Joey would probably call me as soon as he got done talking to Miguel, and I didn't want Miguel to hear what I had to say to him.

Sure enough, a few minutes later, my phone rang. "Hello?"

"Is it true?" Uncle Joey asked, not wasting time on pleasantries.

"Uh... well, the agent seemed to think it looked promising." I told him everything I'd picked up, even the part about the other person the director had liked. "He might want Miguel to sing again so he can compare them, hopefully sometime tomorrow morning before we need to leave."

"Do you think he'll start out as an understudy then?"

"Well, either that or the lead. You have to remember he's an unknown talent without much of a resume, so I think it would be a miracle if he got the lead. On the other hand, the director really likes him and wants to cast him for the part. We'll just have to see what happens."

"I can't believe it," he said. "I thought he might have a chance but... this is all happening so fast." He swallowed and took a breath. "To be honest... I don't want him to go."

His declaration caught at my heart-strings. I knew if Josh or Savannah wanted to move halfway across the country right after high school, I'd have a terrible time. "Yeah, I understand. It's a lot to take in. I think Miguel's a little torn too. Don't get me wrong. He'd love to do the show, but he doesn't want to leave you, either."

"Thanks Shelby. That means... a lot." He cleared his throat. "So... what do you think of Frank?"

"Well... we're having dinner with him and Sylvie in about forty-five minutes, so I'll know more then, but I think he's great. He loves this hotel, that's for sure. Um... he also knows all about your arrangement with Syd."

"He does? Hmm... well, that's good to know. And... keep your ears open for anything else while you're there, okay?"

"Sure," I agreed.

"Good. We'll talk later."

We disconnected, and I sank down on my bed, then stretched out and pulled a pillow under my head. Had Uncle Joey gotten a little teary-eyed there? Whoa. That was something I never thought I'd see. Of course, he understood what a big deal this was. Probably a lot more than Miguel realized.

Things were about to change in their lives, and I was grateful I had a few more years before I had to go through that with my own kids. It reminded me of how I couldn't wait to leave my parents behind and rush out on my own without a thought about how they felt about it.

Of course, on second thought, that was probably a good thing. We all needed to forge our own paths, which meant that change was the one thing in life that was always constant. It was better to get used to it, than try and fight it.

I took a quick shower without getting my hair too wet, then took my time freshening up my hair and makeup. Nearly ready, I even spritzed on some of my favorite perfume. After slipping on my black lace dress, I sighed with gratefulness that I'd brought it. There was something magical about being here in New York and, in this dress, I felt like I fit right in.

But I missed Chris. I wished I could hear him say "oh baby, oh baby" after he got a good look at me all dressed up. But if Miguel got the part, we'd come back, and I could wear it again. With that happy thought, I sauntered into the sitting room.

Miguel waited on the couch, fiddling with his phone. As I stepped into the room, his eyes widened. "Whoa. You look great." He was thinking how lucky he was to have a cousin like me, one that he was proud to be with.

"Thanks," I said with a smile. "Are you hungry?"

"Starved." He hadn't eaten much because of his nerves, but with the audition over, he was finally hungry again. I noticed that he wore the same jacket and jeans, but with a different shirt. He looked great and more relaxed than I'd seen him all day.

We took the elevator down to the lobby and hurried toward the restaurant. Glancing around, I couldn't find Frank anywhere, but the hostess smiled with recognition at our names and led us through the tables to a private room.

She opened the door, and we found Frank sitting at the beautifully set, round table. He jumped up and smiled, relieved to see us. "Come in and sit down. Sylvie will be here in a minute."

As we took our seats, I picked up that Frank was anxious about something. He could hardly look me in the eye, and alternated between uneasiness and excitement. I glanced at the table and realized it was set for five instead of four.

My stomach clenched, and a shiver of dread ran down my spine. "Is Syd joining us?"

Frank's brows drew together, and he wondered why I would think that. He was no relation to us. "Uh... no. But Sylvie's bringing... oh here they are." He jumped to his feet again and ushered Sylvie and another woman into the room.

He stood beside the newcomer, and his face broke into a huge smile. His eyes even got a little moist with unshed tears. What was going on? I listened to his thoughts, and a wave of shock stabbed me in the heart. My breath caught, and my heart began to race, then my eyes bulged, and I even got a little light headed. No! This couldn't be happening. Not this!

"Shelby," Frank said, licking his lips nervously. "I'd like to introduce you to your... your real mother. This is Maggie Manetto."

Chapter 7

Holy hell!

"Are you all right?" Miguel asked, patting my back and placing his hand over my fist where I'd clenched the tablecloth. He was thinking that, from the croaking noise I'd just made, I was probably in a state of shock. I took comfort that at least I hadn't blurted out the 'holy hell' part.

"Here," Miguel continued, "have a drink of water."

He brought the glass toward my lips, and I let go of the tablecloth to take the glass before water spilled down my chin and all over my new dress. After a couple of gulps, I put it down and glanced up. Everyone gazed at me expectantly. Both Frank and Sylvie had the same expression of glee on their faces, thinking they had done something wonderful in reuniting a mother with her long-lost child.

Maggie's lips curved up into a calculating grin. Her wavy, silver hair was cut short, reminding me a lot of Uncle Joey, and she wore very little, if any, makeup. Even without it, she had beautiful bone structure and only a few wrinkles to show her age. With her strong jaw and piercing gaze, there was no question that she was a Manetto through and through.

She also knew I wasn't who I said I was.

"I thought you were a nun," I blurted.

Her face crinkled into a full-fledged smile. "I am a Sister, which is a little different than a nun. A sister is a woman who lives, ministers, and prays within the world, rather than being cloistered in a monastery. I have taken simple vows, so I don't wear a habit, and I go by Sister Mary Margaret.

"Right now, I run a half-way house. I spend my time helping out a few women who have been newly released from prison. Still, I don't go anywhere without this." She grabbed the large silver cross dangling from her neck and held it toward me like I was a vampire and she was using it to send me straight to hell.

At my widened eyes she let it drop, willing to play along with my story until she could get me alone. Then she'd get to the bottom of this charade. If I was lying to con Joe for his money, or anyone else in the Manetto family, I'd be damn sorry I was ever born.

"Why don't we all sit down," Frank said, wiping his perspiring forehead and wrinkling his nose with disappointment that this wasn't the happy reunion he'd imagined. "I can tell that this is a shock to you, Shelby. But I thought you'd be happy to meet your mother."

"Oh... of course... I'm just a bit... surprised, that's all. I never thought this would happen."

Maggie's lips turned up. She thought that at least I wasn't lying about that. "It's okay dear. I didn't either. In fact, you could say that I was just as shocked by the news as you seem to be."

Everyone chuckled, but they all picked up the underlying friction of something-not-quite-right about this reunion.

"Well, I think it's pretty awesome," Miguel said, hoping to break the ice. Besides, he totally understood the shock of meeting a parent this way. That's exactly what had happened to him and his dad, and everything had turned out great, so the same was bound to happen for me.

Frank and Sylvie voiced their agreement, so I nodded and smiled as well. A waiter entered our little room, giving me a reprieve from the shock. But what was I supposed to do now? I swallowed, knowing I needed to take control of the conversation. After the waiter took our drink orders and left, I took a deep breath and jumped right in, hoping for the best.

"So..." I smiled at Maggie, trying hard to sound calm. "Uncle Joey... well, he hasn't told me a lot about you. Do you live here? In New York? He didn't seem to know that."

"Yes I do," Maggie answered with a pleasant smile. "I'm not surprised he didn't know. After we left New York all those years ago, I missed it here so much that I came back." That wasn't exactly true. It was Stan whom she had missed, and she didn't regret one moment she'd shared with him, even if it wasn't long enough.

"I wrote my parents and told them I was in San Francisco to throw them off. I don't know what they told Joey, but I got a few letters over the years until they died. The address in San Francisco belongs to a friend of mine there, and I made sure she forwarded me any mail she received. I remember getting a couple of letters from Joe, so that's why he probably thinks I'm still living there."

"Oh... yeah, that makes sense."

"I only wrote him once, and that was to tell him I was fine, and living the life I wanted." She remembered telling him to leave her alone, and that she didn't want to have anything to do with the family ever again. He didn't know about Stan, so he probably thought she'd betrayed the family, but it was too late to fix it now.

"What I'd like to know is how he found you." Her sly gaze caught mine and she smiled, but there wasn't a lot of warmth involved, reminding me of Uncle Joey when he knew he had me over a barrel.

I chuckled to cover my total lack of such a story, and decided to lie and blame Uncle Joey for everything, since this whole debacle was his fault anyway. "Well... I don't really know much. Uncle Joey's probably the one you should ask. He's the one with all the details. But I'm pretty sure it involved a private investigator and lots of time and money. Maybe he was even looking for you to begin with?" I shrugged and smiled. "So how did Frank find you? Uncle Joey thought it was pretty clear that you didn't want to be found by anyone in the family." Based on her thoughts I figured that was a safe thing to say.

"I guess you could say it was a happy coincidence," Frank answered, jumping in since Maggie didn't. "We went to mass several years ago and happened to see Maggie there. She made us promise not to tell anyone, but we've kept in touch. When Joe told me about you and that you were coming for a visit... well, naturally I had to tell her."

The waiter came back for our orders, and I sighed with relief for the reprieve. Since I hadn't even looked at the menu, I feigned interest while I listened closely to Maggie's thoughts. How far was she willing to go with this? I needed to know if she planned to expose me in front of everyone.

I picked up that she was thinking about what she wanted for dinner since the food here was amazing. Then, after she placed her order, she glanced at Miguel, and the muscles around her eyes tightened. There was something familiar about him, but what? Had she seen him somewhere? Did he look like...

"You miss?" the waiter asked.

"Uh... uh... I'll have what she ordered," I said, nodding at Maggie, mostly to get Maggie's attention off Miguel. "It sounded good."

"Like mother like daughter," Frank said with satisfaction.

Maggie smiled. Her left eyebrow rose and she thought *nicely done.*

"Did you hear about Miguel's audition today?" I asked, totally de-railing her intended interrogation. "He was amazing." I launched into the story, going over how good Miguel was, and how fun it was to be in the theatre. Then I spoke about Times Square and all the sights. After that, I asked them what else Miguel and I should see before we left. By the time we'd finished talking about that, our food arrived, giving me a moment to catch my breath.

As we began to eat, I heard Maggie thinking that I was putting on quite the show. She'd even be proud of me if I'd been her real daughter. A sudden pang of grief shot through her. Grief and pain for all she'd lost nearly overwhelmed her, but she pushed it back before it took hold.

Turning her focus to me, she vowed to get to the bottom of my little scheme. Then it hit her that she could play the part just as well as I could. Why not enjoy this chance to be a mom for a while. After Frank had called to tell her the news, she'd felt more alive than she had in a long time. This whole situation added a little spice to her life, something she'd been missing for a long time.

"How long are you staying, dear?" she asked me. "There's so much I want to know about you."

"Uh... we're leaving tomorrow."

"Certainly not!" she gasped. "After just finding you... you can't leave yet. I need more time to get to know you better first."

"I'm sure Joe wouldn't mind if you stayed a few more days," Frank agreed.

"Well, yeah," I said, trying to figure a way out of this. "But it's not just me. Miguel needs to get back to school. And I've got my family to get back to."

"Your family?" Maggie asked.

"Yes. I have a husband and two kids."

Sylvie gasped and turned her excited gaze to Maggie. "Maggie! You've got grandchildren... two of them! Isn't it wonderful?" Sylvie clasped Maggie's hands, thinking that she'd always felt bad that Maggie was all alone in the world, but now she had a family! What could be better? Tears sprang to Sylvie's eyes and she let go of Maggie's hands to dab at them with her napkin.

Oh hell! This was just getting worse and worse!

"Anyway," I said, trying to gain some control over this fiasco. "How about we get together in the morning? We probably won't leave until early afternoon because Miguel might get a call back to audition again." I glanced at him. "Isn't that right?"

Miguel shrugged. He wasn't sure it would happen, but he wanted to stay a little later just in case. "Hey Shelby, I'm sure if you want to stay one more night, I can work it out. Who knows? It might be a good thing, especially if they want me to come back tomorrow."

"Wonderful," Maggie said. "If we can get together tomorrow I'll take it, no matter how much time you can give me." She smiled and reached for my hand across the table. "I know it won't make up for all the time I've lost with you, but it's a good place to start. Just think! A new beginning for both of us."

"Yeah," I agreed. "It sure is."

She squeezed my hand, then sat back in her chair. "Thank you Frank and Sylvie. I never thought I'd meet my...

my own flesh and blood." She shook her head in wonder, playing it up for all it was worth. "I don't know what to say."

Sylvie leaned toward Maggie and gave her a teary hug. "Hey, we're family. Nothing more needs to be said."

I closed my eyes and tried not to shake my head or roll my eyes or something. Wasn't a nun, or whatever she was, supposed to tell the truth? Of course, if she'd accused me of lying, that might have been worse. But I wasn't so sure this was any better. Why had I ever agreed to this?

Miguel patted my arm to comfort me, but he couldn't take his gaze off Maggie. He marveled that she was his real aunt. Too bad he couldn't tell her. But this was great for me. I'd probably always wondered what my birth mother looked like, and today I'd met her. How awesome was that? This trip was worth it just for that.

I let out a little groan. What was it with these Manettos and their focus on family? It was like there was nothing more important in the whole entire universe. Sheesh! If they really believed that, then why weren't they asking Maggie how she could have abandoned me in the first place? I'd like to hear her answer to that.

Just then, Syd entered the room with a pleasant smile on his face. "Sorry to interrupt, but it's time to go." His gaze traveled over our little group and came to rest on Maggie. His brows drew together, then his eyes got as big as saucers. "Maggie? Holy shit! Is it really you?!"

She smiled, amused at his outburst. "In the flesh."

All sorts of swearing came from Syd's mind, and his mouth gaped open in shock. "How... how..."

Frank chuckled and explained how they'd met at church a few years ago. As the implications set in, Syd glanced at me in wide-eyed horror. Then he turned his gaze to Maggie and realized she was going along with the whole thing. She had to know the truth... so what was going on?

"Sorry to cut this short," I said, standing. "But we'd better get going or we'll miss the show."

Everyone murmured in agreement and stood, giving Syd a moment to adjust from his shock. Then Maggie came toward me and gave me a quick hug. She even kissed me on the cheek. "I can hardly wait until tomorrow to talk to you again, Shelby. There's so much I want to know about you."

"Uh... yeah. Me too," I agreed. "How about we meet in the morning around nine? We could meet here in the lobby and maybe have breakfast."

"That will be perfect."

"Good, see you then."

I grabbed Syd's arm while Miguel said his goodbyes, and led him out of the restaurant ahead of everyone. "Maggie's going along with it," I whispered. "Why's she doing that?"

Syd shook his head. "I have no idea."

"So is she really a nun? What's she been doing all this time?"

"I have no idea," he said, repeating himself.

"Well, maybe you'd better call Uncle Joey while I'm at the play and tell him what's going on so we can come up with a plan."

"Yeah... sure. I'll do that."

Miguel caught up to us, ending our little chat, and we began the short walk to the theatre. The walk helped me calm down, and I was grateful Syd got to be the one to tell Uncle Joey about his sister. I just hoped that didn't mean we had to stay one more night because, as far as I was concerned, that wasn't going to happen.

Syd left us at the theatre entrance and told me to text him when the play ended so we could meet up to walk back. I assured him that I would, and we got in line with our tickets. I turned my attention to my surroundings, and excitement to be at a Broadway play quickly distracted me from my problems.

Inside, the attendant led us to our seats, and I could hardly believe where she took us. Our seats said mezzanine overhang box, but I had no idea it meant that we had our own private box above the stage. "Whoa," I said, glancing around. "These seats are amazing."

"That's just what I was thinking," Miguel agreed.

We stood there for a moment, taking it all in. Our box was positioned over the left side of the stage. It held only two cushioned chairs, so it was quite intimate, and we had a perfect view of the stage and everything on it. We could even see the orchestra below as they got their instruments tuned and ready to begin.

The theatre itself was amazing, with flowing, ornate carvings of flowers and vines framing the stage and interior walls in the typical art nouveau style. Even our boxes were not boxes at all, but round like teacups, with beautiful flowing vines decorating the outside. This lent a flavor of magic and anticipation to the atmosphere, which I hadn't expected.

Just then, the orchestra began to play the intro music, and the lights dimmed. The curtains drew apart, and the Genie of the Lamp opened with a resoundingly enthusiastic rendition of "Arabian Nights." With a delighted sigh, I let go of my worries and settled back to enjoy the show.

I learned several things during the show. First, even though the show was called *Aladdin*, he was not the only star. The genie was incredible. Aladdin and Jasmine had their parts to play but sometimes took a back seat to the genie, and I could tell that it made Miguel feel more comfortable about his possible involvement as the lead.

The actor who played Aladdin gave his character the light, carefree touch of youth, which I could totally see in

Miguel. In fact, the part seemed like it was made for Miguel's personality. Maybe there was a good chance that he'd get the part. From here, my worries that Miguel didn't have the huge resume didn't seem to be that big of a deal.

I picked up from Miguel that he loved the limelight, but he wasn't so sure he could carry a Broadway show. Still, if he got a chance to play any part on the show, he couldn't pass it up. This production was bigger than anything he'd ever seen in his life.

As the show progressed, his confidence grew that maybe he could play Aladdin. There was quite a bit of dancing involved, but he was good at dancing; he'd just never wanted anyone else to know.

It gave him a lot to think about. Was he ready to jump into a production that was functioning at such a high level with his own limited experience? It would be a challenge, but he was more than willing to make it work if he got the chance.

That kind of surprised me. If I was good enough to be in that group, I'd feel pretty intimidated. These guys were top-notch, nothing like a high school play. With all that pressure, I'd probably crack, and tell them I wasn't ready.

But Miguel wasn't thinking that at all. By intermission, he was more excited than ever to be a part of the production. I thought he was a little crazy to even consider it, but what did I know? Some people were born to perform, and he was obviously one of them.

I knew Uncle Joey would be disappointed, but wouldn't Miguel be better off if he wasn't groomed for Uncle Joey's kind of life? Sure, there were bad elements to everything, and the theatre was no exception, but it had to be better than becoming a mob-boss, right?

The special effects mesmerized me, especially with the genie coming right up out of the floor. It was also amazing to see Aladdin and Jasmine flying through the sparkling, night sky on their magic carpet. The scenery and set changes, along with the costumes were also fantastic, especially Jafar's change into the most powerful genie in the world. I absolutely loved it.

Then it had to end, and I couldn't believe the magical journey was over so quickly. I knew one thing for sure: the actors had certainly earned their standing ovations, and I couldn't wait to see it again... hopefully with Miguel playing a part.

After it was over, I sent Syd a text, and we stood to leave. At that moment, an usher hurried into our little box and gave Miguel a note.

I looked over his shoulder and read that the director wanted to speak with Miguel. He asked if we'd wait for him in our box. Miguel caught my gaze, thinking this was unexpected, but excitement bubbled inside of him.

Just a few minutes later, the director came inside the box and shook our hands. "How did you like the show?"

"It was awesome!" Miguel answered. "Something I'd love to be a part of."

"Can you come back in tomorrow for another song or two? I have someone I'd like you to meet."

"Absolutely," Miguel agreed. "What time?"

"Let's say around eleven?"

"Yeah, I'll be here."

"Good. See you then." The director smiled, then hurried out, thinking that Miguel was pretty perfect for the part. He wondered if Alan would think so too.

I caught my breath. Did he just think Alan Menken? The person who wrote the music? Holy cow! Alan was going to be there in the morning to play the piano for Miguel and give the director his opinion. That was incredible. Should I tell Miguel? But if I did, how would I explain how I knew that?

"Wow, that's so cool," I said, glancing at Miguel.

"Yeah... it is." All kinds of things went through his mind, but they were all overshadowed by Miguel's deep desire to participate in the show. His yearning was like a physical thing that filled up his whole body. I'd never felt anything so strong, and I sure hoped his wishes came true.

"Would you be okay if they asked you to be the understudy?" I asked him. "Or maybe part of the cast as a singer and dancer?"

He blinked. "Uh... sure. I'd be happy to do anything. It would be amazing to learn from them and be a part of that. They're the best."

I smiled. "Well then, I hope it happens."

We entered the lobby and passed the gift shop. The cutest t-shirt ever was hanging above the display, and I stopped to admire it. It was black with the skyline of New York City in silver sparkles and stars. On the right side, the word "Aladdin" was all in gold with the words "New York City" in silver underneath. That alone was amazing, but what made it extra special was the reflection in the water. Instead of the New York skyline, it was the city of Agrabah.

"I've got to have that," I blurted, and hurried over to the counter. Miguel followed, not quite sure what I was talking about, but he picked it up pretty fast once I pointed out the t-shirt to the salesclerk, who was happy to take my money.

On a whim, I picked up another one for Savannah, since I knew if she saw mine, she'd probably take possession of it at the first opportunity, and leave me empty-handed. The clerk told me that for only five more dollars, I could have the Aladdin bag, so naturally I bought that too.

We came out of the theatre to find Syd waving from the edge of the crowd. He asked us how we liked the show and listened to our enthusiastic replies. He was also pretty impressed that the director had asked Miguel to come back for another audition tomorrow. We told him all the pertinent details, and arrived back at the hotel before we knew it.

Since we weren't finished talking about the show, Syd motioned us to the lobby; and we sat in the comfortable high-back leather chairs around a circular, glass table. A waiter approached and asked if we would like something to eat or drink.

Wanting to make the night memorable, I glanced at Syd and Miguel. "How about some chocolate cake? Want to share a piece?"

The waiter left to get the cake, and soon returned, setting it in front of us with a flourish. It wasn't big, but I cut it into three small pieces and put it on our plates. After the first bite, I groaned with pleasure. This was like eating pure chocolate, with no cake involved. It was so rich and wonderful that I was grateful to have such a tiny piece.

After we were done, Miguel excused himself to go to bed. He was exhausted and still had tomorrow to look forward to. I was ready to go to bed as well, but I picked up that Syd was hoping I'd stick around, since he wanted to talk to me about his phone call to Uncle Joey, so I told Miguel goodnight and stayed put.

Syd let out a breath of relief and began. "Your uncle took the news pretty well. He wants you to see if Maggie will talk to him on the phone tomorrow when you meet with her. He'll clear it all up then. But you should call him tonight and work out the details."

He was thinking that, after the initial shock, they had both had a hearty laugh about it. Who would have thought? Now he understood what Uncle Joey meant when he said *only Shelby.*

"Yeah... right. Uh... okay. I'll give him a call tomorrow. Thanks, Syd. Wish me luck with Maggie in the morning. Do you have any ideas about what's on her mind?" Was I really asking him that?

He smiled. "Nope... I haven't seen her in years, but I don't think you have to worry she'll do something crazy or anything. After all, she is a Sister."

"True, true. Well, I'm going to bed. I'll see you tomorrow."

While the events of the day came crashing down around me, I made it to my room and could hardly wait to crawl into bed. But I had to call Uncle Joey, and I'd promised Chris I'd call him too, so I called Chris first and gave him a quick update on all the happenings.

"Then you'll never guess what happened... Maggie showed up."

"What? Are you serious?"

I explained that I was meeting her in the morning, and that Uncle Joey knew all about it. "I didn't pick up anything bad from her, so I think it will be okay. But wish me luck."

"Wow. I can't believe it. This family stuff is getting out of hand."

"Tell me about it." We spoke a little longer, then said our goodbyes.

Next, I put the call through to Uncle Joey.

"Shelby," he began. "I had no idea Maggie would show up. I can hardly believe it."

"Yeah... it sure took me by surprise."

He sighed. "Well, if it makes you feel any better, from what I remember of my sister, she's got a good heart. So I don't think you have to worry that she'll spill the beans before you have a chance to explain yourself. Then you can just tell her that it was all my idea."

"Okay. Hey... do you know anything about someone named Stan? She was thinking about him."

"Hmm... not that I recall."

"Well, he's the real reason she came back to New York."

"Is that so? Well... then I think it would be helpful to know more about him. See what you can pick up and let me know."

"Okay."

We spoke about Miguel, but he already knew the news about his second audition, since Miguel had called him. "Don't worry about getting back tomorrow. Let's just see what happens, all right?"

"Sure," I agreed, too tired to argue about anything. We said our goodbyes and disconnected.

A few minutes later, I snuggled under the covers and turned out the light. Just before sleep took me, I heard a man's beautiful voice. He sang a sweet melody that comforted and relaxed me, like he was singing me to sleep. I smiled. I'd have to remember to thank Miguel in the morning.

The next morning I got to the lobby a few minutes early. My chat with Uncle Joey last night had left me feeling more confident about talking to Maggie. Once she spoke with her brother, she'd know I wasn't the one who'd instigated this deception, even though I'd gone along with it.

Still, no matter how hard Uncle Joey's methods of persuasion might be, I wasn't sure she'd continue the charade. He'd probably have to tell her about Miguel, but since she was his sister, he could probably trust her.

Now Uncle Joey wanted to know who Stan was, and what had happened back then. Even if he hadn't asked, I'd want to know, but Uncle Joey asking me to spy on his sister might not be the right thing to do. Maybe she didn't want him to know her personal business, and I'd be invading her privacy. But wasn't that what I did with everyone?

On the other hand, what if explaining things made it better for her and brought the family together? After all these years, it could even give her some closure that would be good for her mental and spiritual health. Wouldn't that be a good thing?

My stomach tightened, and I took a deep breath. There was never an easy answer to these situations, and I'd just have to follow my conscience and hope for the best.

Just then, Maggie entered the lobby with her head held high and her lips pulled into a thin line of determination. She wore a high-collared white blouse with a spring-green colored sweater over black slacks.

The large cross dangling from her neck was the only evidence of her calling as a Sister. Her gaze found mine, and her breath caught with surprise that I actually showed up. All morning she'd been imagining the excuses I'd make to put her off, but there I was.

She was thinking that maybe I was made of sterner stuff than she gave me credit for. Still, she couldn't wait to hear my explanation, and she wasn't about to settle for anything less than the truth.

"Hello Shelby. I've been looking forward to our little chat."

"Me too," I said, even if it was only partly true. "Are you ready for breakfast?"

She shook her head. With all the tension, the thought of eating turned her stomach, and I had to agree with her assessment. Hmm... maybe we were more alike than I thought.

"If it's all right with you," she answered. "I've got something else in mind." She was thinking of the little garden within the church grounds. Even in the middle of the city, it was a quiet place of peace and reflection. It would also be hard for me to lie to her surrounded by statues of saints and standing on holy ground.

"Okay." Wow. She sure knew how to lay it on.

"It's not far. Have you ever been to New York before?"

"Uh... we drove through once when I was a kid."

She smiled. "I love it here, but it can take your breath away, especially with the crowds and how busy it always seems to be."

"That's true. I can't believe how many people there are... everywhere." I sent her a smile, even if she seemed formidable, I found it easy to talk to her. "You mentioned last night that you help run a half-way house. Is that where you live?"

"Yes, at least at the moment. I live there with three other Sisters, and we minister to a few of God's children who have lost their way. The women we take in need structure and guidance. None of them are hardened criminals, so we are quite safe. Most have been through a lot in their short lives, and we try our best to keep them from returning to what they knew before they went to prison. I believe we have made a great difference in their lives, even though we've lost a few."

"It must be very rewarding."

"I find it so," she agreed, glancing my way. My interest surprised her, and she could find no deception in my expression or tone. Maybe there was more to my involvement with Joey than she first thought.

"Most of the women were abused as children and have very little self-worth. They can come across as belligerent and mean, but I've found that they are the ones who hurt the most."

As we walked along, I encouraged her to share some experiences, and she told me a couple of heartwarming success stories before we came to a stop in front of a beautiful church. "Here we are." She climbed up the steps, then opened the door and ushered me inside.

It was cool and quiet inside, especially after the noise on the street. She led me through the church to a door in the back. It opened into a rather large, walled off garden. Several paths wound through the grass-covered lawn, circling a few trees and benches with nearby statues of saints and angels.

I followed her down a path that opened into a private little nook with a wooden bench along one side of the wall, surrounded by trees and flowering bushes. Since it was late spring, the blossoms were just about done, but still carried their color and scent.

"It's beautiful here. I can see why you'd choose this place to talk." We sat on the bench facing one another like old friends. Whoa! When had that happened?

"That's right, but I also wanted to make sure you'd tell me the truth." She caught my gaze with a piercing one of her own and raised an eyebrow, reminding me so much of Uncle Joey that my eyes widened. "We both know I'm not your mother, so what's going on?"

Behind her disapproval, real concern spilled from her mind and pulled at something inside of me. What she had to offer went deeper than knowing the truth. She was concerned about me as a person and, knowing her family, she had a pretty good idea that I'd gotten entangled in something way over my head.

Now that she'd had a chance to talk with me, she didn't believe that I was a con artist of some sort, mostly because she knew her brother couldn't be taken in. Plus, I seemed too kind-hearted to try pulling something off that could get me killed. So what was going on?

"Well, it's kind of a long story," I began, pulled in by the concern and worry in her warm brown eyes. The compassion flowing from her made me want to spill my guts about the whole thing. "It was actually Uncle Joey's idea to tell Frank that I was your daughter."

She nodded her head. "Then he's protecting someone... and it isn't you. So it must be Miguel."

Whoa. She was good, and my hesitation totally gave me away.

"He seems a little young to be Joey's son, but... he's definitely got the Manetto forehead and jaw." She glanced up at the trees and shook her head. "I always felt a little bad for Joe that he didn't have any children. But then I would have felt bad for his children if he did. Still, from the way things look, it doesn't seem like Miguel has been around him long enough to become jaded by all that wealth and power."

I nodded my agreement. "He's a good kid."

"So how did you get mixed up in all this?"

I listened real close to her thoughts, but there wasn't a shred of a hidden motive anywhere. So I began. "It all happened about a year ago when I stopped at the grocery store for some carrots..." I told her that I met her brother because of a woman named Kate, and I began calling him Uncle Joey because she did, and I knew he didn't like it.

I kept to the truth, only leaving out the mind-reading part, substituting that I had psychic abilities brought on by the gunshot wound instead. Her eyes widened, and I knew that she didn't quite believe that part, but she didn't interrupt. Once I got going, the story just poured out of me like a raging river bursting from a dam. It felt good to tell someone who actually understood what I was going through.

"So now," I said, coming to the end. "My children think Uncle Joey is related to us through my father's sister who divorced him. And Miguel truly believes that you're my real mother, and that he and I are cousins. None of it's true, and I feel terrible about all the lies. It's a mess!"

She shook her head, marveling at the scope of it all. With a deep sigh, she let out a breath and chuckled. "Now you know why I stayed away from the family. But in some ways, I guess I'm trying to make up for all the bad things that my family has done."

Her thoughts went to Stan and the tragedy of his death. If not for her and her family, he'd be alive and well today. The old pain stabbed at her heart.

Taking a chance, I decided to probe a little further with my so-called psychic powers. "I'm sensing that there's a lot more to your story, and it involves someone you cared for. Can you tell me what happened?"

Her eyes narrowed. Was I just guessing, or was I the real deal?

"You don't have to tell me, but it might feel pretty good to let it all out. I know I feel better now that you know the truth about me."

She shrugged. "It's a sad story. Are you sure you want to hear it?"

"Yes, but only if you want to tell me."

She glanced at the garden surrounding us, but her eyes held that far-off look of someone lost in another time. "I was young, and I didn't realize how dangerous it was to involve someone with my family. But Stan and I were high-school sweethearts, and we were in love. It was during our senior year of high school that my father insisted on moving away."

Her gaze found mine. "I'm six years older than Joe, so he wouldn't remember much of this. Needless to say, I fought my father with everything I had to get him to let me stay, but he wouldn't budge. You see... I had two older brothers and, by this time, one was in prison and the other one was dead.

"It was a hard time for our family, and I had no idea how bad things were between my father and my uncle. But my grandfather knew. Apparently, he didn't want his sons to kill each other off, so I'm pretty sure it was his idea to send us away.

"Since I had to go, I promised Stan that I'd come back that summer and we'd figure things out so we could be together." She shook her head and swallowed.

"So that summer, I told my dad that I was going back to visit my grandparents for a few weeks. I think he knew about Stan, but he figured a few weeks wouldn't hurt anybody. My grandparents didn't know about Stan, but they figured it out pretty fast. They told me I was too young to marry him, and I needed to break it off before someone got hurt.

"Of course I didn't to listen to them. We were in love, and I couldn't imagine my life without him. Unfortunately, my uncle and cousins noticed him coming around, and one day I introduced them. I made the mistake of telling them how smart he was. I even told them he had a full-ride scholarship to Harvard. I was just bragging because I was proud of him. But it was stupid. I didn't realize the danger I'd put him in.

"My uncle asked him if he wanted to earn a little extra spending money for college, and Stan agreed. It was easy money, and if we were going to move in together while he went to school, we'd need it. Still, I remember that first feeling of unease in the pit of my stomach.

"I told Stan about my misgivings, and that he shouldn't do it. He knew about my family, but he said he'd be careful, and he convinced me that we needed the money if we were going to make a life together.

"You don't know how many times I've regretted that decision." She sighed, and pain washed over her. Still, after all this time, the story came easier than she thought, and she realized that she wanted me to understand her past, so that I could understand the choices she'd made.

"I don't know all the details of what happened that day," she continued. "What I do know is that Stan and one of my cousins were both killed while they were on their way to the bank with a large cash deposit. They were gunned down, and the money was stolen.

"Both my grandfather and my uncle were heartbroken, and they pledged revenge against the family who had done this. It didn't take long before they traced the hit to the Bilottis, and that was the beginning of the war between the Manettos and the Bilottis that basically wiped out both families.

"That war began not too long after Stan's funeral. I was so oppressed with grief that I spent most of my time in the cemetery next to Stan's grave, so I didn't pay much attention to what was going on around me."

She caught my gaze. "I wished I had died with him, and I spent a lot of time talking to God and asking why he would do this to me. I soon realized it wasn't His fault, and I finally began to feel peace. I even thought that maybe I could go on with my life after all.

"But the worst was yet to come." She swallowed and glanced at me, then at her hands before taking a breath to continue. "I came home later that day to find my grandparents... both of them had been murdered. Shot down in cold blood. And the worst thing was... I would have died too if I'd been there."

I inhaled sharply, catching the scene from her thoughts of her grandparents' bullet riddled bodies and sightless eyes opened in death. No wonder she'd left the family and become a nun.

"I retreated from life after that day. I found myself back at the church. I told them I never wanted to leave, and that I would dedicate my life to God if they would let me stay. Of course, it wasn't that easy. I had to prove it wasn't just because I feared for my life. They let me stay and, over time, I proved my desire to serve God.

"To be honest, it took me a long time to forgive myself... and my family, for living the kind of lifestyle that killed Stan, my grandparents, and so many other family members. I guess you could say that I'm still trying to make up for it by being a Sister in the church, but I've also learned a lot about human suffering, and I'm at peace."

She smiled at me, thinking that if Stan hadn't died that day, I could have been her real daughter. But it wasn't meant to be, and she was okay with that.

"After everything that happened back then, my cousin Frank and his family are all that's left of the New York Manettos. As far as I know, they're not in the mob business anymore, so that's good. And they've been able to keep the hotel, which has meant everything to them."

"Um... well that's mostly right," I answered. "I mean... at least it's still in the family, but not quite how you're thinking."

Maggie's eyes widened. "What happened?"

"Apparently, several years ago, Frank was headed into bankruptcy, and he asked Uncle Joey for help. Uncle Joey bought the hotel, and Frank's family is running it. I don't know all the arrangements, but it looks like they're working together again."

Her brows rose in surprise. "Oh, I didn't know. Joey must be doing rather well."

"Uh... yeah." I shrugged. "He seems pretty well off. I mean... we flew here in his private jet. He also wants to talk to you. Would it be all right if I called him?"

The light went out of her eyes, and she glanced away. Being involved with the family again went against her better judgement.

"I understand if you don't want to, but talking to him doesn't mean you're rejoining the family. It can mean as little, or as much, as you want. Besides, he can't tell his big sister what to do, especially when you've caught him lying about you and me. You could even put the fear of God into him if you want."

She smiled, thinking that might be good for him, since it didn't look like anyone else was willing to do it. Wasn't that what big sisters were for? "All right. I'll do it."

I smiled and took out my phone, then called Uncle Joey's cell. He picked up pretty quick. "Hey Uncle Joey... it's Shelby. Uh... Maggie's here and she's willing to talk to you." I handed her the phone.

After taking a deep breath, she brought the phone to her ear. "Hello Joey. It's been a long time."

Wanting to give them a little privacy, I left my spot on the bench and wandered around the garden. I could still pick up bits and pieces of their conversation, but I didn't listen too closely. This was private, and I didn't want to intrude.

I had circled around the garden a couple of times before Maggie found me. Whatever they'd said to each other must have agreed with her, because her face had a happy flush to it.

"Thanks Shelby. It was good to talk to him." She was thinking that maybe the time had come for her to be more involved with the family. Not in an official capacity, but she could have a positive influence in their lives. Knowing Miguel was her nephew helped. And the fact that Miguel might be moving to New York definitely made a difference. He was a good kid, and she didn't want him corrupted by her brother.

She glanced at me with a gleam in her eyes. "So tell me about Miguel. What do your premonitions say his chances are for getting a part in the play?"

"Uh... that they're pretty darn good. In fact..." I glanced at my watch. "I should probably get back. After the play last night, the director invited Miguel to sing for a second audition at eleven this morning, and this time the man who wrote the whole freakin' thing is going to be there."

"Wow. That's impressive. I guess we'd better get going. Um... Shelby... there is one more thing." She caught my hands in hers. "I was thinking... I don't mind pretending to be your mom, if that's okay with you." Her hopeful gaze caught mine. "I mean... only when you're in New York, of course. But if Miguel gets the part, you might come more often."

I squeezed her hands before letting go. "I think that would be great. I wouldn't mind talking more often either. You're the first person, besides my husband, whom I've talked with about this whole thing, and you understand what it's like to be part of a mob family. I have a feeling I might need your advice."

She smiled and lifted her brow. "That's true. I don't know what help I could be, but I used to babysit Joey. I might be able to come to your defense if you need it."

I laughed at the idea of having her on my side. "That would be awesome!"

We made our way through the church, and she walked with me back to the hotel. On the way, she asked me about my family, so I told her about my husband and kids. In front of the hotel, I gave her my card so she'd have my phone number. With a teasing smile, she pulled out her cell phone and entered my number into her contacts list.

"Oh," I said, not realizing Sisters had cell phones. I put her number into my contact list, and we said our goodbyes.

"And let me know how it goes with my nephew," she said, smiling brightly.

"I will."

Chapter 8

Miguel and I arrived at the theatre ten minutes early. We'd left Syd behind since he was busy, and we knew how to get there on our own. On the way, I'd picked up that Miguel wasn't as nervous today. But if he knew that Alan Menken was going to play the piano for him, it would be a whole different story. Good thing I'd kept that little tidbit to myself.

After checking in at the office, we were shown to a downstairs rehearsal room with hardwood floors and sound proof panels on the walls, which were also covered by framed posters of the plays that had been performed on the stage above us. A leather couch nestled along one side, with a grand piano on the other, along with a few musical instruments and a set of drums.

We only waited for a few minutes before the director and Alan came in. While the director greeted Miguel, Alan took his place at the piano, just like an ordinary accompanist. Miguel didn't think anything of it. In fact, if I hadn't picked it up from the director's thoughts, I wouldn't have figured out who he was either.

The director asked Miguel if he'd like to sing *Proud of Your Boy*, and Miguel nodded his agreement. Alan played the introduction and, when Miguel came in, I picked up that Alan was blown away by Miguel's voice.

As the song continued, I heard Alan thinking how impressed he was with the feeling Miguel put into the song. How could such a young person relate to this so well? It was apparent that Miguel knew something of life, and it piqued Alan's interest.

The song ended, and Alan asked Miguel where he grew up. I was afraid Miguel wouldn't want to answer with the truth, but he candidly told Alan his story of growing up without a father in Mexico. Then he explained how his father had unexpectedly come back into the picture, saving him and his mother from a bad situation.

Described in such a way by Miguel made it sound like something from a fairytale. I'd never really thought of how Uncle Joey had taken on a drug cartel for his son. Of course, Miguel didn't go into the details, but it was easy to pick up that Miguel had lived a hard life... kind of like Aladdin.

Alan made up his mind that instant. Miguel was the one. Besides looking the part, along with his incredible voice, Miguel was earnest and humble, not like some of the others who knew they were good and deserved it. Miguel was a diamond in the rough, exactly what they needed.

I smiled to hear that thought. Still, my eyes filled up with tears. How cool was that? I just hoped Miguel could take care of himself in this world. Of course, he had the street smarts from his former life, and there was always Uncle Joey, so maybe he'd be okay.

Plus, I couldn't rule out Maggie and the New York Manettos. They'd watch out for him, too. He'd be fine. Still, that mothering part of me worried about this big change in his life, and how he'd handle it.

I also worried about how it would affect the family. A lump rose in my throat for what it would cost Uncle Joey to lose his son so soon after finding him. I'd known how much Uncle Joey wanted to turn the business over to his son, and now that wasn't going to happen.

On the other hand, wasn't that was a good thing? So maybe it was okay. I took a deep breath and shook my head. What was I thinking? That almost sounded like it was my family I was worried about. I pursed my lips with dismay. I needed to get home to my normal life before I forgot where I belonged.

The director thanked Miguel and told him they'd be in touch. I stood to leave and met Miguel at the door. He knew he'd done a good job and hoped he'd get some small part. As we walked down the hall, he couldn't hold it in any longer.

"Did I get a part?"

"How should I know?"

"Shelby... that's why you're here isn't it? Because of your premonitions? At least tell me if I have a chance."

I smiled and nodded. "All right... there's a pretty good chance, but wait until you know for sure before you tell anyone, okay?"

He grinned, thinking *like you're waiting to tell my dad?*

I chuckled but wisely kept my mouth shut. Just then, the door to the rehearsal room opened, and the director stepped out. "Hey, can you come back for a minute?"

"Sure," Miguel said, thinking this was a good sign. He caught my gaze and wiggled his eyebrows.

I smiled and followed him back. As we entered the room, the director introduced Miguel properly to Alan. Miguel's eyes widened, and he stood there a little tongue-tied until Alan came forward with an outstretched hand.

"I'm sorry, I didn't know who you were," Miguel said.

Alan waved it off. "That was part of the fun. So..." He glanced at the director, then at me, and finally at Miguel. "We'd like to offer you the part of... Aladdin."

Miguel's eyes widened in shock, then excitement spiked through him. "Dios Mio! Oh sorry... I'm just so... overwhelmed." He swallowed, then ran his fingers through his hair. "Uh... I don't know what to say."

"Say you'll take it," Alan offered, clearly delighted with Miguel's excitement.

"Yes. Yes! Of course! I would be honored." Miguel turned to me and, with great exuberance, caught me in a tight hug, lifting me off the ground and twirling us around in circles. He spoke several phrases in Spanish, then set me down and beamed from ear to ear.

Once he had settled down, the director got down to business. "I'll call your agent so we can work out the terms of your contract. Do you think you could stay one more night? We should be able to get everything put together this afternoon for you, but probably not before you have to leave."

"I'm sure that would work," Miguel answered, then glanced my way. "Right, Shelby?"

"Yes, of course. We can work with that."

"Great," the director said. "We should have everything ready to sign later this afternoon."

"Thank you so much," Miguel said. "I won't let you down."

We spoke for a few more minutes, and Miguel thanked them again and again, then we left the room. Out in the hall, Miguel jumped up and down a few times. "I can't believe it! This is so... amazing." He continued his excited chatter all the way out the door. "I need to call my Mom... and my Dad!"

"Yes, you do. Wait." I stopped him. "Stand right there so I can take a picture of you." He stood in front of the theatre with a big grin on his face, and I snapped several photos of him with my phone to mark the occasion. "Now you can send the picture too!"

I took his arm, and we began walking back to the hotel while he punched in his mother's number. As he told her the good news, I kept us moving in the right direction. Her response came back in Spanish, so I had no idea what she said, but he didn't talk long, telling her he needed to call his dad next.

Luckily, we weren't too far from the hotel, and I convinced him to wait until he had more privacy to make the call. We entered the lobby to find Frank and Syd talking together at the desk. Syd took one look at Miguel and knew something big had happened.

He rushed over to us, with Frank and Sylvie hot on his heels. "What's happened?"

"I got the part!" Miguel shouted. "Aladdin!" They all exclaimed and congratulated him amid hugs and pats on the back. "I need to call my father."

"Here son," Frank said. "Come into my office. You'll have some privacy there." Frank pulled Miguel away, and they disappeared into the room behind the front desk.

A minute later, Frank came out wiping his eyes and thinking how proud he was of his cousin, and that this musical talent ran in the family. His grandfather had been a great singer, and now it had been passed on to Miguel.

I glanced across the room to find Sylvie talking to Frank. She caught my gaze and quickly glanced away. So she was the one who'd figured out that Miguel was their cousin, but how? Did she overhear me talking to Syd? Before I could ask her, Miguel came out of the office, his face flushed with excitement.

He caught my gaze and smiled, but Sylvie and Frank practically jumped all over him, both stating that they needed to have a celebration before we left. Syd took my arm and walked us over to their circle so we could be included in the planning.

"We'll have a special dinner tonight," Sylvie said. She glanced at me and smiled, motioning me closer. "Miguel said you were staying another night, so this will be perfect. And let's invite your mother. I'm sure she'll want to come."

"Uh... sure," I agreed.

"We'll set it all up. Where would you like to go for dinner?" She didn't want to suggest the restaurant here, but going somewhere else would be twice as expensive.

"Why not eat here? The food last night was amazing."

"Wonderful. I'll make the arrangements."

Miguel's phone rang at the same time as mine, and I knew it was either the agent, Chris, or Uncle Joey. "If you'll excuse us," I said, grabbing Miguel's arm. "We need to answer these calls." As they waved us off, I pulled Miguel toward the elevator and answered the phone. "Hello?"

"Shelby?"

"Oh, hi Uncle Joey. Hang on, I'm getting Miguel out of here." We stepped into the elevator and I pushed the button for the twelfth floor. "Okay, we're on the elevator, headed to our rooms."

"What's going on?"

I explained the commotion in the lobby, while listening with half an ear to figure out who Miguel was talking to. We exited the elevator and hurried into our room. "Okay. We made it inside our rooms." I let out a relieved sigh and sank into the couch. "So what do you think about all this? Pretty exciting, huh?"

"Yes. I'm glad you warned me, or it would have been... more difficult to take in."

"Yeah... I understand. I think Miguel is talking to his agent right now."

"Yes... the agent called me right after Miguel did, and I told him to send Chris the contract as soon as it was drawn up so he could look it over. They should be finished with it sometime this afternoon."

"That's great. Did Miguel tell you we needed to stay one more night?"

"Yes. That should be fine, as long as you leave first thing in the morning."

Something in his tone didn't sound quite right. "What's up? Is something wrong?"

"It can wait until you get here."

"What is it?"

He let out a breath. "It's this whole thing with Ramos. Things are getting complicated, and I think he could use your help. There's something going down here that has me on edge, and I think Ramos might be taking the brunt of it. He's too involved, and I don't like it."

"You mean like he's being used?"

"Something like that."

"But... does he think so too?" My heart thumped faster in my chest, and dread rolled over me. "I thought... he said he could take care of it. So what's happened?"

"Look, we're handling it for now, and I don't want to ruin your fun. Don't worry about it. You'll be back tomorrow, and we'll figure it out then."

"Are you sure it can wait?"

"Yeah, no problem. Oh... there's one more thing..."

"Yes?" I braced to hear more bad news.

"Thanks for getting Maggie to talk to me. I don't know what you said to her but, whatever it was, it worked. It's been so long, and I didn't even realize that I'd missed her, but it was good to hear her voice. It also makes it easier for me to know she's there for Miguel."

"I agree with you on that. And since we're on the subject, Frank and Sylvie know he's your son. I don't know how they found out, but they're pretty happy about it, so I don't think you have anything to fear from them."

He huffed out a breath. "Hmm... I wonder who told them."

"Well, they're Manettos. They have ways of making people talk. It must run in the family."

He chuckled. "I'll see you tomorrow. And Shelby, take care of my son."

"I will."

We disconnected, and I let out a sigh. Worry about Ramos tightened my stomach, but there wasn't much I could do about it until tomorrow. Hopefully, nothing happened before then.

Pushing my worry aside, I quickly called Chris and heard everything he was doing on his end with the contract. He was excited for Miguel, but not too happy that I had to stay another night.

"I know," I agreed. "But I'll be home tomorrow, for sure."

"Uh-huh."

"Hey... I know what you're thinking. That I've said that before and not come home... but this time it's true."

He chuckled. "Are you sure you can't read minds over the phone?"

"Hmm... well yours may be a little different, since I know you so well, it's like I can read your mind anytime."

"Oh yeah? So what am I thinking now?"

"How much you love me... and miss me." I knew I had him over a barrel with that one.

He chuckled. "You know I do, and I'll be thinking of you tonight... when I'm in bed... all alone."

Now I chuckled. "Don't worry. I'll make it up to you."

"Good. I'll see you tomorrow."

We disconnected, and I let out a happy sigh. Maybe it wasn't so bad to leave on these little trips without Chris. He seemed to appreciate me more, and that was always a good thing.

Miguel was still talking on his phone. From what I could pick up, he was calling just about everyone he knew with the good news. After ending his most recent conversation, he came back into the sitting room area.

"I'm still in shock!" he said. "But it looks like things are going pretty smoothly. If all goes well, the agent said he'd be here around four with the contract for me to sign. Just think! I'm getting paid to do something I've only dreamed about! This is crazy."

"Yeah... for sure. How soon do you think you'll be coming back to New York?"

He took a breath. "That's the other thing. I don't start with the show until the first of July, but they want me back as soon as possible. Chris is checking to see if I can graduate early. Then I can come back in a week or two."

"Whoa, that seems pretty fast, doesn't it?"

"Yeah, but May first is next week, and there's so much I need to learn between now and July. All my finals were last week, and I just took my last one before we left, so there's really nothing left at school for me to do. My dad even said he'd fly me home for graduation if I wanted." Miguel was thinking that he'd rather fly his three best friends here to New York. Now that would be the best graduation trip ever.

I smiled at that thought and wondered how Uncle Joey would handle that.

My phone rang. The caller ID said it was Dimples. Oops. Was I supposed to help him today? I told Miguel I had to take the call and quickly answered.

"Hey Shelby, how was your trip?" Dimples asked.

"Um... well, I'm still in New York. We had to postpone coming home until tomorrow morning."

"Oh..."

"Yeah, so how's the case going?" So much had happened since we'd talked, that I'd nearly forgotten what we were working on.

"We're kind of at a standstill. We started with the girl who gave the drugs to Owen, but she wouldn't tell us anything. We did manage to track down her father. Owen said he was the one who had the drugs in the first place, remember?"

"Uh... sure. What did he say?"

"He hasn't said a thing," Dimples replied, clearly disgusted. "That's why I was hoping you could come down to the station. We could use your special help right now. But I guess that will have to wait."

"Yeah, sorry about that."

"It's okay. So... you'll be back tomorrow?"

"Yes. I'm flying back in the morning. Why don't I call you when I get home?"

"Sure," he agreed. "That should work. You probably don't know this, but the other kid who was in the hospital died this morning. We need to get those pills off the streets before anyone else dies."

"That's awful. I wish there was something more I could do."

"Hey... you'll be back tomorrow. We'll get to the bottom of it then."

We said our goodbyes and disconnected. I let out a big sigh. Between hearing his news, and the news about Ramos, it kind of took the fun out of this morning. And there was absolutely nothing I could do about it.

"What's up? Bad news?" Miguel asked. He'd overheard my side of the conversation, and it worried him.

"Oh... just work."

His brows drew together. He thought that I worked for his father, so what was wrong?

"Uh... I'm a paid consultant for the police, and I'm helping them on a case. That was the detective I work with. A couple of kids died from a new drug on the streets, and I'm helping him track it down."

"Oh," he said, surprised. "I didn't know you helped them." As the implications that I worked for both a mob-boss and the police sank in, his eyes widened. "Does my dad know?"

"Yeah. He's good with it. He knows I'd never turn on him... and you should know that too. We're family, right?"

Miguel nodded, but he thought that would be a hard position for me to be in. I totally agreed with him, but kept my mouth shut. He was also thinking that there was a lot more to me than he knew. What else did I do? It was on the tip of his tongue to ask me, but I was saved by the sound of his phone.

"Uh... I'm going to get a diet soda while you answer that. Do you want anything?

"No, go ahead."

I hurried out, grateful that I'd dodged that bullet. I found a drinks machine and a snack machine standing side by side, so I got a package of Cheetos to go with my soda since I'd missed breakfast.

I got back to our room and Miguel was still talking on his phone, so I stood in front of the big window and looked over the city while munching on my snack. A moment later, Miguel joined me.

"You want to do some sightseeing?" I asked him. "We've got a couple of hours before the agent will be here."

"Sure. Let's do it."

We found Syd in the lobby and asked where he thought we should go. With a shake of his head, he checked his watch and did a few calculations in his mind about what we had time to see.

"Okay... let's take the subway... and then we'll have to walk to a spot where you can see the Statue of Liberty. Then we can make our way back here by way of a few other things like the 9/11 Memorial and The Empire State Building." He didn't think we'd have time to make it to the top, but we could at least check it out.

"Sounds great!"

I was excited to take the subway with an experienced New Yorker and found that it was everything I thought it would be. I even saw a rat on the rails. It was also nice to experience more of New York than just Times Square, although that was still pretty awesome.

I took pictures of the Statue of Liberty and the 9/11 Memorial. We also made it up to the top of the Empire State Building. That was because there were no lines due to the clouds and no visibility, but we didn't care about that. It was fun to be up in the clouds and, with the wind, they moved enough that we still got some nice views.

From there, we rushed around like crazy people, but that made it fun. We barely got back to our hotel rooms before the agent called, saying he'd arrived in the lobby. With a surge of excitement, I accompanied Miguel back to the lobby to meet him.

After chatting for a few minutes, we decided to go over the whole thing in the privacy of our sitting room. Syd caught my eye, and I waved him over, telling him we were going upstairs to sign the contract. He gave me a thumbs-up, and we hurried to the elevator doors.

Inside the sitting room, the agent gave us each a copy of the contract so we could go over it together. As he explained everything, I listened closely to his thoughts to make sure he was being honest and picked up that he was super excited for Miguel and happy that he could represent such a great talent.

I also found out that the agent had already called Miguel's drama teacher to tell him the happy news and to thank him for introducing them. He was pretty sure that, by tomorrow, everyone in Miguel's school would know what had happened, but he had a feeling that Miguel could handle it.

It helped me to know that Chris had already gone over the whole thing and had told Uncle Joey and Miguel in a short phone call that it was good to go.

After everything had been explained, Miguel glanced hopefully at me, ready to sign it. Before I could nod, my phone buzzed. "Hang on, let me answer this."

"Hey Shelby," Syd said. "Sylvie and Frank want to know if they can come up and witness Miguel signing the contract."

"Uh... just a minute. Let me ask him." I told Miguel what they wanted, and his brows drew together in confusion.

"Why would they want to do that?"

"Oh... that's the other thing I didn't tell you. Somehow they found out that you're... you know... Uncle Joey's son... you know... a Manetto?"

Miguel's brows rose. "Does my dad know?"

"Yes. I mentioned it to him earlier, and he's okay with it."

"Uh... okay then, I guess they can come up," Miguel said, shrugging his shoulders and setting down the pen.

I told Syd they could all come, and a few minutes later a knock sounded at the door. I opened it to find not only Frank and Sylvie, but Maggie, Syd, and four other people that I didn't know.

"We brought the whole family," Sylvie said. She introduced her two sons and their wives, telling them all that Miguel was Uncle Joey's son and their cousin. Then she turned to me and introduced me as Maggie's daughter.

My heart squeezed just a bit at the lie, but Maggie sent me a knowing smile and quickly came to my side, offering her moral support. All at once, they descended on me and Miguel, giving us big hugs and air kisses on each side of our faces.

I felt a bit smothered from all the attention and hoped Miguel wasn't overwhelmed by them all. I picked up his delight at suddenly having a huge family, just like he'd always wanted. He caught my gaze and smiled.

After everyone had their turns greeting us, Sylvie shushed them all and motioned for Miguel to sign the contract. With a huge grin, he picked up the pen and signed it with a flourish. Everyone clapped and cheered, just like he'd won the biggest prize of his life.

Maybe he had.

The rest of the afternoon and evening was spent celebrating with the family. At dinner we met Sylvie and Frank's grandchildren who'd been invited to eat with us. All six of them were under the age of ten, and having them there made for an entertaining evening.

After they left to put the kids to bed, things settled down, and I had a moment to talk with Maggie. She told me she'd had another phone chat with Uncle Joey this afternoon. He'd told her that when Miguel came back, he and Jackie were coming too, and she looked forward to seeing him after all these years.

"Telling that lie that you're my daughter may have been the best thing that's happened to me in a long time. I hope you don't regret it."

"Not at all," I said. "Just as long as my mom doesn't find out."

She chuckled, and then she wanted to hear all about 'adoptive' family.

Later, Syd pulled me aside to tell me about the arrangements for our flight home. The plane was scheduled to leave at eight in the morning. That meant we had to be ready to leave by six-forty-five. "I'll schedule a six o'clock wake-up call for both of you."

I nodded, then picked up a wave of satisfaction from him that everything had turned out so well. Seeing me with Maggie had convinced him that Frank and Sylvie needed to know that Miguel was Uncle Joey's son, and he patted himself on the back for doing the 'right thing' even if Uncle Joey might not like it.

"Uh... Syd?" I said.

"Yeah?"

"Just so you know... Frank and Sylvie know you report everything to Uncle Joey."

"They do?" His eyes widened with alarm that was entirely feigned. He knew they knew, and he was thinking that, in this business, it was always a good thing to think each side knew something that the other side didn't. It was part of the delicate balance between the families that kept them in line.

"Yeah," I said, smiling. "But something tells me you already knew that."

He smiled back, but shook his head. "What else do you know?"

"I don't think I'll tell you yet. But someday..." I knew he wasn't ready to hear that I'd picked up his more than casual interest in Maggie. He'd remembered her from all those years ago, and once had a huge crush on her. Seeing her again brought all those same feelings back.

He studied me, thinking that maybe I had a talent for finding out things, and that's why Uncle Joey needed me so much. To be honest, he'd been surprised that Uncle Joey had been so adamant about watching out for me. Miguel, he could understand, but I wasn't part of the family. But Joe sounded like he really cared for me.

After observing me with Miguel, and then Maggie and the whole family, he could see that I had a good heart. There was something about me that he trusted, and he was sure Uncle Joey felt the same. Someday, he hoped Uncle Joey would tell him the story of how I'd come to be part of the family.

Yikes! Was I part of the family? Glancing around the room, it sure seemed like it, and I hoped that was a good thing. Not only was I a cousin to these people, but a niece and a daughter. It was a lot to take in, and it made me a little tired just thinking about it.

Since I had to get up early the next morning, I used that as an excuse to say my goodbyes. Miguel smiled with relief and stood as well. He thanked them all for their support and, amid all the goodbyes, we both promised to stay in touch with everyone. I even got an extra hug from Maggie.

As I left the restaurant, I heard Syd offering to drive Maggie home since it was so late. I picked up a wave of pleasure from her as she accepted, and I was glad she couldn't see my pleased grin.

It was a relief to enter the quiet of my room. After packing up everything, and getting ready for bed, I fell onto the soft mattress with a thankful sigh. This had been a whirlwind trip, and I was ready to get home. But I had to admit it had been pretty awesome as well.

Snuggling under the covers, I closed my eyes and began to drift off. Once again, the sound of Miguel's beautiful singing brought a smile to my lips. Then my brow puckered. What was he doing awake? It had been a long, eventful day, and he should be asleep.

The song sounded like one I'd heard before, but I couldn't understand the words. Then it hit me that the words were in another language. What? Was Miguel singing in Spanish? Why would he do that? Wait. I'd just heard this song recently... but where? Then I realized that I'd heard that exact song in the lobby when we first arrived, and later in Frank's office. It was Italian!

My eyes jerked open, and my breath caught. I glanced around my dark room but couldn't see anything out of the ordinary. I only knew that the beautiful voice wasn't coming from Miguel's room. It was here, right beside my bed. My breath quickened, and I held perfectly still.

Con te partirò.

The resonance from that rich voice sent chills down my spine. The haunting melody swirled around me. Since it was in Italian, I couldn't understand what the words meant, but they were filled with emotion and tenderness. I inhaled sharply as the song soared to a breathtaking height, sending a rush of emotion so strong that it brought tears to my eyes.

Then the notes floated away, carrying the scent of sandalwood and spice. Except for my racing heart, all was quiet. I swallowed and sat up to turn on the bedside lamp. What the freak? Was that a ghost?

I'd left a bottle of water on the nightstand, and I grabbed it to take a few long sips, hoping it would help settle me down.

Then it hit me. Hadn't Frank said something about his grandfather being a singer? He'd even thought that the talent had been passed on to Miguel. Was that who it was? Miguel's great-grandfather? Had he lived here in this hotel?

Since I knew I'd never get to sleep after that, I grabbed my Kindle and started reading a book to take my mind off what had just happened. Around one-thirty in the morning, my eyes were too tired to keep reading. After turning out the light, I settled into bed and closed my eyes. Relaxing, I let out a deep breath. As I drifted off, the low hum of a sweet melody lulled me into sleep.

My wake-up call came way too early. Somehow, I managed to get out of bed and hop into the shower. As I dressed in my comfy jeans and my "I Love New York" t-shirt, I wondered if I'd really heard that beautiful voice last night. It had sounded so much like Miguel. Maybe it was Miguel, and there was some connection between the rooms that made it sound so close? Yeah... right. Who was I trying to kid?

Pushing that thought away, I got down to business and made sure all my toiletries and clothes were packed up. Then I stuffed all the souvenirs on top and zipped up my bags. From the sitting room, Miguel's door stood open, and he was just zipping up his bags. He soon joined me in the room with a huge grin on his face, still amazed at his good fortune and feeling on top of the world.

His contagious happiness brought a smile to my lips. "Hey... did you get any sleep last night?"

"Some," he answered. "But it took a while."

"I'll bet. Uh... you didn't happen to do any singing in your room, did you?"

"Last night? No. Why?"

"Uh... no reason. I just thought I heard something, and I wondered if it was you. Did you hear anything?"

He shook his head, wondering what was going on with me.

Still, I forged on, knowing I couldn't let it rest until I knew for certain. "Do you know any Italian songs?"

This time he smiled. "You know... I do. Remember when we came out of the elevator and into the hotel that first day? An Italian song was playing. I actually learned that same song for my vocal training class. Isn't that nuts?"

"Uh... yeah." My eyes widened and my neck tingled. "I remember hearing that song, but I'm not sure how it went. Could you sing some of it for me?"

"Sure. But it's going to sound a little different from the way I normally sing. You know... more like opera."

"That's okay with me."

"Okay, here goes." He closed his eyes to lose himself in the song and then began singing the haunting melody, sounding so much like the voice I'd heard the night before that chills ran down my spine. Then he got to the *Con te partirò* part, and I knew it was the exact same song. At the end of the first chorus, he stopped singing, leaving me a little breathless.

"Wow," I said, after finding my voice. "Will you promise me that you'll record that someday soon, so I can listen to it whenever I want?"

He chuckled, then shrugged his shoulders. "Uh... sure."

"Thanks. I guess we'd better get going... but... are you sure you didn't sing that last night after you went to bed?"

"Yes. I'm sure." His brows drew together in confusion. "Why?"

"Oh nothing." I shook my head. "I must have dreamed it or something." I moved to the door and picked up that he thought it might have something to do with my premonitions. Maybe I'd had a premonition that he sang that song sometime in the future and it wasn't a stretch to think he'd actually record it. *Wow... wouldn't that be something?*

I held back a smile as we closed the door and got on the elevator. Someday, maybe I'd tell him about his great-grandfather, and how he'd serenaded me last night with that song. I was sure Miguel would be interested to know of the connection, but I'd probably have to keep the serenading part a secret.

The doors whooshed open, and we found Syd standing alone behind the desk in the lobby. As we approached, he greeted us and took our room keys, then glanced between us with a twinkle in his eyes.

"I have something for each of you." He pulled a five-by-seven photo out of a large envelope and passed it over to us. "There's two of them in here."

The photo was from our dinner the night before. Miguel and I sat in the center of the group, with the whole Manetto family surrounding us. Everyone was smiling and happy.

"Wow, this is great!" Miguel said. "Thanks."

"Don't thank me. It was all Sylvie's doing."

Just then Frank came out of his office. "Are you off?" he asked.

"Yeah," Miguel answered. "Thanks so much for everything."

Frank waved his thanks away. "Just tell your dad to come with you next time. I'm sure he'll want to see your Aunt Maggie. And Shelby..." he glanced at me. "Your family is welcome anytime as well. Be sure to bring them to this hotel. We're all family now, and we'd love to get to know them."

"Thanks Frank. I will." He was serious about the offer, and I had a deep desire to take him up on it. It would be a blast to bring Chris and the kids to New York and stay here in this hotel. And now that Miguel had the part, I knew everyone would want to come.

We said our goodbyes and followed Syd to the elevator and then into the parking garage, getting inside that same awesome car for the trip to the airport. Syd started the car up, and Italian music poured from the speakers. He was thinking about changing it to something else for Miguel's benefit, but just then *Con te partirò* began to play, and he hesitated.

"Turn it up!" I yelled, my heart hammering with excitement. I caught Miguel's surprised gaze and picked up that he could hardly believe the coincidence. Then he wondered if I'd had a premonition that this song would be playing.

I chuckled with delight and encouraged him to sing along. After a little prodding, he joined in and my heart burst with exhilaration. What a perfect way to end our visit! Little shivers ran down my neck. Was this really a coincidence?

I listened closely. Besides the performer's and Miguel's voices, there was a moment or two that I thought I could hear one more voice, and my breath caught. As the final notes sounded, goosebumps rose on my arms, and I had to swallow before I could speak. "Whoa! That was amazing."

Miguel smiled, thinking he'd never sounded so good singing that song. All at once, a strong bond seemed to connect him to that particular piece. He'd never felt that before. Was it because of his Italian heritage? He'd never felt connected so strongly to that side of his family before, so that had to be it.

Syd was so moved he could hardly speak. He nodded his agreement, and we all settled back in our seats for the drive, each of us lost in our thoughts. Miguel was right about one thing. He was definitely a Manetto.

Before I knew it, Syd was pulling into the airport parking lot. He jumped out of the car to get our bags out of the trunk. I got out and stretched. Then, with everything in hand, we walked to our gate. Syd made sure all was taken care of before sending us off.

"It's been real nice meeting you both. I expect I'll be seeing more of you in the future. I'll let Joe know you got off okay. He'll have a car waiting for you when you land." Syd was thinking that Uncle Joey would probably be in the car, but he didn't want to spoil the surprise.

"Thanks for everything Syd," I said. "It's been great."

We said our goodbyes and hurried out to Uncle Joey's plane. After getting settled and all buckled in, the plane taxied to the runway for take-off. Once we were in the air, I relaxed into my seat, glad to have some down time to process everything.

So much had happened on this little trip that it kind of took my breath away. Miguel's life was changed forever. He was now playing the part of Aladdin... on Broadway. That huge change was sure to put a crimp in Uncle Joey's plans.

Then we'd met the New York Manettos, including Maggie, and had been welcomed as long-lost relatives. Frank had even invited my whole family back for a visit. But how would that work? Everyone there thought we were part of the family, and I'd have to tell my kids some story so they'd think it was true.

Of course, hadn't I already done that? But how would I explain Maggie? Everyone would be calling her their Grandmother. Yikes! What would happen if Frank and Sylvie, along with my kids, ever found out the truth? As much as I wanted to, I wasn't sure I could bring my family back, and that kind of broke my heart.

To top it all off, there was the singing ghost. What was up with that? I'd have to check into it. Then it hit me. This had to be the same grandfather Maggie had told me about, and he'd been murdered. She never said where it had happened, but I had a sneaking suspicion it was at the hotel. She'd said they tracked the hit to another mob family, but what if they got it wrong? Was that why he was still hanging around?

I vowed to find out what Uncle Joey remembered of him. Maybe on my next trip to New York... if I managed to come... I'd find out more. But now, it was time to concentrate on my real life.

First, I needed to find out what was going on with Ramos. The Jodie McAllister concert was tonight. If Ramos wanted to know if Jodie's daughter was also his daughter, I needed to be with him when he talked to her.

I also needed to find out what Dusty was up to. It had to involve those pills he'd planted in the envelope with the tickets. Had Ramos figured it out? It didn't sound good from Uncle Joey's point of view, and my stomach clenched with dread. Nothing good ever came from drug dealers.

That reminded me of the school kids who had died. Dimples needed my help today in questioning that drug dealer, and I sincerely hoped we could get some answers and maybe find out if it was somehow connected to Dusty.

I also needed to talk to Kyle and his nephew, Keola. Hopefully, Kyle could arrange another time for me to meet with Keola, so I could get to the bottom of what was going on with him. He hadn't thought about drugs, but I couldn't shake the feeling that maybe they were related to Dimples' case.

Closing my eyes, I let out a breath. Sheesh! Just thinking about all of that gave me a headache, so I headed to the back of the plane for a diet soda. As I popped the can open, I couldn't help the tinge of regret to leave New York behind. Things had been so awesome there the last couple of days that now I wasn't sure I wanted to go home.

Chapter 9

The plane coasted to a stop at the airport, and Miguel and I gathered our things. Coming down the mobile stairway, the warm spring air blew my hair back, and sunshine rested on my face. I covered my eyes with my hand and spotted Uncle Joey's limo waiting a short distance away. As we stepped off the stairs, the car door opened and Uncle Joey stepped out.

Miguel smiled and hurried to his side, bursting with excitement. As they embraced, I grinned, happy that Uncle Joey had taken Miguel's success so well. Then Uncle Joey turned to me and enfolded me in a tight hug, taking me off-guard.

"Welcome home," he said, releasing me.

"Thanks. That was some trip."

He chuckled. "I'm sure. You'll have to tell me all about it on the way home."

Just then the driver's door opened and I glanced up, hoping to see Ramos. Instead, it was Ricky who greeted me, and I smiled to hide my disappointment. Soon, he had our bags in the trunk, and we were all loaded up and ready to go.

Miguel and I took turns telling Uncle Joey everything that had happened and all the things we'd seen and done. He took it all in with a jolt of pleasure. He was marveling that this amazing kid was his son and thinking how lucky he was. He didn't regret for a minute that Miguel was going his own way. This business wasn't for him anyway.

Whoa! I never thought I'd hear him thinking that.

He glanced at me, thinking that it was too bad it wasn't for me either. I could make a lot of money, and give my children all the opportunities they needed to succeed in this life... just like he had with Miguel. My eyes widened, and he chuckled.

I huffed out a breath and shook my head. "So what's the plan?" I asked. "Where are we going?"

"I promised Miguel's mother that we'd let him off at her house." He glanced at Miguel. "Is that all right with you?"

"Sure," Miguel answered.

"Good. I expect that she'll want to have some kind of a celebration. Maybe we can arrange a get-together at our house tomorrow night." He caught Miguel's gaze. "If it's what you want. Talk it over with your mom and let me know."

"Okay." Miguel thought that might be fun, but not with his mom and dad in the same room. He was pretty sure they'd both be happier celebrating his success separately. But he'd figure it out. At least he could invite his friends over to the house. Then he could invite my family as well, and just thinking of that brightened his mood.

We pulled up in front of a beautiful, hacienda-style home which I knew Uncle Joey had paid for. The front door opened and Carlotta stepped onto the porch, waiting for Miguel.

"I won't be long," Miguel said. As much as he loved his mother, she could be a bit overbearing, and he could only handle so much.

Uncle Joey nodded. "There's no rush. Ricky can come back when you're ready."

"Okay. I'll call." He jumped out of the car and hurried into the house.

We watched as he waved and disappeared inside. "He loves her," I said. "But he's really glad he has you."

Uncle Joey caught his breath. "Thanks Shelby."

"Sure."

"Do you need to go home first, or can you come to the office?"

"The office is fine. I've actually arranged to meet Chris at work for lunch today." On the plane ride home, I'd called both Dimples and Chris to work out a schedule. Since Chris wasn't available until one or one-thirty, that gave me plenty of time to question the drug dealer with Dimples. Of course, I wasn't about to tell Uncle Joey that part.

"Good," he said, letting out a relieved breath. He told Ricky our destination, and we pulled away from the curb. "So how was New York, for real?"

I chuckled. "It was great. I don't think you have anything to worry about with Frank and Sylvie. They even invited their sons and wives with all the grandkids to a celebration dinner to meet Miguel and me. Maggie came too, and it was one big happy family. Oh... I even have a picture."

I pulled the envelope out of my bag and pointed out who everyone was. "Have you ever met them all?"

"No. The last time I was there was when I bought the hotel six or seven years ago." He studied Maggie's face and tried to remember the last time he'd seen her, probably when he was a teenager. "Did you ever find out what happened to her?"

"Yeah," I said, sighing. "It's a sad story, and it all happened about the same time as when your grandparents died. Do you remember much about that?"

He shook his head and pursed his lips. "Only that it devastated our family... but mostly my father. He wouldn't let us go to their funerals, and he didn't tell me much about what happened. To be honest, I've tried to forget that time, but I picked up enough to know that it was a hit by another family. Frank could probably tell you more.

"My father flew to New York for their funerals and was supposed to bring Maggie back, but she never came home. Next thing I know, she's a nun, and it's like she never existed. But I always knew that she didn't want to be part of the family anymore. So what happened?"

"She was in love with her high school sweetheart," I began. "She went back that summer to be with him. Then he got involved with the family and was killed, along with one of your cousins, over some money. It broke her heart.

"Your grandfather and uncle took it upon themselves to avenge their deaths, and I guess it started a war. She was at the cemetery when your grandparents were killed, or she would have died with them. It was the catalyst that drove her to choose a vastly different way of life."

Uncle Joey nodded, finally understanding why she had rejected him and their parents. He never knew she'd lost so much, and a wave of sympathy washed over him.

"Anyway... now she wants to keep pretending she's my mother. How crazy is that? I told her it was okay, but... it's making things really complicated. I mean... I'd love to take my family back to New York to see Miguel in the play, but how would I explain all of this to them?"

Uncle Joey smiled. "Oh, I'm sure we could figure something out. We'll worry about it when the time comes." He glanced at the picture, inordinately pleased that Maggie was going along with the charade. It meant she was getting something out of the arrangement. He handed the picture back and glanced my way, thinking it was me. Wasn't that something? Maybe knowing his extended family wasn't such a bad idea.

"Hey... she's getting Miguel too," I said.

He chuckled. "Yes, that's true. She told me she was excited to get to know him. So I guess that means she'll watch out for him in New York, and that's even better. Anything else I should know?"

"Uh... well, Frank knows that Syd reports to you, and Syd knows that he knows, but they all seem okay with it."

"Did you figure out who told Frank that Miguel was my son?"

Should I tell him the truth? "Uh... yes, I did, but he had his reasons, and I think it all turned out for the best."

Uncle Joey's eyes narrowed. "It was Syd, wasn't it?"

I smiled, knowing it was a lost cause to keep anything from Uncle Joey. "Yes. But to be honest, I think he's loyal to both of your families, and he just wants things to work out between you. None of that power struggle going on like before, you know?"

Uncle Joey was thinking that he knew very well, but he wasn't sure Syd had done him any favors.

"Uh... the thing is," I continued, knowing I had to explain it better. "Frank doesn't know that Syd knows he knows. So in a way, Syd is still in the driver's seat. Syd told me that it's a great way to keep the checks and balances between the two of you. But, now that you know Frank knows, I guess it might not work as well. On the other hand Frank doesn't know that you know, so it might be okay."

Uncle Joey shook his head at all the double-speak. "It's fine. I'm not changing a thing. Forget about it."

"Okay." I snorted just a little, mostly because of the license plate in my bag with that exact same phrase on it.

"Is something funny?"

"Uh... no... not a thing. So where's Ramos? I thought he'd be driving."

"He hasn't come into the office yet."

"Why not?" Alarm tightened my chest. "Did something happen?"

"No. He was out late last night, but he should be there by now." He was thinking that Ramos better be there. This whole thing from Ramos' past was taking up too much of his time. It needed to be solved so Ramos could get back to business.

Yikes. That sounded a little harsh, but I also caught an undercurrent of worry along with Uncle Joey's irritation, so it didn't bother me too much. "Uh... I hope I can help."

"I'm sure you can." He glanced at me, glad that I was back. And glad that I cared about Ramos enough to help out.

We pulled into the parking garage of Thrasher Development and parked in Uncle Joey's reserved spot. I got out, taking my purse with me, and followed Uncle Joey to the elevators. On the way, I managed a quick peek around the support column where Ramos parked his motorcycle. All that shiny goodness sent a little thrill through me, and my shoulders sagged with relief to know he was here.

As we walked into the office, Jackie smiled with pleasure. "Hey Shelby! How was New York?"

"Awesome. Isn't that something about Miguel?"

"Yes. I can hardly believe it."

We spoke for a few seconds before Uncle Joey interrupted us. "Is Ramos here?"

"Yes," Jackie said. "He came in just a few minutes before you and went into the apartment to change his clothes."

Just then the door at the end of the hall opened and Ramos stepped out. He wore his usual jeans with a button-down shirt and blazer. His hair was wet, so he must have showered, but the darkness along his jaw showed that he didn't have time to shave.

With a slight scowl on his face, he exuded danger along with that sexy predator vibe he carried so well. He glanced up and caught me staring at him. His scowl turned into a smirk, then a lopsided grin. Then he did a little head nod in my direction and thought I looked cute in my "I Love New York" purple t-shirt.

"Good. You're here," Uncle Joey said. "Let's go into my office, and you can tell us what happened last night."

At the mention of last night, Ramos' grin faded into a dark scowl. I listened real close to find out what was bothering him, but his thoughts were shut up tight. The only thing I could pick up was discouragement and a hefty dose of annoyance.

I waited for him to come to my side before we both followed Uncle Joey to his office. "Not going so well?"

"You could say that." As much as he didn't want to involve me in his problems, he couldn't see a way around it. "I'm afraid I need your help."

"Is that right?" It was on the tip of my tongue to chew him out for being 'afraid' to ask for my help, but I kept my mouth shut. Still, it rankled just a little that he'd asked like that. "I'll see what I can do."

My tone caught him by surprise, and he realized he was taking me for granted. He was so used to me wanting to help, and sticking my nose where it didn't belong, that he never imagined I'd turn him down. Then he realized I'd just heard that and did a mental head slap.

"It's okay, Ramos. I know this whole thing is frustrating, but we'll figure it out."

"Yeah... sure. Uh... sorry."

"Fuhgedaboudit," I answered, then couldn't help snickering. Ramos lifted an eyebrow, so I shrugged. "It's how they say it in New York."

He shook his head, but the tension left his shoulders, and he cracked a smile. "How did it go?"

"Well... let's just say it was a little crazy."

"You'll have to tell me about it sometime." He'd heard that Miguel got the part, and that I'd met the family. Since that was a new development, he thought the crazy part was probably an understatement.

"Yes it was," I agreed, nodding my head as we entered Uncle Joey's office. Uncle Joey sat down behind his desk, while Ramos closed the door behind us. Then we took our seats.

"So what did you find out?" Uncle Joey asked Ramos.

"I haven't been able to track Dusty down, but I found out those pills he gave me are homemade. They're fake pain pills made with fentanyl. That's a synthetic opioid that resembles powdered heroin. My source told me that just one kilogram of fentanyl can be made into a million phony pain pills. And they sell for a lot of money."

"You think Dusty made them?" I asked.

"Yes. And it gets worse. I've been asking around, and I found out the pills are out on the streets here. Dealers from some of the gangs are selling them like hotcakes. I found out Dusty is Jodie's road manager. So last night, I went to the arena where Jodie's performing, hoping to track him down. All the trucks for her show are there, along with a few motorhomes, and I managed to slip inside the gate, but nobody seemed to know where Dusty was.

"Then as I left, this dude pulled a gun on me and asked me why I'd missed the drop. When I didn't answer, he said he'd give me twenty-four hours to get the money. If the money wasn't at the drop by midnight tonight, he said he'd kill me and anybody I cared about."

"What?" I sat up straight. "What does that mean?"

"I don't know... only that I've been set up. And it's all because of Dusty."

Uncle Joey hadn't said a word, but I picked up his fury that someone had the audacity to come into his city and set up shop without his permission. Most people knew better than to come into his territory without a proper introduction.

Just thinking that one of Dusty's men had the gall to threaten Ramos brought his blood to the boiling point. Threaten Ramos? How dare they? They might as well have threatened Uncle Joey and his whole organization. Well... he wasn't going to stand for it. They'd gone too far.

"I think Dusty's crossed a line," Uncle Joey said. "And we need to teach him a lesson." He glanced at me, not sure he wanted me to be privy to how he was going to do that. "I think Shelby should go with you to the concert tonight. You can corner Dusty and find out what the hell is going on. No more beating around the bush. I want to know everything."

Ramos nodded, convinced that was the only way to handle it. He glanced at me. Was I in?

As much as I hated the idea of violence, I agreed that someone needed to stop Dusty from spreading his drugs. It only surprised me that it was Uncle Joey, and not the police, who would be doing the stopping. "What time do you want to go?"

"The meet and greet is before the concert," Ramos replied. "But I'd like to show up earlier than that so we can have some alone time with Jodie. Probably around six o'clock. After that, I'm hoping she'll help us track Dusty down."

"Okay. I'll meet you here at the office at about five-forty-five."

Ramos nodded. "That should work."

"Now Shelby," Uncle Joey said. "If you'll excuse us, we have some planning to do."

"Uh... sure." They both kept their minds blank while I exited the room, and I was grateful to be out of the loop. There were just some things I didn't want to know, especially since my next stop was the police station.

I said my goodbyes to Jackie, telling her I was off to visit Chris. She reminded me about my luggage in the trunk of the limo, so I told her I'd be back to get it after lunch.

Next, I sent a text to Dimples and told him I was on my way. He replied that he'd meet me in the parking lot, because we were going to the drug dealer's house. Did that mean this was a surprise visit? I couldn't imagine that Dimples had made an appointment. So I hoped the guy was there and this wasn't a waste of time.

I also hoped I could find out more from the police that might help Ramos and Uncle Joey with their side of things. Hmm... did that make me a double-agent? Maybe... but it was all for a good cause, so it couldn't be a bad thing, right?

Since it was a beautiful, sunny day, I didn't mind the short walk to the precinct. As I reached the precinct parking lot, Dimples waved me over to his car. He smiled, but it wasn't enough to make his dimples do their magic dance, so I knew something was bothering him.

"What's up?" I asked.

"Get in. I'll tell you on the way." I listened real close to his thoughts, but all I got was that he was worried about something. "So how was New York?"

"It was great. I got to see *Aladdin* on Broadway and the Statue of Liberty and some other great things."

"Nice," he said, only half listening.

"Yeah it was. Okay... spit it out. What's bothering you?"

He chuckled. "Can't keep much from you, can I? Okay, here's the deal. Billie's freaking out a little about the wedding. I was wondering if you could talk to her."

"What's the problem?"

"Well," he said, scratching his chin. "It's only five weeks away. I think she's finally realizing that three months to plan a wedding wasn't enough time. It's kind of scary because she's the most organized person I know. If anyone could pull it together, it would be her, right? But she's all stressed out, and it's starting to stress me out."

"I can understand that."

"Do you think you could talk to her?"

"Uh... yeah... I can do that."

"Thanks Shelby." He let out a relieved breath. "Maybe you could go to lunch with her, so you can pick up if there's something else besides that, you know?" He was hoping it wasn't him, but he didn't know for sure, but I'd know and could tell him what it was. Then maybe he could do something about it.

I smiled. "I'll do that, but try not to worry too much. I'm sure it's not a big deal."

"Yeah, I'm sure you're right. Thanks, Shelby." He sent me a smile of gratitude. A few minutes later we pulled up to the curb. "Here we are." I glanced out the window to see an older, red-brick, single-family home, probably built in the nineteen-forties.

It was just off a busy street and close to the ball park on the west side of town. A front porch with two windows on either side of the front door was littered with several empty beer cans, newspapers, and a couple of cheap plastic chairs.

I followed Dimples to the door, noticing that the screen door was crooked and hanging off the top hinge. Dimples pulled it open and knocked on the wooden door, which promptly squeaked open. He froze with alarm, then held up his hand to warn me. "Stay back."

My breath caught, and fear raced down my spine. As he pulled his gun, my heart sped up, and I froze in place. With practiced ease, he held the gun in front of him and pushed the door open. He disappeared inside, shouting that he was the police, and I suddenly wished I could back him up like a real partner. What if someone took a shot at him; what was I supposed to do then?

A crash, followed by a yelp, came from inside, then a gunshot exploded. My heart jerked in my chest, and I dashed inside without thinking. I ran through the living room toward the back of the house and found Dimples slumped on the floor and rubbing his head.

"Are you all right?" I couldn't find any blood on him, but that didn't stop my knees from knocking together.

Just then, a man-sized shape bolted out the back door, slamming it open in his haste to get away. Dimples lurched to his feet, thinking that he needed to run after the guy. He swayed with dizziness. "I need to... stop him."

I caught his arm to steady him. "I'll go." Since I was his partner, I knew it was up to me. I just hoped the guy didn't have a gun.

Before Dimples could hold me back, I ran out the door, grateful I had on my comfy jeans, t-shirt, and running shoes. I rushed around the corner of the house as fast as I could go, and caught sight of the guy on the other side of the street.

He shoved the gate open into the neighbor's backyard and disappeared. I ran after him and made it into the backyard in time to see him climb over the chain-link fence, and land on the other side. Great! I wasn't sure I could make it over, but I ran to the fence anyway and started climbing.

I got to the top and grabbed the bar, then used my feet to push me up the rest of the way. I got a toe-hold in the chains and glanced up to see how far ahead of me he'd gotten. At the same time, the guy turned to see how close I was, and I caught a glimpse of his face. Shock lodged in my chest. I knew that kid.

"Hey! Come back here!" I yelled.

Keola's eyes widened as he recognized me, and he stumbled a little. I knew I had to hurry if I was going to catch up with him. I pulled my body up and threw one leg over the top of the fence, but those darn twists at the top of the chain dug into my pants and caught hold.

Stuck, I pushed up on the bar and tried to swing my other leg over the fence. Instead of getting clear, the twisty part of the fence chewed a hole in my pants and twisted the fabric, making it worse. Desperate, I lowered my leg, which left me straddling the fence with the chain still caught in my pants.

My arms started shaking with exertion, and visions of major damage to my tender parts sent terror racing through me. In a panic, I decided to try going back the way I'd come, knowing I'd just have to catch up with Keola later.

With a mighty heave, I shifted my balance and pulled my leg up, hoping to get over without drawing blood. The stupid chain wouldn't let go. In desperation, I jerked my leg over the top and lost my grip on the pole. Falling head first, I heard a big ripping sound and stretched my arms out to the ground so I wouldn't land on my head.

I hung there suspended upside down, with my legs poking up and my hands inches from the ground. Then my pants started to slide off my hips, and I frantically grabbed at them, worried they'd come right off.

Hanging upside down, I pulled and struggled with them, then heard another ripping sound. All at once, the material gave way, and I flopped onto the ground like a rag doll, landing on my back. I sucked in a few deep breaths and lay there winded and dazed.

"Shelby? Are you all right?" Dimples stood over me, worry tightening his eyes. "What happened?"

"Oh... I'm okay." I sat up, still clutching my pants, grateful I hadn't left them on the fence. "I got caught on the fence and it ripped my pants."

"Here. Let me help you up." He held out his hand and pulled me up.

Once on my feet, I took stock of the situation. My New York t-shirt was a little dirty and roughed up, so I was grateful I hadn't worn my Aladdin shirt. My pants had a big hole in them just below the crotch closer to the front. At least it didn't look as bad as I would have thought. I dusted the dirt off my knees and straightened, then tried to look at my butt but couldn't see anything from this angle.

"Holy sh... uh..."

"What? Am I bleeding? It doesn't hurt too much."

"No, no. I don't see any blood, just a few red marks. You're fine." But he was thinking that was a pretty big rip in my pants and... he sucked in a breath and tried not to think about anything.

Suspicious, I reached back and touched my jeans just below the back pocket. An inch further down and my fingers touched bare skin just above my back thigh, obviously exposing a big chunk of my butt. The gaping rip went all the way across my leg, then split at the side, and continued down my pant leg all the way to the back of my knee.

Yikes! I couldn't even feel my panties. Had they ripped too?

"Uh... here, take this." Dimples took off his jacket and handed it to me.

I grabbed it and wrapped the arms around my waist and tied them in a knot. "Uh... thanks."

He scratched his head and nodded, trying hard not to smile. "I guess he got away." The image of me hanging upside down popped into his head, and he held back a snort of laughter.

"You saw that?" I asked, groaning with mortification.

"Yeah. But... I won't tell anyone. Hey... at least you're not bleeding. Could you imagine getting stitches on your... uh..."

"Yeah... I got it." He was having way too much fun, and it was his fault I'd run after the kid in the first place. "What about you. What happened back there? Did he have a gun?" After he'd laughed at me, it was tempting to rub it in.

"No." Humiliation flowed over him in waves. "He... uh... hit me with a frying pan."

"Oooo... I'll bet that hurt."

"Yeah." He shook his head, sighing with disgust. "And it was my gun that went off. I'm glad the bullet didn't hit anyone."

He reached down, picked up my purse, and handed it to me, hoping I wouldn't rub it in. As I slipped my purse over my shoulder, his gaze caught mine and his lips turned down. "Uh... I won't tell anyone about the fence, if you won't tell them about the frying pan."

I chuckled at the irony of our mishaps and smiled. "Deal."

He let out a breath. "Thanks. Let's get back."

Just then, two police cruisers pulled up, followed by a white van that had "Crime Scene Investigation" on it. "Why is that here?" I asked.

"Because I found our drug dealer... and he's dead."

"What? You think that kid did it?" Would Keola really kill someone?

"I don't know, but the dealer's been dead a while. It probably happened during the night sometime. Maybe the kid came to buy drugs and found him dead. But whatever happened, if he didn't kill the dealer, he might know who did, so we need to find him."

"Uh... right. Well, that might be easier than you think."

"What do you mean?"

"I recognized him... he's the nephew of one of my clients."

"What?" For a second, Dimples wondered why I hadn't told him that sooner. I wasn't sure about that myself, so I acted like I hadn't heard that part.

"Yeah. I can get you his contact information and everything." Keeping Keola's identity from the police wouldn't help him, and if he was in trouble, it was the right thing to do.

"Uh... great. Come on, we need to get back to the house."

We crossed the street, and I was grateful to have Dimples' jacket around my waist. Still, even with it on, I felt a big draft back there. "Are you sure I'm covered up?" I asked, before we got to the house.

He glanced at my backside, thinking that the main parts were covered up. There wasn't much he could do about the piece of pant leg flapping in the breeze unless he tried to fix it. But he wasn't touching that with a ten foot pole. "Yeah, you're good."

I let out my breath. Now that the adrenalin rush was gone, my legs were a little shaky, and I needed to sit down.

As we started across the lawn to the front porch, another car pulled up and Detective Bates jumped out. "Whoa, what happened to you?"

I quickly turned around before he could look too closely, and realized that my deal with Dimples wasn't going to work for me. "Uh... I was chasing a suspect... and..." I stopped talking because Bates was thinking that I had no business chasing a suspect. I was a civilian, not a cop. What was I thinking?

"Yes?" Bates prompted, wanting to hear the whole story.

"Dimples got hurt and asked me to chase the kid who hit him, so I did. I just didn't expect to have to climb a fence." That sounded a little lame, even to me.

"A fence? You did all of that just from climbing a fence?" He swallowed a laugh, holding it back behind tight lips, his eyes crinkling with mirth.

I rolled my eyes, and then turned around to head toward the house, needing to sit down in one of the plastic chairs before my legs gave out.

Bates and Dimples watched me climb the stairs. Bates watched carefully, hoping for a glimpse of how far up the rip went. Dimples hoped not to see more skin, but even then, he couldn't pull his gaze away from my bare leg. As soon as I sat down, they both started moving and hurried inside.

I slumped into the chair, sighing with relief, then realized I could feel plastic on my bare skin. Yikes. I jumped to my feet, deciding that I should wait in the car. Or, even better, borrow Dimples' car for a quick drive home to change. I could be back before he was done here, right?

But first I had to talk to him. Knowing it wouldn't get any easier, I hurried inside the house. Unfortunately, he was in the bedroom with the body and all that blood. The man was lying on his back with his dead eyes open, and a bullet hole right in his forehead. Ugh!

Something about him looked familiar, but I couldn't place it, and I quickly turned away before I got sick. Dimples noticed me and thought *I'll be done soon. Just wait a few more minutes.*

I nodded, also picking up that he didn't want me to go until I'd given him the kid's name and address. Taking deep breaths, I shuffled back out to the porch. Pulling down on Dimples' jacket loosened it around my waist, but at least it was between me and the chair before I sat down.

Then it hit me that I'd seen the dead man at the same bar where I'd met up with Keola and Kyle.

Chapter 10

Now it made sense that Keola had been here because of his ties to the Polynesian gangs. I should probably let Ramos know since the gangs had an understanding with Uncle Joey. It also might help him figure out where to look.

Giving Dimples Keola's name and address would be okay too, since it would be helping the police without crossing the line between what he did and what Uncle Joey was doing. So it was a win-win for everyone, and I wouldn't get in trouble with any of them... I hoped.

Fifteen minutes later, Dimples still hadn't come out of the house. I checked my watch for the hundredth time and fidgeted in my chair. I'd stayed glued to that plastic chair for obvious reasons, but I was tired of waiting.

It was almost time to meet up with Chris for lunch, and I didn't want to miss it. I mean, here I was, home from my trip, and I hadn't even seen him yet. If he knew I was sitting here with my torn pants showing my backside, he'd want to come and get me, right?

I pulled out my phone and put the call through. "Hey honey, I'm sort of stuck at a suspect's house, and my pants are ripped. Can you come and get me?"

"What?"

I explained what had happened and made sure to include that I had Dimples' jacket around my waist so it didn't sound quite so bad.

"Oh man... that's too bad," he responded. He hesitated, and then let out a big sigh. "Um... the thing is... I'm not sure I have enough time to come. Things have been crazy with this case, and I was only planning on taking a few minutes to eat lunch here in the office. But... I could send Elisa to come and get you. Would that work? I've already ordered us a couple of sandwiches."

My heart sank. How could he think I'd want Elisa to see me like this? Even worse, how could he think I'd want to go to his office with my backside showing? "Um... listen that's okay. I'm not going to come to your office with my pants all ripped up. I'll wait and have Dimples take me home. You go ahead and eat without me."

"Hey... I'm sorry honey. I wish I could come. I hate letting you down."

"No it's okay. I'll wait for Dimples. It'll be fine." We said our goodbyes and disconnected. I tried not to be too disappointed that he couldn't come. Things like this happened, and I shouldn't get too upset. Besides, wasn't I going to a concert with Ramos tonight? I was pretty sure Chris wouldn't like that much, so it was best to stay on his good side.

Another van pulled up, and some people wearing blue jumpsuits pulled out a gurney and took it inside the house to transport the body. Since I didn't want to see that, I decided to wait until they were done before I found Dimples to remind him that I was still there.

Several minutes later, a cop holding a roll of crime-scene tape came out, ready to put it up. He glanced at me, wondering how I'd gotten onto the porch. "Uh... ma'am you're not supposed to be here. You need to get off the porch while I secure the crime scene."

Before I could answer, another van with the lettering "Channel 2 News" jerked to a stop. A man with a big TV camera jumped out, and a woman with a microphone quickly stood at the edge of the property and began talking. Just then, the people with the gurney holding the black body bag came out of the house and began to roll the gurney down the porch steps toward the crime scene van.

"Ma'am, you need to move," the young cop said again.

"Okay." Since I didn't want to be caught on camera, I jumped up to run into the house. With my abrupt movement, Dimples' jacket came loose and slipped right off my waist. I froze in horrified shock.

The young cop jerked in surprise. "What the..."

I didn't even try to grab it. With a little yelp, I ran inside the house and plastered my backside against the wall. Oh hell! How could this be happening? My yelp caught the attention of most everyone in the room, and they all turned to stare at me.

The young cop followed me inside, carrying the jacket. "Uh... you dropped this." He didn't want to look at my pants, but he couldn't help it. Then he let out his breath, relieved that there wasn't anything to see from the front... but what a view from the back. He replayed the glimpse of my bare bum in his mind, and I groaned in mortification.

"I'll take that!" I grabbed the jacket out of his hand to snap him out of it and held it in front of me like a shield, worried that if I moved a muscle everyone would catch a glimpse of skin.

Once I was properly covered, the cops went back to their jobs, and I turned my attention to the young cop. He flushed under my steady gaze but wasn't sure what to do about me. "Go get Dimp... uh... Detective Harris. I'm with him."

I realized that without my trusty lanyard and badge around my neck, he didn't know who I was, so I cut him some slack. He nodded, grateful for something to do, and left to find Dimples.

I stayed glued to the spot, enduring all kinds of speculative thoughts from the cops around me. One of them had no idea who I was, but the other two put it together when I mentioned Dimples. They didn't say a word, but exchanged meaningful glances, thinking that once I left, they could hardly wait to tell the others what they'd seen... snicker, snicker.

I closed my eyes and threw up my shields before it got any worse. A moment later, Dimples came out, his eyes wide and his face filled with guilt that he'd left me alone for so long... and had his jacket really fallen off?

"Uh... I heard what happened. Here... I'll stand in front of you while you put the jacket around your waist." He turned around, blocking most everyone's view, and I quickly slipped the jacket around me.

"Okay. I'm done," I said.

He glanced back then said, "I've got an idea. Come with me."

I held the jacket securely around my waist and legs and followed him through the house to a back bedroom. A twin sized bed with a lavender bedspread stood on one side, with a dresser and mirror on the other.

"This is his daughter's room," Dimples said. "I thought maybe you could find something of hers to wear until we get you home."

I let out a relieved breath. "That sounds wonderful. I'll take a look."

He nodded. "I'll stand outside the door until you're done." He didn't want to take a chance that someone might walk in on me after everything that had happened.

Once the door closed, I pulled open the drawers one by one but only found socks and underwear. Next, I pulled the closet door open and found discarded clothing lying all over the floor in little piles, like she'd taken them off and just left them there.

I rifled through them, hoping for some sweats, but only came up with a pair of jeans. They looked on the small side, but I thought they might work. After dropping the jacket and pulling off my shredded pants, I slipped them on.

I don't normally wear skinny jeans because they're so tight, and these fit my legs like a glove. I got them zipped up and buttoned without too much trouble, even if they hung a little low on my waist.

Glancing in the mirror above the dresser, I wasn't sure it was a big improvement. They fit so tight that they didn't leave much to the imagination. But they had to be better than bare skin, right?

I gathered my jeans and Dimples' jacket and pulled the door open. True to his word, Dimples was still there. "Here's your jacket. Thanks for this. I'll return the pants."

"Don't worry about it," he said. "I'm done here, so I can take you wherever you need to go."

I checked the time. It was barely after one-thirty. I might still be able to make lunch with Chris, or at least get the sandwich from him and take it home to eat. "I'm supposed to meet Chris at his office. Can you drop me off there?"

"You bet."

At the front door, Dimples stopped short, noticing that the reporter and cameraman still stood outside. "I don't think you'll want them to see you."

"You got that right." Sudden worry tightened my stomach, and I sure hoped they'd missed me earlier.

"Hey Bates," Dimples called. Bates came to his side. "Do you mind making a statement to the media?"

"Sure. I'll keep it simple." He glanced at me, thinking that he didn't mind being the face of the police department for a change, and was glad Dimples had asked him.

We waited until Bates was on camera, then dashed around them to Dimples' car. My breath whooshed out with relief to sit down on a comfy seat, and have more there than bare skin. And if I was careful, I was pretty sure the too-tight pants wouldn't rip open.

Dimples pulled the car away from the curb, and I fastened my seat belt.

"I need the name and address of that kid."

"Oh, right," I said. "Let me call my client and I'll get it for you."

I called Shannon instead of Kyle, since I didn't want him to think he'd given up his nephew by telling me anything. I also hoped he wouldn't think that I'd betrayed them, even if it was for Keola's own good. Shannon answered, and I kept it simple, telling her that I thought Keola might be in big trouble. With that explanation, she was more than willing to give me his home address.

I wrote the information down and handed it to Dimples. "Uh... I don't want anyone to know you got this from me, so can you keep my name out of it?

"Sure."

"Thanks." I sighed. "He's just a kid, you know?"

Dimples nodded with understanding. "That's why we need to step in before he gets hurt. It's the right thing to do, Shelby. You know that, right?"

"Yeah. I know."

"Good."

"Let me know if you find him. I can help with the questioning and all that." I hoped he'd find Keola before anything bad happened to the kid. I also felt bad for Kyle and Shannon. Now I'd have to tell them what I knew, and I was pretty sure they wouldn't like it much.

"I will. Thanks."

A few minutes later, Dimples pulled the car over in front of Chris' office. I thanked him and got out, grateful he hadn't asked for my help to track Keola down. He'd thought about it for about three seconds but figured I'd had enough for one day.

He was definitely right about that, and the day wasn't over yet. I hurried into the building. Since I was hungry from all that excitement, I looked forward to eating my sandwich. I also couldn't wait to see Chris, mostly because after seeing that dead body, I needed a hug something fierce.

The elevator let me out on Chris' floor and I stepped inside, giving the receptionist a friendly wave. She smiled, not recognizing me at first, thinking I looked like a teenager in my skinny jeans and "I Love New York" t-shirt.

Then her breath caught. Was I the person on the porch with the ripped pants from the news report? I wasn't wearing them now, but that purple New York t-shirt along with my blond hair was hard to miss. The fifteen-second shot had been posted on social media, and it already had about five thousand hits. She thought for sure it would go viral. Of course, if she hadn't seen me just now, she never would have known it was me.

I felt the blood drain from my head, and I got a little dizzy. Then I heard her thinking that it was a good thing my face wasn't recognizable in the video, because at least no one would know it was me.

Relief nearly sent me to my knees, but I managed to hold it together until I got around the corner and couldn't hear her anymore. Still... what the freak! At least this day couldn't get any worse.

I hurried down the hall before anyone else saw me, and came to Chris' office. Elisa wasn't at her desk, so I glanced inside Chris' office and found her sitting on the couch. Even worse, she was eating my sandwich.

Holy hell! And here I thought this day couldn't get any worse. Chris wasn't sitting right next to her while they ate, so that was good... but still.

Standing in the doorway, I must have made a sound, because they both glanced up at the same time. With a guilty start, Elisa dropped her sandwich onto the table, and her mouth froze in mid-chew. She was even trying to decide if she should spit it out.

Chris' eyes widened and he said my name, but with his mouth full it came out like, "Shelb." He stood while swallowing his last bite, and hurried to my side, chagrinned that he'd given my sandwich to Elisa. "Honey, I didn't think you were coming, and Elisa hadn't had lunch yet so..."

"It's okay," I said, remembering that I needed to be forgiving so he'd do the same for me. "No big deal."

Elisa wrapped up the rest of her sandwich and stood, but found it hard to look me in the eyes. "Uh... Hi Shelby. How was New York? Hey... that's a great t-shirt. You look... really good."

She was thinking that, for a middle-aged person, I rocked the skinny jeans. "Uh... I'll leave you two alone. I'm sure you've got some catching up to do." She glanced at Chris and opened her mouth to tell him thanks for the sandwich, but wisely decided against it, and closed the door behind her.

I caught Chris' gaze, and a laugh escaped my lips. "That was awkward."

He let out a breath and shook his head, then rested his forehead against mine and took hold of my hands. "I'm glad you came. What's this?" He stepped back and took in my t-shirt, then noticed my skinny jeans and how tightly they hugged my body. "Uh... um..." Sudden desire flooded over him and he swallowed. "Where did you get those pants?" He glanced behind me. "Those aren't the ones..."

"No. Dimples let me borrow these from a closet at the suspect's house. They're a little snug, don't you think?"

He huffed out a breath. "Uh... yeah. I'm not sure you should be wearing them. I mean... they look great, but they're... you know... tight." I pulled the torn jeans from my purse and he gasped at the huge hole.

"I think these are a total loss, don't you?"

"Uh... yes. That must have been one big fence." He examined the large rip that took out most of the leg, imagining how that must have looked on me. Then he hoped no one really got to find out, since it looked like most of my backside was totally exposed.

I couldn't bring myself to tell him about the TV camera and subsequent posting, so I quickly threw them in his trash can. Chris smiled and caught my gaze, then gathered me against him. His lips brushed over mine in little teasing kisses, something he'd wanted to do as soon as I'd walked in.

Then he thought that if he deepened the kiss, he wasn't sure he could stop. That was all the impetus I needed to kiss him good and hard. Kissing him like this quenched a deep thirst inside of me that I'd forgotten I had, and all the rest of my troubles fell away.

Breathless, he pulled his mouth away from mine. "You're killing me, here."

I smiled, pleased that I had that effect.

He took a breath and put a little space between us, glancing out of his office windows toward the hallway and hoping that no one had seen us kissing.

"I guess I'd better go," I said, sighing with disappointment. "But that was nice."

"Yeah... it was. I've missed you."

"I've missed you too. I brought you something from New York."

"Oh yeah? What?"

"You'll see when you get home."

He chuckled. "I'll look forward to it. I should be home around six."

It suddenly hit me that I wouldn't be there, and my heart sank. "Oh crap. Um... remember that I told you about the Jodie McAllister concert?"

His gaze narrowed. "Uh... yeah. You told me you might have to go with Ramos. Why? Is it tonight?"

"Uh-huh," I nodded.

He shook his head, and I caught a few choice swear words coming from his mind. "Why do you have to go?"

"Well... I said I would. She's Ramos' old flame, and her brother told him that her daughter might belong to Ramos... as in... his kid. I need to go in order to find out if she's telling the truth. And... there is one other thing..."

Chris raised his brow, thinking that he wasn't going to like it.

"Uh... yeah... you won't like it. Do you want me to tell you anyway?"

He huffed out a breath. "Of course I do."

"Okay... here it is... Ramos thinks that Dusty has a drug ring going. Worse, he thinks that Dusty is setting him up. Naturally, Ramos wants me to be there when he talks to Dusty... hopefully at the same time that he talks to Jodie. It should work out pretty slick since we've got a special backstage pass to see Jodie before the concert. And it might not even take too long."

Chris let out his breath and rubbed his forehead like he always did when he was upset. "You're right, I don't like it."

"I don't have to stay for the concert... I'll come home right after we talk to them, so I won't be out late. But I'm meeting Ramos at Thrasher around six, so... I'll probably miss you. But hey... I should be home by eight. That's not so bad, right?"

This was the part of my life that Chris hated the most. He hated that I was at Uncle Joey's beck and call, and now it seemed to have transferred to Ramos as well. But what could he do? Not a damn thing. He could be angry over it, but he'd learned that didn't help. But a drug dealer? What if something went wrong?

"Uh... we're meeting at the concert... so there will plenty of security and stuff. Plus, Uncle Joey and Ramos are making plans to take care of the drug part without me, so I won't be involved in all that stuff either. I should be fine."

Chris caught my gaze, thinking he'd heard that before. "I really don't like this."

"Yeah. I know."

He pulled me into his arms. "You still owe me for that extra night in New York. Now you'll owe me double." He was thinking that, for as much as I owed him, it would have to be something big.

I let out a sigh and caught his gaze. "Yeah, but I don't mind owing you so much. Uncle Joey maybe, but never you."

He let out a big breath, and then nodded. "All right. Um... I'll try and get home before you leave. But if I don't, text me when you can, so I know you're all right."

"I will."

He gave me one more kiss, then pulled away. "How are you getting home, anyway?"

I shrugged. "Oh... my luggage is in the limo, so I was going to see if Ricky could take me home."

"You're going back to Thrasher?" He didn't like that idea too much, especially in the pants I had on, and the fact that Ramos might see me wearing them. Maybe he should take me and reschedule his two o'clock appointment.

Just then, Elisa knocked on the door and opened it. "Sorry to interrupt, but Mr. Fletcher is here for your two o'clock."

Chris pursed his lips and sighed.

"Hey," I said. "It's no big deal for Ricky to take me home. Besides, I need my luggage and all the souvenirs I got for everybody."

"Okay. I'll see you later. Be careful and stay safe." He squeezed my hand one last time and watched me leave with a sense of foreboding. I wanted to reassure him, but Mr. Fletcher walked inside, so I missed my chance.

Still, it bothered me that he was so worried, mostly because it started to make me worried too, and I didn't like that much. Besides, I was going to be with Ramos. I'd be fine. Nothing bad was going to happen. Sheesh!

Elisa closed Chris' door behind me and hurried to her desk, still feeling guilty that she'd eaten my sandwich, especially since she'd basically lied, and had already eaten her lunch when Chris offered it to her.

I sighed and shook my head. Was everyone a liar when it suited them? Last time I checked, a half-lie was still a lie.

Lately it seemed everyone lied, or at least didn't tell the whole truth, and hardly felt guilty at all.

But was I any different? Not really. In fact, I was probably worse than most, considering the whole family thing with Uncle Joey. Lying to my kids... how was that right?

"Uh... did you need something?" Elisa asked, since I made her nervous just standing there.

"Oh... no. Just lost in my thoughts. How are you doing anyway?"

"Good, thanks. Uh... sorry I ate your sandwich."

"That's all right. You had no idea that I'd just show up like that after I said I wasn't coming. So how's the job? Still liking it here?"

"Yes. It's the best. I'm learning a lot." She was even thinking about taking the LSAT again. She'd totally tanked it the first time, but she'd learned a lot working here. Then she thought about asking Chris where he thought she should start, and what books he'd suggest studying from his library.

Right then, she was thinking of how much help he could give her, and I could see the wheels turning in her brain about how that would open the path for more involvement with him. I tried not to give her the evil eye, but something about my penetrating stare and raised eyebrow brought her up short, and her eyes widened.

I leaned in close and lowered my voice. "I hope you know how lucky you are to have this job."

She swallowed. "Uh... yes I do. I love working for... uh... here."

"Then I'm sure you won't do anything to jeopardize that, right?"

"Uh... no... of course not." She was a little offended that I thought she'd go beyond her professional boundaries. Sure

Chris was a hottie, and she loved looking at him, but that's all it was. She'd never... he was off-limits... she knew that.

"Good, because I have a favor to ask."

Her eyes widened with curiosity and apprehension that I was going to tell her off, even if she didn't deserve it.

I leaned in closer. "I think Ethan is spying on Chris, and it worries me. I was doing a little digging and found out that Ethan knows the police chief. And... there's something he's hiding. If you spend some time with Ethan... and maybe get to know him a little, he might tell you what's going on. What do you think? You'd be doing it for Chris, but he doesn't need to know about that. Let's just keep this between us. Okay?"

"Sure," she agreed. "I can do that."

"Good." I straightened and smiled. "That's a huge help. Maybe we can talk again next week or the week after and you can let me know if you find out anything."

"Okay, sure."

"Great. Thanks Elisa. It's nice to know you're helping me with this."

"No problem."

We said our goodbyes, and I turned down the hall, hoping that spark of curiosity Elisa possessed could be turned into something good and help keep her mind off my husband. I listened real close and picked up that she thought there must be something to my suspicions, since I was a bona fide private investigator. Then she thought about all the times Ethan had asked her questions about Chris' clients, and her curiosity sparked even higher. What was Ethan up to?

I turned the corner and lost her thoughts, but I'd heard enough to know that I'd made the right call in asking for Elisa's help, and I was almost glad she'd been thinking about Chris and goaded me into it.

It hit me that I should be cultivating friendships like that all the time. Knowing what people really wanted could tell me a lot about what buttons to push to motivate them to do what I wanted. There was so much I could do with my abilities once I got people pushed in the right directions. It would be a little like Uncle Joey, only on the good side.

Wait... what? Did I just compare myself with Uncle Joey? Holy cow! He was really rubbing off on me. But he wasn't all bad, right? Still, having something in common with a mob-boss should be a red flag of some sort, and maybe I'd better do something about it. Like... pray harder.

It was nice to get back outside into the warm sunshine and cool breeze. And the walk to Thrasher helped clear my head. I took deep breaths and managed to feel a little more settled by the time I walked into Thrasher Development.

Jackie was the only one there at the moment, but she put a call through to Ricky and said he'd be there in a few minutes. She asked me about New York, and then told me that she could hardly wait to visit. "How are the New York Manettos? I've never met them."

"They're great... just like one big happy family. You'll love them."

The elevator dinged, and Ricky walked in. I said my goodbyes to Jackie and followed him into the hall. On the ride down, he noticed me in my skinny jeans and immediately thought about his girlfriend and wondered if she could fit into such tight pants.

Yikes! I quickly put up my shields and hoped my face didn't turn red with embarrassment. Still, I caught that he thought I looked good, so maybe it wasn't too bad, but I certainly didn't want to hear any more.

The ride home passed quickly. And stepping into my house filled me with relief. Even though it was nearly three o'clock, with the time change it felt like it was a lot later. All I wanted to do was lie down for a minute.

After unpacking, I succumbed to the temptation and lay down on the bed. Just minutes later, Josh and Savannah came home, so I stumbled up and rushed down the stairs to greet them.

We spent the next little while talking about Miguel and New York. Savannah noticed my New York t-shirt, so we all tramped back upstairs for their souvenirs. "We'll have to go back," I said. "Maybe this summer for Miguel's first performance."

It was still hard to believe he had the part, and the kids thought so too. So what was I going to tell them about the Manetto family? I sighed and decided not to worry about that until I needed to.

Savannah loved her stuffed animal, especially after I told her that Miguel helped me pick it out. But she squealed over the Aladdin t-shirt, and I was glad I got it for her. Josh wasn't as thrilled with his baseball, but he smiled and told me thanks anyway.

After I showed them the license plate with "fuhgedaboudit" for Chris, Josh laughed, then caught my gaze, thinking *that's it*, and my heart sank. Crap! Had I just given him the biggest clue about Uncle Joey, or what? How stupid was that?

I listened real close and picked up that it suddenly made sense to him. His eyes widened as he put it together. The house, the plane, all the money, the private school for Miguel. Was Uncle Joey a mob-boss? And did I work for him?

As he tried to think things through, his brows scrunched together. How long had this been going on? He hadn't paid much attention until he'd met Uncle Joey, but he knew I'd started working soon after the bank robbery, where I'd been shot in the head. Wasn't that when I got my premonitions? Was Uncle Joey really related to us? And didn't Dad work for him too?

"Mom?" Savannah asked. "Did you hear what I said?"

I jerked my attention to her, not having a clue that she'd even been talking. "Oh... uh, sorry. No... what did you say?"

"I just wondered if I could call Miguel and congratulate him."

"Oh... of course. I'm sure he'd like that."

She smiled, and a pulse of excitement shivered through her. "I need his number."

"Oh... right." I pulled out my phone and found his number. At the same time, I listened in to Josh's thoughts and picked up that he wasn't so sure it was a good idea to encourage Savannah. Couldn't I see that she had a huge crush on Miguel? The son of a mob-boss? Shouldn't I discourage her?

I had to literally bite my tongue to keep from replying, especially when he thought Miguel probably wasn't really our cousin at all. What else had I lied to him about?

The enormity of it all sent his head spinning, and doubt crept in. Maybe he was just making it all up? How could it be true? Miguel was cool. He wasn't a bully or anything like a mobster's son. Maybe his imagination was just running wild. Yeah... that was probably it.

"I'm hungry," he said, and promptly left the room.

Savannah danced out too, punching in Miguel's number and heading into her bedroom. As her door shut, I sank down onto my bed, completely shell-shocked. I didn't have a clue about what to do now. I probably should do something but, for some reason, I couldn't think what that could be.

Chris. He would know. I grabbed onto that hope like it was the only thing keeping me from getting swallowed up by quicksand. We'd talk it over. We'd figure it out together. Maybe we'd tell Josh everything... no, not about my mind-reading, but it was clear we'd have to tell him something.

But whatever it was, we'd do it together, and it would be what was best for our kids.

My stomach gurgled from all that anxiety, reminding me that I'd missed lunch, and I'd better eat something before it got worse. But how could I eat now? Sighing, I hurried downstairs needing to find out if Josh was all right. I entered the kitchen as he popped the last of a PB&J into his mouth, and lifted the milk jug to his lips.

"Josh! Stop! Get a glass."

He hesitated with the jug partway to his mouth, and his lips twisted up into a smile, reminding me so much of Chris that my breath caught. His gaze found mine, and he started to raise the jug anyway.

"Hey!" I stormed to his side to grab the jug, but he held it away from me, turning his body and holding it up high so I couldn't touch it.

"All right, all right," he said, thinking that he'd been drinking out of it for two days now, so it didn't really matter anyway, but whatever. He quickly pulled a glass out of the cupboard and filled it up. "There. How's that?"

Only he didn't say 'there, how's that' out loud, so I just shook my head. "Have you been drinking out of that jug the whole time?"

His guilty gaze caught mine. "Uh... maybe."

I sighed, then moved to the fridge to grab a yogurt. I sat at the table and ate it while he finished his milk, eavesdropping on his thoughts. I didn't pick up anything about Uncle Joey, and I let out a relieved breath.

Instead, he was thinking about dinner and what I was going to fix. They'd had eggs and hash browns last night, since that was about the only thing Chris knew how to cook, and he was hoping for some enchiladas or something good like that.

"What do you think we should have for dinner?" I asked him. "I was thinking enchiladas. Does that sound good?"

"I was just... yeah... that sounds great." A knock sounded at the kitchen door, and Josh glanced at me. "Oh... I forgot to tell you that Chloe was coming over to do homework. Is that okay?"

"Um... sure."

He let her in, and we exchanged pleasantries before they headed into the living room. I let out a breath, relieved they hadn't gone downstairs, since I kind of wanted to keep an eye on them. Then I tried to look on the positive side. At least Josh wasn't focusing on me and Uncle Joey right now. That was good, right?

Just then, Savannah came into the kitchen, a happy flush covering her face. Among other things, she was thinking that Miguel was the coolest person in the whole world. Visions of them together in all kinds of romantic situations floated across her thoughts at a dizzying rate. Whoa. She had it bad, and a spike of alarm threatened to overwhelm me.

Maybe she could set the table for dinner. That might take her mind off Miguel for a minute or two. With a jolt, I suddenly realized that I had to leave in an hour, and I wouldn't be home for dinner. Crap! I was a terrible mother. Here I'd been gone for two nights, and now I was leaving again.

My breath whooshed out. Before despair overcame me, I clenched my teeth with steely resolve. Sure, I might be leaving for a couple of hours, but I could still make dinner for my family. I jumped up from the table and grabbed some chicken out of the freezer, then rolled up my sleeves and got to work.

Half an hour later, I was nowhere near being done. The chicken was still partly frozen, and there was no way I could stuff the tortillas and get them into the oven in less than twenty minutes. Plus, I still had to get ready for the concert.

In defeat, I turned off the stove and called for pizza delivery. Then I put the half-cooked chicken in the fridge, along with the rest of the ingredients. At least it wasn't a total loss. I could still make the enchiladas for dinner tomorrow.

I ran upstairs, trying to figure out what to wear. Since I was going with Ramos, it should probably be black, so I slipped on my black jeans and black boots. Wanting a little bling, I wore a different t-shirt that I'd picked up in New York. It was a fitted light blue tee with depictions of the Statue of Liberty and all the tall buildings. On top of that, sparkly rhinestones accented the words *New York City*.

A little thrill of excitement, combined with a touch of nerves, washed over me when I realized I was actually going to meet Jodie McAllister. Besides being a huge star and totally gorgeous, she was Ramos' ex, which made it a big deal. I didn't want to look like a washed-out wallflower next to her, so I added a little darker eye-shadow to highlight my eyes, and freshened my lipstick.

Next, I shook out my hair to get that wind-blown look, and spritzed it with hairspray. On impulse, I also sprayed a touch of my favorite French perfume to my neck and wrists. My leather motorcycle jacket was a little rough around the edges after my exploits in Paris, but that added a touch of character that totally worked with the look I was going for.

Ready to go, I glanced in the mirror, and my lips tilted up in a sassy grin. Yup. I looked pretty hot for a middle-aged person, and now I could meet a gorgeous music star with confidence.

Chris hadn't made it home yet, but it was time to go, so I found Josh and Savannah to explain that I had to help a client tonight, and that both Chris and the pizza would be there soon.

"But wait for your dad before you eat the pizza. And Chloe, you're welcome to stay if you want."

Since they were all hoping she could, I figured I might as well grant them their wish. Plus, letting her stay distracted them enough that they hardly noticed I was leaving.

"I'll be back in a couple of hours." With a quick wave, I made sure the VIP pass Dusty had given me was tucked inside my purse before I hurried out to my car.

To get in the mood, I listened to Jodie McAllister's breakout album on the drive to Thrasher Development. Now that I knew it was all about Ramos, I enjoyed it more than ever. I even played *Devil Rider* about three times before I pulled into the parking garage.

I got out of my car, totally in rock star mode and singing the chorus out loud. Before reaching the elevator, I checked around the corner to see if Ramos' motorcycle was in its usual parking place. Yup. There it was all shiny and gorgeous.

A secret hope that we'd take the bike rose in my heart, mostly because of the whole *Devil Rider* thing. I mean, Ramos was the actual guy in the song, and if he showed up at the concert on his bike, it would be like the song had come to life. How cool was that? Just thinking about it sent shivers down my spine.

Caught up in the moment, I started singing the first verse. "He came riding into town they say... like thunder crashing on a cloudless day. Demons chasing him from the past... riding behind, coming at him fast. Bringing the storm, bringing the rain, stirring the breeze, flowing with pain... You love me, then leave me... you devil rider. Hold me close, don't let go... you devil rider. Break my heart, take my soul... you devil rider. You broke my heart. You took my soul...."

The sound of someone clearing their throat stopped me cold. With wide-eyed mortification, I jerked around to find Ramos leaning against the pillar with a crooked smile on his face.

"Babe."

"Gah! What are you doing here? I thought we were meeting upstairs."

He lifted an eyebrow and shook his head. "I saw you in the security camera and came down." He'd seen me staring with glazed eyes at his bike and had arrived just in time to hear me singing the song Jodie had written about him. Priceless.

"You weren't supposed to see that." I grabbed onto my indignation like a shield to cover the horrible embarrassment that I was sure had turned my face a bright red. Of course, my show of anger didn't faze him one bit.

"It's okay. I won't tell anyone."

I huffed out a breath and shook my head, unsure of how to respond to that. He chuckled and turned to his car, then popped open the trunk and pulled out two motorcycle helmets. He held the smaller one toward me and cocked his brow, hoping I'd take it and be a good sport.

I took the helmet and did a mental head-slap. Why did this happen to me? Why did I ever sing that song out loud? At least he hadn't thought I'd sounded bad, but still... how embarrassing.

Ramos pulled his leather jacket from the trunk and shrugged it over his muscled shoulders. As he slipped on his dark glasses, the whole devil rider persona just rolled off him in waves, and I tried not to shake my head. How did he do it?

He took in my outfit and smiled, thinking that as much as I tried to look as bad as him, it didn't quite work. Mostly because I still had that wholesome freshness about me that came from always trying to do the right thing, even if it killed me.

Was that a compliment? I glanced at him, and he caught my gaze, wondering why I hadn't put on my helmet yet. Since I didn't want to tell him it would ruin my hair, I shrugged. "Uh... what's the plan? I mean... nothing's changed, has it?"

"No."

"Okay. Uh... did you find out any more about the drugs?"

He nodded. "Yeah, we've got a pretty good idea that Dusty's been distributing them, so it's important that we find him and have a little chat. I'm hoping Jodie will help out with that."

"Are you going to tell her what he's doing?"

"It depends..." He was thinking that she might not want to talk to him at all. He was pretty sure Dusty hadn't told her that he was coming tonight. He figured Dusty had gone to all this trouble just to set him up, and that it had nothing to do with Jodie or her daughter. He'd only used them to lure him in. Too bad it had worked.

He shook his head and sighed. True or not, he really did want to know if she was his, and having me along was the only way to solve both problems at the same time.

"There was a drug dealer that was killed today... or sometime last night," I said. "Someone shot him in the head." I pointed to my forehead, seeing the vision of that dead body all over again. My stomach twisted with nausea. It didn't help that, in my rush to make dinner, I'd forgotten to eat again. "He looked familiar... like someone from the Tiki bar."

"Part of the gang?" Ramos asked.

I shrugged. "I think so."

"Dusty must have been using him, but I can't imagine that Dusty would kill someone. He's not a killer."

"Yeah... that doesn't make sense to me either, but the police had questioned the man earlier. Maybe Dusty thought he'd crack and rat him out."

"Maybe," Ramos said, unconvinced. It still didn't sound like something Dusty would do. "There must be more going on than we know."

"If it helps, don't forget that Dusty seemed nervous when he met with you in the club. He also thought someone was watching him, but he had a plan in mind."

"That's right," Ramos agreed. "He was setting me up and wanted to make it look like I was agreeing to sell his drugs. So when I didn't bring the money to the drop, the guy watching would have a reason to kill me. I just don't understand why he'd go to that much trouble."

"Yeah... that doesn't make sense. I didn't pick up that he hated you that much, especially since he seemed sort of happy to see you."

Ramos shrugged. "Whatever the reason, I'm hoping you'll figure it out." He straddled the bike and slipped on his helmet. "Let's go."

I let out a breath and followed his lead, slipping on my helmet and climbing on the bike behind him. He started her up, and we roared up the ramp and out to the street. I held on tight, and my stomach did that little flip-flop it always did.

Then we were on the road, and I tried to enjoy the ride. Still, I couldn't stop the flutter of unease that tightened my stomach. A set-up or not, since Ramos couldn't take any kind of weapons through security, it felt like we were walking into a trap.

Chapter 11

The venue for the concert wasn't too far, and we arrived long before I wanted the ride to end. Ramos pulled into the parking lot across the street from the arena and paid a hefty amount to park there. Parking the bike close to the attendant, he locked our helmets to the ring under the seat.

We crossed the street to the arena and showed our tickets and VIP passes to the attendant. After passing through security, we were led to a lounge room and told to wait in a short line behind a roped-off area. Since we'd arrived early, there were only a few people ahead of us.

Naturally, Ramos caught the eye of the woman running the show, and she couldn't resist stopping by to tell him hello. I caught from her that Jodie was in her dressing room getting the final touches on her make-up and hair, but it would still be a while before she came out, and this woman might as well enjoy herself.

After exchanging pleasantries, Ramos pulled a card out of his pocket and held it up for her to see. "I have a favor to ask," he said, his voice low and sultry. "Could you give this to Jodie? She'll want to know I'm here."

The woman froze at the sight of the card with the ace of spades on it. She raised her brows, then locked gazes with Ramos, sizing him up and trying to decipher his meaning. She'd been with Jodie long enough to know the story of Ace, the man who'd become the subject of Jodie's hit song. Besides herself and Dusty, not many people knew him by that name.

Her curiosity got the best of her and she took the card. "I'll show her, but that doesn't mean she'll want to see you." With that, she turned on her heel and hurried out of the room, thinking that Jodie could get a good look at him from the surveillance camera over the door.

I mentioned that to Ramos. With a nod, he turned toward the camera to make sure he was visible and waited. It wasn't long before the woman came back out. "Come with me." She motioned him to the front of the line and unclasped the rope for him to pass through.

I followed behind him, hoping she'd let me in too, but she stopped me in my tracks. Not about to let that happen, Ramos grabbed my hand and pulled me to his side. "She's with me."

The woman hesitated, then shrugged and let me in with a shake of her head. She was thinking that she'd never seen Jodie so flustered at the sight of a man before. She'd even said "Ace" like a prayer or something. She hoped my presence would discourage Jodie from throwing herself at him and ruining her life all over again.

As we followed her down a hall, her thoughts centered on Ramos, mostly since he was like a legend to anyone who knew the story. She had to admit he'd rattled her. Usually the real thing wasn't half as impressive as the story, but this guy... nothing could have prepared her for him in real life. No wonder Jodie got her heart broken.

She opened a door to a room and preceded us inside, then held it open for us to pass through. She inhaled as Ramos passed, catching his scent, and I tried not to roll my eyes. After I entered, she left, shaking her head and closing the door behind her.

The room was larger than I first thought. On the far wall, there were four TV monitors showing real-time images of the stage, the room we'd just been in, and a couple other places I couldn't make out.

A couch sat in front of the monitors against the wall, and a table and chairs with snacks and drinks stood on the other side. Now that the time had come, Ramos began pacing, his nerves finally getting the best of him.

"I think I'll sit down on the couch," I told him. He sent me a quick nod, and I wandered over to the couch and sat down in the corner. The intensity of this whole encounter ratcheted up the tension, and I wished I could turn invisible.

I mean, here they were, two star-crossed lovers meeting for the first time in years, and here I was watching the whole thing. Maybe if I didn't make any noise, they'd forget about me, and I could do my job. To reinforce that image, I got out my phone and started playing a mindless game.

Just then, the door opened. Jodie stood frozen in the doorway, dressed to the nines in a dazzling short dress that showed off her toned body and wearing classic cowboy boots to match. Makeup artfully accented her beautiful large eyes, and her curly blond hair fell in waves to her shoulders.

"It's really you," she said.

Ramos stopped in his tracks. "Jodie."

She inhaled sharply, and I picked up how the sound of his voice brought back a rush of memories she'd tried to forget. They stared at each other for a few seconds before he broke the spell.

"Are you going to come in?"

She let out her breath and stepped inside. Closing the door behind her, she leaned against it for support, clearly shaken to be this close to him. She was thinking that he looked even better now than she remembered, and that was saying something.

She hadn't remembered how his presence filled a room. His whole body seemed more muscular and toned, and his face had taken on that hard edge of someone who'd lived through more trouble than most. The way he stood exuded danger and intimidation, making it easy to tell he wasn't someone to cross.

"Your hair's shorter," Ramos said. He thought she looked smaller and more fragile than he remembered. Maybe that was because of the vulnerability pouring from her dark eyes. Then she straightened and regained her composure, and he saw the strength that wasn't there before.

Memories flooded over him. The late nights after her show when he'd taught her how to play poker. The first song she ever wrote about him, and how she'd sung it during a performance, but how it felt like he was the only person in the room.

Her struggles to help her brother, and turning to him for guidance. The late-morning motorcycle rides into the mountains, and the time they got caught in the rain. The tenderness and love they shared that made him feel cherished and whole. So many little things they did together. It was a simpler life before trouble caught up to him.

I felt my face heating up. They were so caught up in each other that they didn't even notice me, which was fine, only I felt like I was eavesdropping on something way too personal. I slid a little lower onto the couch, wishing it would swallow me up.

"I never thought I'd see you again," Jodie said. Then she shook her head, angry that he still had the ability to hurt her. "Look. I know why you left, but... you could have at least called to say goodbye."

She thought of all the times she'd waited for her phone to ring. All the times she looked for an email or a letter... anything. But it never came. Not one damn thing. He just disappeared from her life like he'd never been there. It had devastated her. She thought she meant more to him than that.

Ramos sighed with obvious regret. "I can't excuse it, only to say that I thought it would be easier not to. I couldn't stay, but I'm sorry about the way I left." He stepped toward her, invading her space. "Can you forgive me?"

Her gaze sprang to his with surprise. She hadn't expected that and, after all this time, she found that she really wanted to let go of the anger and hurt. She'd held onto it for too long and finally realized that the only person she'd hurt was herself.

"Yeah. I forgive you." A shock of relief rolled over her, and she smiled for the first time. It changed her whole countenance to one of warmth with a little cocky thrown in.

"I'm finally over you," she said, surprised. "I mean... I can't be too upset. When you left, I thought my world had ended. But it was actually the best thing that could have happened for my career. My breakout album was all about you. Did you know?"

His shoulder lifted in a careless shrug, but a gleam of satisfaction came into his eyes, and his lips tilted into a seductive smile.

"Of course you did." She let out a dramatic breath and rolled her eyes. "So why are you really here?" She hoped he'd say it was because he'd wanted to see her and apologize, but that didn't happen. In the silence, her gaze locked with his. From the set of his lips, she knew there was more to it, so she hid her disappointment behind a chuckle. "It's all right. You might as well tell me."

Ramos let out a breath and stepped away from her, knowing he'd disappointed her again, which was why he wasn't good at relationships and avoided them at all costs. "Dusty came to see me. I think he's in some kind of trouble... and he told me about your... daughter."

Her breath caught. "My daughter?" Then she realized that Dusty would have told Ramos about her for only one reason. "Oh... I see."

A knock sounded at the door, and her assistant stuck her head inside. "You've got five more minutes before you need to meet with your fans."

"Okay, thanks." The door closed and she glanced at Ramos, knowing she needed to tell him something. "So... did Dusty tell you she was yours?"

"No. But he implied that she might be. Is she?"

Jodie shook her head, not quite ready to share the whole story. "No. She's not."

Ramos breathed a sigh, but he wasn't sure if he felt elation or disappointment. Maybe a little of both.

Jodie sighed as well and glanced away from Ramos. She caught sight of me sitting on the couch, and her eyes widened. "Who's that?" A spike of jealousy and anger went through her. Why the hell would Ramos bring another woman with him to this intimate moment?

I smiled and sent her a little wave, but I didn't want to get too close in case she clobbered me. "Hi, I'm Shelby... uh... Ramos' friend. It's so nice to meet you. I love your stuff."

She nodded politely and then looked between us, trying to figure out what our relationship entailed. She didn't think we were a couple, but why was I there? Was Ramos trying to tell her something? She wasn't going to fall for him again if that was what he was afraid of.

"Dusty invited me," I said, hoping to calm her down.

"You saw him, too?" she asked. At my nod she turned to Ramos. "So what kind of trouble do you think he's in?"

"He's selling drugs," Ramos said, knowing the truth was the only way to get through to her. "That's why he came to see me, only I think there's more to it. I need to talk to him and find out what's going on."

Her mouth dropped open in surprise. "He can't be. He hasn't done that for years. You must have it wrong." She shook her head in disbelief, not wanting to hear any more about it. "I've got to go." She stepped around him to leave, but he caught her arm.

"Jodie. Please. I'd never lie to you."

She wrenched her arm out of his grip but, beneath the anger, worry spiked through her. Was that why Dusty had been on edge? Just yesterday they'd had a fight over Lacie's tutor, Stephanie. She thought Stephanie was doing a great job, but now she wondered if Dusty's concerns had merit. Dusty had even been adamant about keeping Lacie with him tonight during the concert.

"Dusty has Lacie tonight." Her brows puckered together with concern. "He's been worried about her spending so much time with Stephanie... her tutor. He insisted Lacie stay with him tonight."

"Is that unusual?" Ramos asked.

"Not entirely. She usually stays with Stephanie, but Dusty and Stephanie haven't been getting along lately." Jodie shook her head, unconvinced that Dusty could be selling drugs. He'd changed. Still, some of the tension he'd been exhibiting worried her.

A knock sounded at the door, and the manager popped her head inside again. "It's time."

"Okay, just give me a second." Jodie glanced at Ramos, unsure of what to do. "Can we talk after the show? You're staying aren't you?"

Her pleading gaze was hard to resist, and Ramos didn't want to disappoint her again. "Sure."

She let out a relieved breath. "I'll let Kristin know... she's my assistant. She'll take care of you, and we can meet back here after the show."

"What about Dusty?"

She shook her head. "I'll talk to him. I'll tell him he needs to come back here. We'll straighten this out then." She was thinking she didn't have time to call Dusty, but she'd make sure Kristin arranged it for her.

Ramos pursed his lips, thinking that if Dusty had a heads up, he might not come at all. Instead of telling Jodie this, he nodded his agreement.

"Good." Jodie smiled with relief. She had a sudden urge to throw her arms around Ramos, but she pushed the impulse away and hurried out the door. I caught her thoughts of excitement to have Ramos here, along with relief that she could see him at least once more after the show. Maybe she could hug him then. There was so much she wanted to....

The door closed, but I knew that she wanted to tell him about her life, and she wanted to know about his. She might not be in love with him now, but she still had feelings for him.

Ramos took a deep breath. That had been harder than he'd thought, and he wasn't sure staying was a good idea. Maybe he could find Dusty long before the show ever started. If he got what he needed, he wouldn't need to stick around here. Sure, it would disappoint Jodie, but it was better that way. Of course, that all depended on Lacie, and if Jodie had told the truth that Lacie wasn't his daughter.

He glanced my way, realizing that he'd put me in the middle of it all. It embarrassed him just a little for me to witness this whole thing and see him so vulnerable. Good thing I knew what kind of a person he really was and that he could trust me. "So... is Lacie my... daughter?"

I took a deep breath and let it out. "Well... that's hard to say. Deep down, she really wants Lacie to be your daughter, even if she's not. But she's not really sure, whatever that means. There must have been someone else right after you left. Maybe it's the guy she married?" I shrugged, sorry I couldn't give Ramos a better answer.

The door opened and Jodie's assistant, Kristin, came in. "Jodie said you were staying for the concert?"

Ramos nodded. "Yes, but she was going to find Dusty so I could talk to him right away. Did she tell you that?"

Kristin's brow puckered. "Uh... she told me to call him and have him come here. Maybe that's what she meant. I'll give him a call." She pushed in his number and shook her head, thinking that she was too busy to babysit Dusty all the time. After five rings, he finally picked up.

"Hey Dusty, Jodie wants you to come back to the arena. There's someone here who wants to talk to you." Kristin glanced at Ramos, and I picked up that Dusty was describing him and asking if he was there. "Yeah, that's him."

He said something else and she rolled her eyes, then handed her phone to Ramos. "Here. He wants to talk to you." Ramos took the phone and held it to his ear.

"Yes." He listened for a moment, then his gaze caught mine, and he shook his head. I only picked up a small part of the conversation, but from what I could tell, Dusty was asking for Ramos' help, and he sounded kind of frantic.

Ramos closed his eyes and inwardly groaned. "I'll come." Then he handed the phone back to Kristin. "Thanks."

"No problem. So... are you staying for the concert?"

"Yes," Ramos said. "We wouldn't miss it."

"Okay. Give me a few minutes and I'll come back to take you to your seats." At Ramos' nod, she left.

As soon as the door closed, I turned to him. "What's going on?"

"Dusty's begging me to help him, and he says that Lacie might be in trouble, too. He wants me to meet him by the storage trucks and equipment behind the arena. He said there's a couple of motorhomes there, and he and Lacie are in one of them."

"Why?"

"He didn't say."

I shook my head. "Of course he didn't. I don't like it. How do you know it's not a trap?"

"I don't." He was thinking that he didn't trust Dusty past the end of his nose, but since he had Lacie with him, he wasn't sure he could risk not going.

"How can we even be allowed back there?"

"He told me there was an exit on the south side of the building. We just need to go left when we leave this room and keep left until we come to an exit."

"This seems way too contrived to me," I said, my stomach churning with tension. "First, he lures you here to talk to Jodie, then, once you're here, it's no big deal to ask you to meet him in the parking lot. Then, if you go out there you're totally at his mercy with no one on your side to help."

"I know what it looks like," Ramos said, clenching his jaw. "And maybe it is a trap, but Dusty was more concerned about Lacie than himself. How can I chance it? Even if she's not my daughter, she's just a kid."

"Well... I guess you can't. But, hey... at least you'll have me. I just wish I had my stun flashlight or you had your gun handy."

Ramos mentally agreed with me. He also wasn't sure that he wanted me to help him, but it was only because he worried for my safety, and not because he thought I was incompetent. At least that was positive.

"Come on," he said. "We've got to go before Jodie's assistant comes back."

"Okay."

He opened the door and checked the hall, then motioned for me to follow him out. I held my breath, worried that at any moment the assistant, or even Jodie, would come around the corner and catch us. We came to another hallway, and Ramos stopped to glance in both directions. To our left were several people wearing black t-shirts and carrying equipment, like they were part of the stage crew.

To our right, the hall opened into more of a concrete lane that sloped down into the bottom of the arena. Ramos straightened and turned toward the people, walking with purpose, and thinking *act like you're supposed to be here* for my benefit.

He nodded at one guy but, for the most part, ignored everyone else. I followed his lead and let out my breath as we reached the end of the long hallway without any trouble.

We turned left again to find an exit sign over a double-door at the end of the hall. Ramos hesitated at the doors while I caught up with him, then he pushed them open and we stepped out.

The sun was still shining, but on its way toward dusk, and we could see most of the semi-trucks from here. I was amazed at how many trucks it took to run a big show like this. I counted at least eight, but there were probably three or four more. At least there weren't any people around. They were probably all busy with the concert.

"Where are the motorhomes?" I asked.

"Let's try that direction." Ramos nodded toward the right, and we circled that way. "Be on the watch for security. There are probably a couple of guards around here somewhere, and we don't want to get caught."

I nodded, picking up that he didn't want to hurt anyone, but he would if he had to. Hearing that got my heart racing a little, and a knot of fear curdled my stomach. I let out a quick breath and managed to keep up.

We rounded one of the trucks and stopped short, finding two motorhomes parked next to the building. "Which one is Dusty's?"

"I don't know," Ramos said, ushering me out of sight behind the truck. "He said he'd be here waiting, but since he's not, let's sit tight and watch before we make a move."

I nodded and stepped out of sight behind the truck, letting Ramos do the watching. I kept my senses open for movement of any kind in case someone approached, but so far, things stayed quiet. Then I heard a door open, and Ramos stiffened.

"That's him. He just came out." He caught my gaze. "Can you pick up anything from here?"

I concentrated on Dusty and picked up a few words, but I needed to get closer before they made any sense. I shook my head. "Not really."

"Okay, let's go."

I followed Ramos around the truck and picked up a blast of relief from Dusty. He met us half-way. "Thanks for coming." He glanced at me and his brows puckered. What had happened to my black hair?

"It was a wig," I answered.

"Oh." The fact that I answered his thoughts threw him a little, but he didn't have time to waste. "Uh... come inside and I'll explain everything."

We got to the steps of the motorhome, but I didn't want to go in there if it was a trap, so I grabbed Ramos' arm to stop him. "I think you can tell us out here. I'd rather not go inside if that's all right with you."

Dusty paused before opening the door and turned to face us. He let out a breath and came back down the stairs, ushering us toward the back of the RV.

"Fine." He glanced at Ramos and swallowed. "Look man, I know you're probably thinking that I set you up the other day, but I had no choice, and it didn't work anyway."

He glanced around the area, hoping no one could see us, and rubbed his nose. "I did it all to keep Lacie and Jodie safe, you have to believe that."

"Where is Lacie?" I asked, suddenly worried.

"She's fine, she's in the motorhome."

"What did you do?" Ramos folded his arms and sent Dusty a hard glare.

Dusty swallowed, thinking that we only had a certain amount of time to stop Luke, and if it was going to work, we needed to leave now.

"Who's Luke?" I asked, just to get things moving along.

Dusty's eyes widened, and his mouth dropped open.

"Answer the question," Ramos said.

"He's been... he's the one who's behind this mess I'm in. He's been forcing me to sell his drugs." At Ramos' narrowed eyes, he continued, "I thought if I made it look like you had agreed to sell the drugs, but double-crossed him, he'd come after you and you'd kill him. But I've run out of time and he's... well, he's out of control. He's already killed one person, and the contacts we've made in the city have all dried up. It's like nobody will do business with us except for a few gang members."

I picked up that there was a lot more to it than that. "Is he threatening Lacie... and Jodie?"

He let out a breath, surprised that I'd picked it up so easily. "They don't know anything, but he's holding that over my head if I don't do what he wants." He shook his head in disgust. "Lacie's fine for now, but I could use your help to stop Luke before he follows through on those threats."

"You mean like kill you?" I asked, since that's what he was thinking.

He nodded. "Yeah... something like that. Look, I know this is all my fault." He shook his head in disgust. "But I want to make it right."

"Is he the one who's been following you?" I prodded. "And the one who threatened Ramos the other night?" Dusty lowered his eyes and nodded. "Where is he now?"

"He went to do a drug exchange, and I know where he is. If we don't go after him now, we'll miss our chance. He'll come back here, and who knows what he'll do then." He sent a pleading gaze to Ramos. "Will you help me?"

Ramos glanced my way, silently asking if Dusty was telling the truth. Unfortunately he was, so I nodded. Ramos' mouth turned into a grim line before he answered. "All right, I'll help you, but what about Lacie? Is she safe here?"

"Yeah, Stephanie's with her, so she's fine for now."

"Are you sure?" I asked. "It seems like you have a love-hate kind of thing going on with Stephanie. Why is that?" I needed to know before I agreed to leave Lacie there.

"I never said that." Dusty sent a suspicious glance my way, then took in Ramos' scowl and decided to answer the question. "Okay. She found out about the guy Luke killed, and she's just as freaked out as I am. We don't exactly agree on what to do about it, but neither of us wants to go to jail."

"So... you're together?"

He shook his head and let out a deep breath. "It's complicated. But she's great with Lacie."

I shook my head, something didn't add up. "So who's Luke? Is he part of your road crew?"

Dusty closed his eyes and shook his head. "He's Jodie's... boyfriend."

"What?" I could hardly believe what I was hearing. From the swearing going on in Ramos' mind, I knew he thought the same thing.

"I told you she doesn't have much luck with men," he said, glaring a little at Ramos. "Look, I know where he went. If we can stop him from coming back here, it will all be over. I know I'm asking a lot of you, but you're the only person I know who could kill someone and pull it off."

So that's what he'd wanted all along. He knew Ramos was a killer, and he thought that if he brought Ramos into the picture by setting him up, Ramos would kill Luke, and his troubles would be over.

"What does he have on you?" I asked.

Dusty shook his head. "Look, it doesn't matter, and we don't have a lot of time. If you're going to help me, we need to go now."

Ramos turned to me, thinking there were all kinds of ways to take care of a person like Luke, and I didn't need to know about any of them. "Why don't you stay here and make sure Lacie's safe? I'll come back for you."

"I'll tell Stephanie you're staying," Dusty hurried to the door and bounded inside, elated that Ramos had agreed to help him, and thinking that maybe he could get out of this alive after all.

I caught Ramos' gaze. "I don't like this. It's all happening too fast."

"Is he telling the truth?"

"Yes. I just wish I knew more about what was going on."

"I know... I do too." Ramos shook his head. "But I'd better check it out. I'm not saying I'll kill the guy, but I'll handle it." He was thinking there was plenty of time to get to the bottom of it once Luke was incapacitated.

"Okay. Be careful." He nodded with a reassuring smile, just as Dusty came back to the door of the motorhome and motioned me inside.

The super luxurious space was just what I'd expect for a star of Jodie's caliber. Dusty quickly introduced me to Lacie, who sat at the table coloring a picture. He told her I was a friend and would be staying with her for an hour or so. She glanced up shyly, then went back to her coloring.

"Stephanie's in the bedroom," he said, thinking that Stephanie wasn't too happy with him. He'd told her about his plan, and she hadn't liked it much. He basically shut her down, telling her that he didn't have time for her objections, and now she refused to come out and meet me.

"I'll be back soon," Dusty said, loud enough for Stephanie to hear.

Just then, Stephanie opened the door and glanced at Dusty, then noticed me standing beside him. Her lips turned into a tight line, and she slammed the door shut. Dusty sighed and turned to me. "Sorry about that. Uh... I'm sure she'll be fine." He kissed Lacie on the top of her head. "Hey kiddo... I'll be back soon." Lacie nodded and he left.

I let out a breath and sat beside Lacie, a little worried about Stephanie. The only thing I'd picked up from Stephanie was that she was furious, so I hoped she calmed down soon. Or... she could just stay in her room... that would be fine with me.

I turned to Lacie and asked her about her coloring book. She was a little shy at first, but eager to share her passion for art. Behind that, she seemed relieved for the diversion from the constant bickering between Dusty and Stephanie. She hated that they fought all the time, so having me there came as a relief.

"This is an adult coloring book," she said, wanting me to know she wasn't a little kid. "Have you ever heard of them?"

"Yes. My daughter has a few, but I've never seen markers like those before."

"These are totes awesome. I'll show you how they work."

"Great."

We spent the next few minutes coloring together, and I had to admit, the markers were amazing. They worked with tips that would turn the colors lighter or darker so the color would look shaded on one side and totally professional. I decided then and there that I needed to get Savannah some.

Seeing my enthusiasm, Lacie handed over another book, and I got to work coloring. It was kind of nice to focus on something creative and forget about dirty drug dealers for a while. About five minutes later, I totally understood why Lacie and all kinds of people liked it so much. Maybe I'd get one for me?

The bedroom door popped open, startling me out of my happy place. Stephanie stepped out. Her face was a little splotchy like she'd been crying, but the gaze she sent my way held nothing but ice. A shiver of pure dread rolled down my spine. She held a gun in front of her and pointed it straight at me.

Chapter 12

"Lacie, honey," she said. "This is a bad person. I need you to come over to me."

Lacie's eyes widened. She'd never seen Stephanie holding a gun, or seen that crazy look in her eyes before. There were times Stephanie scared her, but never like this. She glanced at me. I was a lot like her mom. I didn't seem dangerous at all. What was going on?

"I'm not a bad person," I blurted. "I'm here to watch out for you Lacie, and to protect you." I turned my gaze to Stephanie. "You should be protecting her, too. So why are you doing this?"

"Don't listen to her Lacie. She's lying. She's only saying that to confuse you. I'll keep you safe, but I need you to get up and go into the bedroom and lock the door. Don't come out, no matter what happens, or what you hear. I promise I'll keep you safe."

Lacie glanced at me with widened eyes, and slowly slid out from behind the table. She didn't think I was bad, but Stephanie had a gun. Scared out of her mind, she could hardly walk. With quick breaths, she slipped past Stephanie and scurried into the bedroom, then closed the door and locked it.

Stephanie visibly relaxed once Lacie was out of the room. She glanced at me, trying to figure out what to do. She couldn't take the chance that I'd sit quietly while she followed Luke's instructions. So she needed to put me someplace where I couldn't make trouble.

Or she could just shoot me and be done with it. She'd tell everyone I'd tried to kidnap Lacie. But could she actually kill me? Maybe not like this. But if I made any trouble, she could pull the trigger. Raising the gun to point at my head, she said, "Get up."

She was thinking I'd fit into the space under the seat just fine. It only held a few blankets and pillows, but she could take enough out to carve a place for me. The tricky part would be getting me inside without a struggle. But if I made a fuss, she'd just shoot me in the leg or something. That would work.

Yikes! I tried to keep the panic from consuming me and raised both hands. With shallow breaths, I slowly stood, then inched my way out from behind the table.

"Hey! I never said to move."

I froze in place and swallowed, hardly daring to breathe. She examined me, noting that I had a purse slung over my shoulder, and thinking it could have a phone in it.

"Put your purse on the table."

With a sinking heart, I pulled my purse over my shoulder and set it down.

"Now empty your pockets... nice and slow."

"There's nothing in my pockets." I patted them down to show her I was telling the truth. "See?"

"Fine. Now lift up that seat cushion, and take out whatever's under there."

I nodded and moved in slow-motion so I wouldn't startle her. With trembling fingers, I lifted the cushion off the seat. For a moment, I contemplated using the cushion to take a swing at her gun hand, but with her twitchy fingers, that probably wasn't a good idea. Instead, I set it down and pulled a couple of blankets out of the top, and set them to the side.

Knowing that she wanted me in there, I made sure to leave a blanket in the very bottom, along with a small pillow for my head. Still, I wasn't sure I'd fit. I might be small, but that space was tiny.

"Get in," she ordered, motioning with the gun.

Taking a deep breath, I stepped inside. After sitting down, I scrunched into the space, and laid my head down on the pillow, but that left my knees poking up too high for the cushion.

"Turn on your side," Stephanie said, growing anxious that I was taking too long. "Hurry up."

Knowing she was strung tight, I quickly turned onto my side and pulled my knees up toward my chest, barely managing to fit.

Stephanie let out a relieved breath and leaned over me. "Don't try to get out. I'll hear you moving under there, and you'd better believe that I'll shoot you. And don't make any sounds, either." Satisfied, she slid the cushion into the slot and lowered it until it fit just above my cramped body.

In the dark, I heard her move away. I waited a few seconds before raising the cushion to find out what she was up to. I may not be able to see her, but I hoped with the cushion raised a little, I could still pick up her thoughts.

I knew one thing for certain; she was totally freaked out and desperate. Not someone I could reason with. But she had a plan. I listened real close as she moved to the driver's seat. Setting the gun on her lap, she started up the motorhome.

She was thinking that it was close, but at least she'd warned Luke before Dusty and the scary guy got to him. It was a good thing the motorhome walls were thin, because she'd been able to hear Dusty asking that guy to kill Luke. How had this gotten so out of control?

Luke told them that he'd had to kill that drug dealer because the police were onto him, and he couldn't risk the dealer spilling his guts. But it had freaked Dusty out. It bothered her too, but she never expected Dusty to go after Luke.

When that scary dude had agreed to kill Luke, her heart had nearly stopped, and she knew she had to do something. But things were unraveling fast, and she didn't have a lot of time.

Now she had to play her part carefully and do what Luke said. If they got caught, they were both going to prison, and that couldn't happen. Doing what Luke told her was the only way out, even if that meant shooting me.

My breath caught, and my stomach tightened. How was I going to get out of this mess?

She pulled out of the parking space, thinking that she still had to get the security guard to open the gate. That might be tricky, but she hoped he'd let her out without any trouble, since she didn't want to shoot him either.

I let out a breath and tried to decide what to do. Should I try and sneak out while she was busy talking to the security guard? I was scrunched in so tight, I wasn't sure I could get out easily, let alone in a hurry. Still, I pushed the cushion up and got ready to jump out.

I heard her roll the window down. "Hi there. I'm just headed out to get some ice cream for Lacie. Can I get you something?"

"Oh... no, I'm good. Uh... don't you normally take the car for stuff like that?"

"Yeah... normally... but Dusty took it, and I don't want to wait around." She paused, then continued in a lighter tone. "Hey, I'm fine driving the motorhome. I've done it before, and I'm not going far."

"Okay. I'll get the gate open."

"Hey thanks. I owe you one. See you in a bit."

A few seconds later, the motorhome began to move, and I'd missed my chance. Maybe that was a good thing since she might have shot us both, but if another opportunity came along, I had to take it.

She turned onto the street and then picked up speed. Through the bumpy ride, I caught that she was relieved to get away so easily, but that didn't mean she had a lot of time. If she didn't make it back within half an hour or so, the security guard would probably sound the alarm.

She needed to find the building where Luke had told her to meet him, and get back to the arena before that happened. Luke would know what to do with me after that, and he'd take care of this mess. She couldn't figure out what had gone wrong. Dusty wasn't supposed to double-cross Luke. Not with what Luke had on him. Dusty had ruined everything.

Anger simmered, and she hit the steering wheel, deciding she'd make Dusty pay. He never should have underestimated her. If he thought leaving me there with her was enough to keep her from taking matters into her own hands, he was sadly mistaken. Of course, he didn't know she had a gun and was willing to use it.

Only, if she didn't get back in time, it could all unravel. There was still the option that she could blame it all on me... that I'd forced her to drive away because I was kidnapping Lacie for some ransom money.

Right now, I was the only one besides Dusty who knew that she was working with Luke. She could say that I'd kidnapped her and Lacie. Since she'd sent Lacie into the bedroom for her own safety, Lacie wouldn't know any different.

Then she'd be in the clear, and everything would work out just fine. Luke would kick Dusty back into line, and it would all go back to the way it was. A sense of relief flooded over her, along with the thought that I'd have to die, but Luke would take care of that, too.

My stomach clenched with dread, and I let the cushion down. I knew her plan, but what was I supposed to do about it? Even if I managed to crawl out of this box without her hearing me, she wouldn't hesitate to shoot me, mostly because she wanted me dead anyway, and it fit in with her plans.

An idea popped into my head and I lifted the cushion again. My purse was still sitting on the table. Maybe I could reach it and use my phone to call for help? With renewed energy, I pushed the cushion up, and levered my body to reach across the table, hoping to snag my purse strap.

Just as my fingers touched the strap, the motorhome made a sharp turn. My purse went flying off the table to crash against the other side of the motorhome, and my face hit the edge of the box. Then the motorhome turned in the other direction, and I fell back into the box, hitting the back of my head against the side.

Inwardly cursing, I touched my cheek for damage. It stung a little, but at least there wasn't any blood. Sheesh... and she thought she could drive this thing?

What about Lacie? Was she okay back there? Since I didn't hear any crying or moaning sounds, I took that as a good sign. The cushion had fallen to the floor, but I left it where it was and tuned into Stephanie's thoughts.

She'd nearly missed the turn, and she was a little confused about where she was going. Then she found the building Luke had told her about, and pulled behind it, relieved to find an empty parking lot with a small water canal at the back, out of sight from the street.

Luke wasn't there yet, but this was the perfect spot to meet. Relief washed over her that he was on his way. She turned off the engine, thinking that she needed to find the gun since it had flown off her lap when she'd made that sharp turn.

My breath caught. This was my chance! I pushed myself up and scrambled to get out of the couch. She heard me coming and doubled her efforts to reach the gun before I got out. Knowing I didn't have much time, I lurched to my feet and jumped over the edge of the couch.

I nearly fell, but caught my balance on the table and rushed toward the front seat. From her thoughts, I knew the gun was on the floor of the passenger seat. I found Stephanie sprawled over the middle console, reaching for the gun. Hoping to stop her, I leaned over her back and grabbed her arm, but not before her fingers closed over the gun handle.

She twisted and elbowed me, then brought the gun up and pulled the trigger. The bullet flew above my head and went straight through the ceiling. I cringed and fell backwards, then scooted away until I hit the side of the motorhome next to the door.

Stephanie brought the gun around and aimed it at me, ready to pull the trigger. Just then, the bedroom door opened and Lacie stuck her head out. Stephanie quickly lowered the gun, and took in a couple of deep breaths, then she moved from the front seat to stand over me, holding the gun in my direction.

"It's okay, Lacie. Get back in your room and close the door."

"I want my mom," she shouted.

"I'm going to call her right now. I've got this. Go back in the room where it's safe."

"Not until you call her." Lacie's chin jutted out in defiance, but tears ran down her cheeks.

Stephanie sent a murderous glance my way before taking out her phone. She set it on the table where she could push the buttons with one hand, not willing to put the gun away with me so close.

The call went through and she held it to her ear. "Hey... something's happened and I need you to come right now. We're at the address... yeah... behind the brick building. How soon can you get here? Okay, we'll sit tight."

She ended the call and glanced up at Lacie. "Help's on the way. Now please go back inside, and close the door."

Lacie couldn't figure out what Stephanie was up to. It didn't make any sense. Why had she come here? Still, she nodded and closed the door.

After the door shut, Stephanie glanced at me with narrowed eyes, thinking that if Lacie hadn't opened the door, she would have shot me. "You're one lucky bitch."

I swallowed, but kept my mouth shut. It wouldn't do me any good to talk to her, since I already knew that Luke was the one she'd called, so I had to think of another way out of this.

Suddenly drained, Stephanie stepped over to the couch and sat down on the edge, still pointing the gun in my direction. I stayed where I was, mostly because my purse happened to be in the corner right behind me. The next time she looked away, I planned to grab my phone.

She kept her gaze pinned on me, thinking that maybe it was time to get out of the drug business. Between her and

Luke, they'd made almost seven million dollars. That was enough to live comfortably for a while.

They could stash their equipment in a storage unit until they needed it and disappear. Luke should have all the cash they'd made from this city by now, and they could cut their losses and leave. She hoped he'd agree with her. This scam had been profitable, but maybe it was time to go off the grid.

"So you're the one who made the pills?" I asked. "I thought it was Dusty." Her gaze narrowed, so I shrugged. "Hey... if I'm going to die, it wouldn't hurt for you to tell me." She didn't say anything so I continued. "So who are you scamming anyway? How does that work?"

She drew in a breath. How had I known about that? "Are you with the police?"

"Um... no. I came tonight to help Dusty. He's not much of a friend, though. I mean... I never thought this would happen." I hoped that was enough to get some sympathy from her so she'd open up a little. "How does this scam of yours work?"

She smirked, thinking I was going to die anyway, and she might as well tell me, as long as we spoke softly so Lacie wouldn't hear. "It was kind of an accident, actually. Luke caught Jodie's attention and they started seeing each other."

I raised my brows. Stephanie was okay that Luke was with another woman? She noticed that look and shook her head. "You've got it all wrong. Luke's my brother. He's a big time con artist, and has been for years. He thought with this con we'd hit the mother-load. Since Jodie was getting ready for her big tour, he saw an opportunity to sell our little pills at each tour stop.

"He thought since we wouldn't be around for more than a few days in each place, it was the perfect cover. He even managed to bring me on board as Lacie's tutor. That way I could be his eyes and ears and help out with the operation."

She let out a breath. "I'd already made most of the pills by then, so I finished up, and after that it was a simple case of distributing them. Only we hadn't planned on Dusty. It fell to me to distract Dusty from what Luke was doing, so I started dating him."

She shook her head. "He has no idea that Luke's my brother and that we're in on it together. I just never thought he'd try to kill Luke. Did you know he wanted to do that?"

"No. I didn't know anything about it."

She narrowed her eyes, thinking I was lying. I'd come with the scary guy, so I probably knew more than I was saying. Worry tightened her mouth. Maybe she shouldn't have said anything. They certainly didn't want that scary guy after them. She'd have to warn Luke since he might have to kill him, too.

"Luke will know what to do," she said, mostly to calm her fears. "He always does."

She was thinking that, in the last five years, they'd never been caught or even questioned. Luke had the charm and the good looks, and he was smart as a whip. He thought of everything and never made mistakes. He even had contingency plans for everything. The fact that this had happened just wasn't right.

As if on cue, the sound of a car pulling into the parking lot sent a chill down my spine. Stephanie let out a breath of relief and stood. The door opened, and Luke glanced inside, his gaze taking us both in before settling on me.

He had that scruffy look down, wearing jeans and a denim jacket, with a short dark-brown beard and longer hair curling around his ears. If I'd have seen him any other time, I would have thought him extremely good-looking, but not tonight.

"So this is Shelby." His rich baritone voice rolled over me, but his dark eyes held contempt. "What are we going to do with you?"

"I've got an idea," Stephanie said. "But let's take her outside."

Luke stepped off the stairs and swung the door open, gesturing with his arm that I should follow him out. Stephanie pointed the gun in my direction, so I got to my feet and stepped out the door. With Stephanie following, I hoped she wouldn't notice the phone that I'd managed to slip out of my purse and into the waistband at the back of my jeans.

The sun had set, but there was still enough light to see by. Luke led the way to the other side of his car and popped his trunk. He rummaged inside, then pulled out a piece of rope, and my heart rate spiked. My hopes sank as he grabbed my wrists and tied them tightly together behind my back.

Stephanie explained her idea of blaming me for everything, but Luke thought she was dreaming to think it would be that easy. "I don't think it's going to work. You don't know her." He glanced at me. "Or her connections. She could be a cop for all we know."

"She said she wasn't..."

"You think she'd tell you if she was?"

Stephanie dropped her head in shame. "Fine. So what are we going to do now?"

He stepped close to her, then raised her chin until their gazes met. "You're going to take the motorhome back to the arena. Take Lacie inside and tell her she needs to stay with Kristin while you get things sorted out. Then you're going to clear out your things and take a taxi to the nearest bus station. Buy a ticket on the first bus that's leaving town, and when you get there, call me."

He took out his wallet and handed her a wad of cash. She took it, remembering that this was the plan they'd always talked about if anything ever went wrong. "Okay." She swallowed and glanced up at him. "Be careful, all right?"

"I will. Now get going before they think you ran off with Lacie."

Stephanie nodded, then hurried to the motorhome. With a wave, she started it up and pulled out of the lot.

Luke waited until she'd driven away before turning to face me. He shook his head, thinking that the stop in this city had ruined everything. He'd never had so much trouble selling drugs in his life.

Now it looked like he had to cut his losses and run. That meant leaving without a lot of his money, but he didn't have any other options. At least the cops would never pin anything on him. That's what Dusty was for.

But what was he going to do with me? Killing drug-addicted dealers wasn't the same thing as killing someone like me, even if that didn't change the fact that I had to die.

He did have one other option. He could get someone else to kill me. And if he played his cards right, it just might work.

He opened the back car door and shoved me inside. "Time to go."

I fell onto my side, but managed to scoot over and get my feet into the car before he closed the door. Luke started the car, and I got a whiff of something that smelled like sweat and blood. My nose wrinkled, and I glanced at the pile of clothes on the seat beside me.

In the dark, it was hard to make out more than a shirt and blanket. But the splotches of reddish-brown certainly looked like dried blood, and the smell definitely came from there. In revulsion, I moved closer to my door and worked hard to loosen the rope around my wrists.

Luke's idea of getting someone else to kill me had my stomach turning into knots. I listened real hard to find out who he thought that was, but he started singing a rap song about it being his world and doing what he wished to, and left me in the dark.

I tugged and twisted at the rope, but it didn't seem to get any looser. With a disgusted huff, I sat back in my seat. What was I going to do now? My phone wouldn't do me any good if I couldn't use it. Frantic, I felt for it in my waistband and then struggled to pull it out. If I could set it on the seat where I could see it, I might be able to send a text.

"What you doing back there?"

My gaze jerked to the rearview mirror where Luke stared at me with raised brows. I froze before my anger got the best of me. "What do you think? I'm trying to get out of this rope so I can get away before you kill me."

He hadn't expected the truth, and his brows turned into a frown. "I'm not going to kill you."

"Maybe not. But you're planning on getting someone else to do it, so what's the difference?"

He sucked in a breath. How the hell did I know that?

"Who is it anyway? I know it's not the mob. You're too much of a light-weight criminal to be involved in the big leagues. So who are you going to con into doing it?"

Just then, a low moan and a twitching movement came from the blanket beside me. I jumped and screamed a little, then plastered myself against the door. The mound of clothes shook, then the blanket fell from a face I recognized, even if it was bruised and bleeding.

Before I could say his name, Luke pulled over to the side of the road, sending me crashing into the front seat, and jumped out of the car. He opened the back door on Keola's side and knocked him in the head to shut him up.

Then Luke covered Keola with the blanket, and glanced at me. He thought he might have to do the same to me if I didn't shut up, but since I looked scared to death, he decided against it... unless I opened my mouth again.

I swallowed and tried to catch my breath. That was enough for me to keep my mouth shut. From what I'd seen of Keola, he looked pretty bad. One of his eyes was swollen shut, and he had several gashes on his face and lips. Luke had just knocked him out again, and he looked bad enough that I hoped he wasn't dead.

I certainly didn't want Luke to do that to me. I'd rather die all at once than get beaten up like that.

Luke took a deep breath and slammed the door shut, then hurried back to his seat. He started up the car and even put on his seatbelt. Frustrated, he thought that he didn't have time for this, and maybe it would be faster if he just killed us both himself. Then he shook his head. No. That might backfire. He needed to be smart, and taking me to them would do the trick.

He signaled, then pulled back onto the street. He started singing the same rap lyrics in his mind about doing what he wished to, since that always calmed him down. I tried to pick up where he was taking us, but the only thing I came up with was a gloomy, dark place that didn't do much to calm my nerves.

Still, if he was going to try to get someone else to kill me that meant that there was a small chance that I could talk them out of it before it happened. That gave me a little hope, but I still had my phone, and now was the time to use it.

I closed my eyes and tried to keep my features calm so Luke wouldn't notice how hard I was working to get my phone out of my pants. The moment it came free, it fell onto the seat, but that didn't matter.

With my fingers, I pushed it toward the side of me closest to Keola where I had some light and kept my gaze lowered. Hoping Luke wouldn't notice, I shifted my gaze to where it sat without moving my head. Then I shifted my body so I could actually touch the phone with my hands.

After several tries, my hands and wrists started to ache. Who knew pushing a button could be so hard? At last, I managed to turn it on and the screen lit up the whole backseat.

Crap! My breath caught, and I glanced to the rearview mirror. Luckily, Luke had his eyes on the road and didn't seem to notice the light. Still, I moved a little in front of it, hoping to block the glow. With my heart pounding, I swiped it open, and glanced to see where the contacts button was. I managed to push that and scrolled down until Ramos' name popped up.

With trembling fingers, I pushed on his name a couple of times before it worked, and his contact information came up. With my wrists and arms aching from the strain, I decided to hell with a text message, I'd just call him instead. Even if I didn't say anything, he'd know I was in trouble and needed him.

As my fingers reached the call button, Luke swore and swerved off the road, slamming the brakes and sending me crashing into the back of his seat again. My phone went flying, along with Keola. After the car came to a stop, Keola's head and shoulders had fallen onto my lap, and my phone was somewhere on the floor.

Luke turned in his seat to glare at me, shocked that I'd had a phone. He began searching for it and finally found it lying on the floor by Keola's feet. He let out a breath and glanced my way. He wanted to hit me something fierce, but time was running out. With Keola in my lap, there was no way I could retrieve the phone, so he left it there and pulled back onto the street.

Tears burned at the back of my eyes, and my throat got tight. I'd been so close! Just one more second, and the call would have gone through! Now what was I going to do? Before despair could completely overtake me, I remembered that I still had one more resource. My watch.

Once Ramos realized I was in trouble, all he had to do was check the tracker in my watch and he'd know where I was. I wasn't sure how much time had passed, but I hoped that by now he'd know something was up. I pushed away the panic and blinked back the tears, then took a calming breath.

There was still a chance I could get out of this alive... as long as Ramos found me in time.

Chapter 13

My phone began to ring. It was the song I'd programmed in for Chris, and I couldn't help the tears that came into my eyes. What if I never got to see him or the kids again? Luke swore a blue streak in his mind but didn't say a word.

A few minutes later, the ringing started up again, and Keola stirred. He moaned a little, then his eyes opened... or at least one of them did. He turned his head until his gaze found my face, and I felt confusion coming from him before his eyes closed and he drifted back to unconsciousness.

I glanced up as Luke pulled into a parking space behind a building. In the dark, I wasn't sure where we were, and my heart lurched with fear. Luke got out of the car and opened the door on Keola's side.

He reached in and pocketed my phone before pulling Keola out. The movement woke Keola up, and Luke managed to get him standing on his feet. He put Keola's arm around his shoulders, then grabbed him around the waist.

"I'll be back," he said to me, then closed the door and used his key pad to lock the car.

He walked Keola to a door in the back of the dark building, opened it, and dragged him inside. The door swung shut behind them, and I didn't waste any time trying to get the car door open. The unlock button was by the door handle, so I stood up in the cramped space and leaned over, using my fingers to feel for the button.

Countless seconds ticked by before I finally found it and pushed down. I didn't hear the click of the lock opening, and my hopes sank. Had he put the child-safety lock on? I felt for the door handle and pulled it, only to have nothing happen.

That meant I had to get to the front seat and try unlocking it from there. I glanced out the window, grateful there was no sign of Luke coming back, and moved to the center console. I twisted sideways and got my shoulders between the front seats. I pushed as far as I could go, and then fell onto the passenger seat, landing on my right shoulder.

I kicked my legs into the air and wriggled forward until I got them over the seat, then used my legs and shoulders to push me into a sitting position. Next, I brought my legs into the passenger side and twisted again so I could push backwards over the middle console and into the driver's seat.

After a lot of groaning and wiggling, I made it over and fell into the seat, pushing with my legs until they rested on the driver's side floor. Gasping a little, I managed to sit up and take a look at the buttons until I found the one I wanted.

With hope surging through me, I turned around, and felt for it with my fingers. All the buttons felt the same so I started pushing each one. Then came the sound of the lock releasing. Yes! I grabbed for the door handle and yanked it hard.

The door popped open, and I twisted back into the seat, then pushed it all the way open with my legs. With my heart pounding, I got my feet on the ground and managed to stand. Just then, the door on the building opened, and Luke came out.

I took off running, but didn't make it past the car before he grabbed me around the waist. He jerked me against him, squeezing me so tight I thought my ribs might crack.

"You never quit, do you?" Luke said, his mouth next to my ear.

I gasped for breath, and he finally loosened his hold. Then he grabbed my arm and started pulling me toward the door. "Come on."

I couldn't get my feet under me fast enough and started to fall, so he stopped to get a better hold. He clamped one hand around the back of my neck, and held my arm with the other, then began to push me forward. He could hardly believe that I'd almost gotten away.

Lucky for him, I hadn't, and things were working out the way he'd wanted. It seemed that turning in a traitor to these guys put them in a conciliatory mood, and they were more than happy to do him a favor in return. With relief, he opened the door and pushed me inside.

I stumbled through the doorway, then down a short hall. We came to a staircase and started down. I slipped a few times, but Luke kept a tight hold on me until we came to the bottom and a closed door. He pushed the door open and shoved me into a smoke-filled room with a low-hanging light over a pool table.

Other than that one light, it was dark enough that I couldn't see into the corners, but I picked up several people's thoughts and knew they were observing me from the shadows.

Luke pushed me into the light and let me go, then stood back with a satisfied smirk. "Nice doing business with you."

He turned to leave, but someone stopped him. "This is the haole you want us to kill?"

I jerked my gaze to that familiar voice, and my heart nearly burst. Big Kahuna held Luke's shoulder in a tight grip. His gaze locked with mine, and he took in the bruise and scrape along my cheek, along with my wild eyes and disheveled hair. His lips turned into a frown, and anger burned in his chest.

In that moment, I knew I was safe, and my legs nearly gave out.

Big Kahuna was thinking that this haole had just made the biggest mistake of his life. It was bad enough that he'd beaten up Keola... even if the kid deserved it for doing business behind their backs. But asking them to kill me was laughable. This guy was obviously not from around here.

Sensing trouble, Luke jerked out of Big Kahuna's grasp. "Hey, if you won't do it, then I'll take care of it. But I get the kid. He owes me." Luke reached inside his jacket, ready to pull out the gun that he kept there.

Big Kahuna smiled and raised his hands in a placating manner. "No problem, man. I hear you. I just have one question."

"What's that?"

"Do you know someone by the name of Joey 'The Knife' Manetto?"

"No," Luke said, sensing danger. "Why?"

"So you're not one of his associates?"

"I said I didn't know him."

"Good to know." Big Kahuna's smile widened. Moving faster than I thought possible for such a big guy, Big Kahuna landed a solid punch in Luke's stomach. Luke doubled over and would have fallen to his knees, but two men grabbed his arms to keep him upright.

While Luke coughed and gasped, Big Kahuna took the gun from Luke's jacket and handed it to another man. Then he patted Luke down, coming up with two phones and a wallet, along with a stash of pills. After taking the money out of his wallet, he returned it to Luke's pocket along with the pills.

Big Kahuna glanced at me. "Does one of these phones belong to you?"

"Uh... yeah."

Before he could bring it to me, everyone froze at the sound of someone rushing down the stairs. Big Kahuna stepped back as the door burst open and Ramos rushed in. He took in the scene, finding Luke restrained before his gaze came to rest on me. His heart filled with relief to find me alive.

"I was wondering when you'd get here," Big Kahuna said.

Ramos leveled a dark stare his way, and his lips turned down. "Then why is she still tied up?" Before Big Kahuna could answer, Ramos came to my side, flipped open his knife, and sliced through the rope.

Relieved to have my hands freed, I let out a soft moan. Ramos rubbed my hands between his, noticing the red rope burns on my wrists with barely controlled anger. He cupped my scraped cheek in his hand and couldn't figure out how leaving me with Lacie had gotten me into so much trouble.

"It was Stephanie. She's in on it."

"The tutor?"

I nodded. "Yeah. She's his sister." A spike of alarm went through Ramos. Was Lacie still with Stephanie? "Lacie should be fine," I continued. "Stephanie was supposed to take her back to the arena and then take off for parts unknown, while Luke... uh... took care of me."

Ramos turned toward Luke with his lips drawn into a tight line. "So this is Luke."

At the mention of his name, Luke shook his head to clear it from the pain, and let out a groan. Breathing heavily, and with his arms restrained behind him, he straightened up enough to glance at Ramos.

He took in Ramos' hard eyes and stone-cold features, and sudden fear lanced into his heart, turning his arms and legs into jelly. He'd never stared death in the face before, and his mouth went dry.

"This is all... a misunderstanding. I can... I can make you a deal. I've got money. Lots of it." He swallowed. "Take it... and you'll never see me again. I swear."

Ramos shook his head. "What about Jodie and Lacie? You've been deceiving them for a long time. How do you plan to make it up to them?"

Luke knew he couldn't go down that path, so he turned to his anger instead. "What's it matter to you? A killer like you isn't any better than me."

Yikes. I wanted to tell Luke to shut up, but it was too late for that. I knew he had hit a nerve, but Ramos brushed it off, thinking it hardly mattered anymore. He took a step closer to Luke and clenched his fists.

"Who says I want to be better?" Ramos asked, a devilish gleam in his eyes.

"I didn't say that. I meant that we're... alike... we're the ones who make the deals. We make the arrangements that benefit everyone, regardless of who it hurts. I've got plenty of money. I'm better to you alive than dead."

Ramos chuckled. "You think I care about money? After what you've done?" He really wanted to kill Luke, but since I was standing in the room, he held back for the moment.

I ground my teeth together and clenched my jaw, feeling that same deep desire to kill Luke that Ramos had. It scared me just a little, since I normally didn't want to kill people. But this guy... he really got my blood boiling.

Then I realized that maybe I wasn't thinking rationally, because pretty much everyone else in the room had that same burning desire. Maybe that's where it was coming from, and I wasn't such a bloodthirsty person after all.

"I should go," I blurted. That caught everyone's attention. And like a collective sigh, the tone in the room lightened just a bit. I mean... they still wanted to kill Luke, but maybe not tear off his arms and legs and then take turns stabbing him to death.

Ramos caught my wide-eyed and pale face. He straightened and then came to my side. "Sure, babe."

My shoulders sagged, and Ramos steadied me. I leaned into his chest, letting his warm strength comfort me. He held me tightly in his arms, and I took in a few deep breaths to calm my nerves and regain my equilibrium. A few seconds later, it amazed me how much better I felt. Stronger, I straightened, and Ramos tucked me under his arm.

We moved toward the door but, before leaving, Ramos turned to Big Kahuna. "Don't kill him before I get back."

A big grin split Big Kahuna's face. "We'll wait bro." He patted Ramos on the shoulder, then handed me my phone.

"Oh... thanks," I managed.

"Sure. And... next time you come, let's play some pool. I'll have a Diet Coke with a lemon ready just for you." His pleased grin caught me by surprise, and I smiled back.

"Okay."

Ramos held me close, and we walked up the stairs together. Outside, I took a few deep breaths of fresh air, grateful to be alive. Ramos walked me over to his bike and handed me my helmet. "Do you mind if we go to the arena first? I want to make sure Lacie's safe."

"That's a good idea. Where's Dusty?"

"He stayed at the arena in case you guys showed up. We waited at the drop point, but when it became clear that Luke wasn't going to show up, we came back to the arena and found the motorhome gone, so I left Dusty there and came looking for you."

"I'm glad you found me."

He shook his head. "Yeah... that tracker has sure come in handy. But I'm still a little confused about how you happened to be here. I mean... how did you get him to bring you to Big Kahuna?"

I chuckled. "I wish I could take the credit, but I had nothing to do with it." As I put on my helmet, I explained how Luke wanted them to kill me in exchange for Keola's life. "He wanted them to do his dirty work for him. Plus, I think he was worried that I was a cop or something, and he didn't want the police after him for my death."

Ramos frowned, thinking that, in a way, I was the police. Would that change anything? Would he have to leave Luke alive? He brushed it aside for now. "Ready to go?"

I nodded and got on the bike behind him, grateful to hold him close after what I'd been through. It also gave me time to think. I knew that Ramos and the gang wanted to kill Luke. Part of me was okay with that, but another part wanted him to be held accountable.

Not only had he killed that drug dealer, but his drugs had killed two kids. The only problem I could see was proving it. But what if we couldn't prove it, and he got off? Was it better if he was dead? Well... he wouldn't be selling drugs anymore. Still... I wasn't sure what to do.

We arrived at the arena, and Ramos pulled around to the back, looking through the fence for Dusty and the motorhome. The security guard came to the gate.

"Did Stephanie come back?" Ramos asked.

"Yeah. She came back about twenty minutes ago." He studied Ramos. "You're Ace, right? Dusty told me to let you in if you showed up."

"That's me," Ramos said.

"What's going on?" he asked.

"It's Stephanie," I told him. "She's armed and dangerous, so be careful."

The guard's eyes widened, then he nodded and opened the gate, thinking that he'd better let the security team know something was up. After letting us in, he put in a call over his radio to alert the others.

Ramos wasn't real happy I'd spilled the beans, but I figured I owed the guard, since I was pretty sure Stephanie wouldn't hesitate to shoot him if he didn't let her out.

Ramos pulled through the gate, taking the route toward the motorhome's parking space. We found it parked in the same spot, but it was crooked, like she'd been in a hurry. Dusty's car was also there, parked close to the back of the motorhome, and blocking it in. Without the lights turned on inside it didn't look like anyone was there.

Ramos stopped and pulled off his helmet before turning to me. "What was Stephanie's plan again?"

I pulled off my helmet and answered. "She was supposed to take Lacie inside and leave her with Jodie's assistant, then get her stuff and take off. Maybe we should check the motorhome just to make sure she's gone?"

Ramos nodded, even though his first instinct was to head inside and make sure Lacie was all right. He shut off the bike. In the quiet, we both heard a faint gasping sound. I scrambled off the bike, and followed the sound to the other side of Dusty's car.

To my surprise, Dusty lay on his back with a dark stain of blood spreading over his chest. I knelt down beside him, frantic that he'd been shot. With blood pouring out of his chest, it didn't look good. "What happened? Did Stephanie do this?"

He took in a quick breath to speak. "Yeah... Lacie..." His eyes closed, and his breathing slowed.

"What about Lacie?" Ramos asked, kneeling at his side. "Where is she?"

"In... inside. But Stephanie..." He tried to draw in another breath, but it never happened. The light went out of his eyes and he died.

My eyes filled up with tears, but I caught his last thought, and it wasn't good. "He was thinking that Stephanie's still around here somewhere."

"Is Lacie okay?"

I blinked the tears away and nodded. "Yeah... I think so, but it's a little fuzzy. Stephanie might have taken her inside, but I don't know if it was before or after she shot Dusty."

Ramos let out a breath and stood. He glanced around the parking lot but could see no sign of Stephanie or Lacie. "I need to go inside and find them."

"Yeah... okay. I'll call nine-one-one and see if I can find the security guards."

With a grim nod, he ran toward the arena doors.

I let out a breath. Watching Dusty die sent a cold chill through me, and I got a little lightheaded. Still, I needed to pull it together and call the police. I took a deep breath and stood. With the helmet in my hand, I laced my arm through the neck and face so it would rest in the crook of my arm. Then I pulled my phone out of my jacket pocket.

With shaking hands, I fumbled just a little before I got it turned on. Taking a breath to place the call, the click of a cocking gun sounded right behind my left ear, and I froze.

"Drop it," Stephanie said. Since she was ready to shoot me, I lowered it to the ground. "Where's Luke? How did you get away?" Her voice shook with desperation.

"He's fine," I said. My heart raced, and I could hardly catch my breath. I slowly raised both arms and turned to face her. Then I backed up a couple of steps since she had the gun pointed right in my face, and her hand shook like crazy. I picked up that she didn't believe me, so I scrambled for a reasonable explanation.

"I'm telling you the truth. He let me go. Call him if you don't believe me."

"Don't you think I've tried?" Her gun hand shook even more, and spittle flew from her mouth. She glanced at Dusty's sprawled body and realized she'd killed him. Panic grabbed her chest, and her eyes bulged. What had she done? She pulled her desperate gaze back to mine. "Where is he? Where's Luke?!"

"He's at a bar not too far from here."

Stephanie's brows drew together in confusion, so I quickly continued, "He had a deal with the Polynesian gang who runs it, and he went to pick up the rest of his money. The gang members there know me, so we worked out a deal. I'm sure he's still there. I can take you if you want. Then you'll see that I'm telling you the truth."

She didn't want me taking her anywhere, but she needed to get out of here... now. She glanced at the car, but Dusty's body was in the way, and she didn't want to touch it. Then she noticed Ramos' motorcycle, and the helmet hanging off my arm. She didn't know how to drive it, but maybe I did.

"Can you drive that?" She pointed to the bike.

"Uh... yes," I lied. "Yes I can."

"Okay. Let's go." She thought that sitting close behind me was ideal for keeping the gun at my back, since she didn't think for a second that I would take her to Luke. But as long as I got her away from here, it didn't matter where we went. It was ideal since everyone would be looking for her in the motorhome or Dusty's car. Then, the first chance she got, she'd just shoot me and ditch the bike, and then call a taxi or Uber for a ride to the bus station.

Swallowing my fear, I led the way toward the bike, knowing this was the only way out. I slipped on my helmet and snapped it up tight, since I was pretty sure I'd crash it right off the bat. In his haste, Ramos had left the keys in the ignition and his helmet on the seat.

Stephanie grabbed Ramos' helmet and put it on, grateful for the extra layer of obscurity it offered, and thinking no one would know it was her.

Letting out a deep breath, I straddled the bike like I knew what I was doing. Stephanie got on behind me, then poked me in the ribs with her gun. I planted my feet on the ground and managed to stand the bike up, but it was a little heavy for me, and I wasn't sure I could pull it off.

Instead of kick-starting it like Ramos liked to do, I pulled in the hand clutch and pushed the little red button. It started right up, surprising me that I'd made it this far. With my heart racing, I revved it up like Ramos did and knew this was my moment of truth.

I wasn't sure what gear Ramos had left it in, mostly because I had no idea how to work the gears. I also knew that if I tried to lift my foot off the ground we'd probably tip over without some forward momentum.

So... that left letting out the hand clutch and giving it some gas and hoping that somehow it moved forward. After that, I had no clue what to do, except maybe scream a little and jump off. That reminded me that the brake lever was above the gas handle, and maybe I should pull that at some point.

Stephanie began to wonder what was taking me so long, so I said a quick prayer and let out the clutch while giving it some gas. To my astonishment, the bike started forward.

Surprised, I lifted my feet and managed to get them onto the pedals.

In the excitement, I accidentally pulled harder on the gas without realizing it, and we shot forward, heading straight for the back of the building. We gained speed and, sensing immediate death, Stephanie screamed, reaching some part of my brain that told to let up on the gas.

Pure survival instinct kicked in, and I turned the wheel and leaned to the side, then pulled on the brake and put my foot down to stop us from falling over. In the momentum, Stephanie flew off the seat, and the bike spun out beneath me, turning almost completely around before pivoting to a stop.

The engine died, and I gasped for breath, shocked to still be alive. It started to tip over, so I put both feet down, but it was too heavy for me to hold. As it began to fall over, I screamed a little. Holding tight to the handlebars, I tried to get my leg out of the way, but the bike came down on top of me anyway.

"Shelby!"

Before I could register any pain, Ramos lifted the bike off me. He set it up on the kickstand and knelt by my side. "Are you hurt?"

"I don't know." It came out a little garbled, so I sat up to take off my helmet. Ramos helped me get the strap undone, and I pulled it off. Taking a deep breath, I blurted, "Where's Stephanie?"

"It's okay. The security guard's got her. He just put her in handcuffs."

I let out a breath of relief, then glanced at Ramos with a wince. "Sorry about the bike."

He shook his head, thinking that seeing me trying to drive that thing had nearly given him a heart attack. He thought for sure I was going to crash right into the building. Then I executed a nearly perfect one-eighty and promptly fell over. He was still speechless.

"You saw that?"

"Uh... yeah."

Wanting to stand, I moved my leg and groaned, mostly because of the big rip in the knee of my favorite black jeans. "Damn! That hurts."

"Don't move." Ramos proceeded to run his hands down my leg from my thigh to my ankle. "I don't feel any broken bones, but that doesn't mean you don't have any."

I swallowed, embarrassed that his touch had sent my heart racing. Plus, I was talking more about the rip in my pants than my leg. But now I had to play along. "Um... I think I might just have a few bruises. See? I can wiggle my toes just fine, although my ankle hurts a bit."

"Let's see." He pulled up my pant leg and found a dark bruise forming along my ankle bone. "Why don't you try moving your ankle?"

I rotated it in a circular motion. "Uh... yeah. That only hurt a little."

"What about your knee? Can you bend it?" He took hold of my foot and raised it toward my body to test my knee. It hardly hurt at all, and a spasm of guilt rocked through me. Here he was being so concerned that I was hurt, and I'd probably put a few scratches and dents in his bike. Still, maybe I shouldn't complain and should just enjoy it, especially since I'd been through a lot in the last hour or so.

"That didn't hurt much," I said, trying to keep a straight face. "I think it might be bruised, and a little swollen. But that's it. I want to stand up on it just to make sure."

His eyes narrowed, and he wondered if I was pulling his leg. "You sure?"

"Uh... yeah."

Ramos helped me up, thinking that if I was pulling his leg, he didn't mind too much. That made it easier to hold me in his arms, because he was sure grateful I wasn't dead. He slid his arms beneath mine and lifted me up against his body, startling a gasp out of me.

My feet dangled off the ground and his lips were mere inches from mine. He held me close, then reluctantly lowered me to the ground without kissing me the way he wanted to. Satisfaction gleamed in his eyes that he'd left me breathless and shaken.

"Can you walk?"

"Huh?" His smirk woke me up, and I quickly backed away from him. "Uh... yes. Of course." I took a few more steps back, and stumbled over the edge of the sidewalk.

Ramos grabbed my arm to steady me, and I got a little dizzy. "I think I need to sit down."

Alarm widened his eyes, and he helped me to the sidewalk where I could sit and lean against the back of the building. He studied my pale face, and his brows drew together. "I thought..."

"I was teasing?" I finished. "No... uh... well yeah... but then you... and... I think it all caught up to me. I'm fine now... and I really hope your bike's okay too."

He let out a breath and sat beside me, shaking his head and thinking the bike was the least of his worries. "What a night."

"Yeah... you can say that again."

The security guard trotted over. "The police are on their way... just thought you'd like to know."

Ramos tensed. He still had Luke to take care of but, with Dusty dead, and Stephanie in custody, he wasn't sure how that was all going to play out. "Uh... maybe I'd better go." He didn't want to leave me to fend for myself, but he also didn't want to be involved with the police.

"I'm not sure you should go. Stephanie saw you, and so did the guards. But I think I can help you out. You know I've been working on this case with Dimples. Why don't you go inside and watch the rest of the concert? That's why you came. I'll tell Dimples what happened and ask him to keep you out of it."

Ramos narrowed his eyes. "You think he'd do that?"

"Yes. I do."

"What about Luke?" He really wanted to kill the bastard for everything he'd done, but if we did things my way, he wouldn't be able to, and it might tarnish his image.

I shook my head, but I managed not to roll my eyes since he was mostly kidding. "I know... but he killed a Polynesian gang member, and his drugs killed two kids. Then Stephanie killed Dusty. We need to let the police handle it. Trust me, it will all come together."

He let out a breath. "All right. But where do they find Luke?"

"Let's leave him where he is. Dimples and I will pick him up at the bar later tonight. Just give them a heads up, and tell them it's something I worked out with the police. I promise they won't get in trouble... you know... since they saved my life?"

He shrugged. Big Kahuna might not like it, but if Ramos told him to do it, he was certain they would. "Are you sure?"

"Yes."

"Okay. But I'm moving my bike out of the way." He grabbed both helmets, then rolled the bike close against the building. Securing the helmets, he took the keys and pocketed them, thinking that maybe he'd better teach me how to drive it, even though it was way too big for me. Hmm... considering what had just happened, maybe that wasn't such a good idea...

Just then, two police cars pulled into the parking lot. With a pang of regret at leaving me to the cops, Ramos sent me a nod before slipping inside the doors. As the police took charge, I leaned my head back against the building, knowing it was going to be a long night, but grateful to be alive.

Chapter 14

Lucky for me, Dimples was the first detective to arrive on the scene. As he recognized me sitting on the concrete, surprise rolled off him, followed by disbelief, and then resignation. How did I get involved in these things? He quickly came to my side, noticing my bruised cheek and my torn pants, along with my pale face. "Are you okay?"

"Yeah," I said, sighing. "It's been awful, but I think it's over now. I'm glad you're here. I can explain all of this and tell you what's going on with the whole drug thing. I can also tell you who murdered that drug dealer we found today."

His eyes widened. "That's good."

I pursed my lips and nodded, hating to ask him for a favor, but I needed his assurance to leave Ramos out of it before I told him the whole story.

"Why do I get the feeling there's something else going on that you don't want to tell me?"

"Wow. You caught that? You're good."

He chuckled. "I think I know you better than you give me credit for."

This time, I held his gaze and smiled. "I guess that's why we make such great partners." I took a breath, then let it out. "There is something that I need from you. There's a certain someone I'd like to leave out of this if it's possible. This person didn't do anything but help, which you might find hard to believe, but it's true."

"Well... you certainly have my attention."

"Can you promise me you'll consider it? You know I wouldn't ask if I didn't think it was the right thing to do."

Now it was Dimples' turn to let out a breath. "Fine. I promise I'll do everything I can to leave him out of it." The fact that Dimples had a good idea it was Ramos should have surprised me, but I was too relieved to care.

"Great. Thanks. Uh... can I text Chris first? I need to tell him I'm all right." He nodded, a little perplexed as to why I hadn't already done that. "Oh... my cell phone's over by the... the dead body behind the car over by the motorhome. Can you get it for me?"

His brows rose at my request, and he glanced in that direction. None of the cops had gone over there, so he figured they didn't know about the dead body. He hurried that way and took in the scene, pocketing my phone before he called a police officer over.

After giving the officer instructions to secure the scene, he called the precinct and asked for the crime scene unit, then came back to my side and handed me the phone. "You know the dead guy?"

"Uh... yeah. He's Jodie McAllister's brother, Dusty. It was Stephanie over there who killed him." I pointed out Stephanie, who was now sitting in the back of a police cruiser. "Thanks for getting my phone." Since Dimples had a hundred questions to ask me, I quickly continued. "I'll just send a fast text, and then we can get down to business."

Dimples shook his head, but waited patiently, so I sent a text telling him that I was fine, but things had gotten complicated, and I needed to stay a little longer to help Dimples. It was a cowardly way to tell Chris about all the trouble I'd been in, but if I actually heard his voice, I knew I'd turn into a blubbering idiot.

"Do you want to sit in my car?" Dimples asked. Since that was much better than the hard sidewalk, I quickly agreed. He helped me up and I took my time, testing out my leg to make sure it was okay.

Sitting in the car came as a relief. Then my little reprieve was over, and it was time to tell Dimples everything. I wasn't sure how much of Ramos' story to share, so I did my best to leave him out of it, saying that Dusty and I had a mutual friend who, in his concern for Dusty, asked me to help because of my premonitions.

Dimples shook his head at that, since he knew my premonitions got me into all kinds of trouble. Then he wondered if this 'friend' knew I could read minds.

I decided to ignore that thought and continued my narrative, telling him that when I found out about the link to the drugs, I decided to follow up.

"Naturally, one thing led to another, and I ended up meeting the person responsible for the drugs." Here, it was easy to talk about staying with Lacie in the motorhome, while Dusty went after Luke, and all the events that happened afterward, up until and including Stephanie killing Dusty, and our little motorcycle ride.

Dimples had noticed the bike because... well... who wouldn't? It was a beauty. "You drove that? Oh my hell!"

"Hey. It turned out okay. I don't think it's scratched up too much." I'd only seen a few scratches, and maybe one little dent. "That can be fixed, right?"

Dimples closed his eyes and shook his head, then came back to the matter at hand. "Okay... so we need to go get this Luke person from the bar where the Polynesian gangs hang out?"

"Yeah... actually, he's in the basement. But I made a deal with them, so he shouldn't be dead yet, but we might want to hurry."

Dimples sighed, then he jumped out of the car to tell the other detectives and officers where we were going and that we'd be back soon. He asked me for the address, so I pulled it up on my phone from the time I'd been following Kyle.

Once we arrived at the bar, I directed him to pull around to the back parking lot, and we got out of the car.

Not knowing what else to do, I knocked on the back door and waited. A moment later, someone pulled the door open and peeked out. "We're here for Luke," I said.

The guy nodded and shut the door. A moment later, two burly Pacific Islanders opened the door and shoved him out, throwing his gun after him. Luke stumbled to the ground, but his hands weren't tied. He rose to his feet to get away, but Dimples slapped a pair of cuffs on him.

"Hey... you can't do that!"

As Dimples read him his rights, Luke spotted me, and the color drained from his face. He cursed a blue streak in his mind while despair rushed over him. He should have killed me himself, even if I was a cop. He could have gotten away. Then he cursed some more.

It didn't sound like he appreciated the fact that he was still alive. He should be thanking me. All in all, I thought he got off pretty well with just a bleeding lip, lots of swelling under his eyes, and bruises covering his jaw.

After securing Luke in the back seat, Dimples put on some gloves and bagged the gun as evidence. We drove away in silence. Luke was determined not to say a word, which suited me just fine, but with all the swearing going on in his thoughts, I had to put up my shields.

That's why it came as a surprise that Dimples had decided to return to the arena. I sat tight while he transferred Luke to a regular cop car and had a couple of police officers take him in. I took in the scene, noticing that the coroner had loaded Dusty's body into the van, and it was just about time for the concert to end.

"Okay. I think I have everything straight," Dimples said, sitting back down in the car. "Stephanie and Luke made the pills and recruited Dusty into selling them. Somehow you got involved through a 'client' of yours and followed the clues to the concert. When Dusty left to find Luke, you stayed with Stephanie and Lacie, not knowing Stephanie was in on it. She kidnapped you and met up with Luke. He took you to the gang in exchange for the life of one of the gang members he had in the car and asked them to kill you."

He was thinking it got complicated after that. "For some reason, they knew who you were, so they turned the tables on him and let you go. You returned here and found Dusty dying. He told you Stephanie shot him before he died. Then Stephanie snuck up on you with a gun, asking where Luke was since he was supposed to kill you. You told her you'd take her to Luke on the bike. That's when you crashed, and the security guard caught Stephanie."

"Yeah... that's pretty much what happened," I said, impressed with his skills.

He was thinking that everything was a little convoluted, and he wasn't sure about including the gang part in his report. But it did make sense.

"If you want, we can leave the gang part out and just say that I got away and came back here. Would that work?"

Dimples sighed. "I think we've got all the evidence we need to make both murder charges stick, especially if we find the machinery they used to make the pills."

"Yeah... I heard Stephanie thinking about it, so I have a good idea where we can find it."

"Good. With what we've got, we can probably get them on the deaths of the two kids as well. So... we'll just stick to the facts and go from there. And I think we can leave out your friend, since I really don't know what he did anyway."

"Thanks."

Just then, the building's exit doors opened, and several people came out. One of them was Jodie. A police officer held her back, and Dimples frowned. "I need to tell her about her brother. It might help if you come along."

He got out of the car and I followed behind, not looking forward to this at all. Both Luke and Stephanie were long gone to the police station, but the coroner's van hadn't left yet, and there were enough police cars with lights flashing that she'd know something bad had happened.

Dimples reached Jodie's side and took her back inside. He motioned for me to follow along, and I did, even though I knew this would be bad. Not only was Jodie's brother dead, but he'd been shot by her daughter's tutor. Even worse, her boyfriend was behind it all. How was she going to cope with that?

We ended up right back in the same room where Ramos and I had met Jodie earlier. Lacie was there with Kristin, and she jumped up with happy surprise to see me safe. Without thought, she ran to me and threw her arms around me.

"I'm glad you're okay," Lacie said. "I didn't think you were bad. Are you a police officer?"

I hunkered down to squeeze her back. "I'm glad you're okay too, and... yes... I work with the police. Everything's okay now. You don't have to be scared anymore."

"What happened to Stephanie?"

"She's been arrested, so you'll never have to see her again."

Lacie let out a relieved sigh. She'd never liked Stephanie much... maybe that was because she was a phony, and was always sneaking around and leaving her alone.

"Let's go sit down." I took Lacie's hand and led her over to the couch. "Your mom's going to have a hard time in the next little while, so I think she's going to need your help. Can you do that?"

She nodded, picking up that something bad had happened, especially when Jodie started crying. "What is it?" She glanced at me, knowing it was bad, but wanting the truth.

"I'm sorry Lacie, but... it's your Uncle Dusty. He got shot... and he... he died." Her eyes widened, then she shook her head, not sure it was true. "Go to your mom. She needs you now."

Lacie didn't hesitate and rushed to her mother's side. Jodie pulled her into a hug, and they clung to each other. When their tears had subsided, Jodie held Lacie on her lap, growing even more upset to find that Luke and Stephanie were behind the whole thing. She berated her judgement, thinking that she was an idiot, and now her brother was dead.

Just then, a knock sounded at the door. Dimples hurried to the door and opened it slightly, speaking to an officer outside. Then he opened it wider, and a handsome Latino man came inside.

"Daddy!" Lacie cried. She flung herself into his arms and held him tightly. Jodie stood, hardly daring to believe that

Emil was standing there. He glanced over at her and held out an arm. Jodie ran to his side, and he pulled her close.

"I'm here," he said. "I'm here now... and... I'm here to stay." Jodie pulled away and glanced into his dark eyes, hardly daring to believe what he said. "I mean it. I'm here to stay if you'll have me."

Jodie's eyes filled with tears. As they fell down her cheeks, she nodded. "Yes." She'd always nourished a small hope that Emil would find his way back to her. That it had happened now at such a terrible time seemed like an answer to her prayers.

Emil was thanking God that Dusty had tracked him down and had explained what was going on a week ago. Emil had always wanted to come home to Jodie but was just waiting for the right time. That it had happened at this moment came as a shock, especially now that Dusty was dead.

Then there was Lacie... he hated being away from his daughter, and now that would all change. She pulled away from his neck, and they held each other with their cheeks pressed together. In that moment, they looked so much alike that I knew she was his daughter.

Movement outside in the hall caught my attention, and I hurried to the door. I glanced into the hall and caught sight of Ramos walking away, picking up that he'd heard and seen everything. I was just about to tell him to wait for me, but the words got stuck in my throat. Then he disappeared around the corner. I still had the option to run after him, but I wasn't sure what to do.

My heart ached for him, and tears pricked at the back of my eyes. As he'd left, I'd picked up a gut-wrenching pain that sort of hit him all at once. Witnessing Jodie and Lacie so happy to see another man struck a nerve. The realization that Ramos was alone, without family ties, or anyone to hold onto, left him empty with a deep ache in his heart.

I hated to know he felt like that. But what could I do to help him? From his thoughts, I'd picked up that he wanted... no, needed to be alone, so I let him go and hoped that, maybe tomorrow, he'd be willing to talk to me about it.

With a heavy heart, I turned back to the room to find that most everyone was enthralled by the happy reunion. Someone laughed and broke the spell. After that, people began to talk again. It struck me how much Emil and Jodie loved each other, and I wondered what had happened to break them up.

Then I realized that it was probably the ghost of Ramos in their relationship that did it. So maybe it was a good thing that Ramos had left without talking to Jodie. Who knew what would have happened if he'd been in the room.

Nearly two hours later, after I collected my purse from the motorhome, Dimples dropped me off at my house.

I hurried inside, eager to be with my family. As soon as I came into the kitchen, Chris stood from the table and enfolded me in his arms, then showered kisses all over my face. While I'd waited for Dimples to wrap things up and take me home, I'd called Chris and told him everything. I didn't know how relieved he was until now.

I winced after he kissed my bruised cheek, which caused him to pull away. "You're hurt," Chris said, his brows drawn together. "Why didn't you tell me?"

"It's just a bruise." The concern and worry in his gaze sent a wave of guilt through me. "Hey... I'm okay. Just... kiss the other cheek, or how about my lips... or maybe my neck? That would be nice."

Chris let out a breath and pulled me close, thinking that I would be the death of him. Hearing what had happened to me tonight had probably taken twenty years off his life. He'd already found three more gray hairs in his head just since this morning.

"You have not!"

He pulled back, sending that sexy grin my way. "It's true. I'm just glad it's not falling out." Then he thought that, if it ever did, he could always blame me for it, and I couldn't complain.

I shook my head, but smiled, grateful to have such an awesome husband. My stomach chose that moment to growl, reminding me that I had hardly eaten all day.

"Whoa! Sounds like someone's hungry. Too bad all the pizza's gone." At my crestfallen expression, he quickly continued, "Good thing I saved you a piece."

At my huff, he chuckled and pulled me toward a kitchen chair, then warmed up the pizza in the microwave, and handed it over. The kids came up from the basement, surprising me that they weren't in bed yet. Then I realized it was Friday night, and they'd wanted to stay up until I got home.

"So mom... how was the Jodie McAllister concert?" Savannah asked. "Dad told us that's where you were." She couldn't quite figure out how going to a concert was helping a client like I'd told her earlier, and her mind buzzed with curiosity.

Since I hadn't seen it, I was ready to lie and say it was great, but something stopped me. I was suddenly tired of lying to my kids about everything I did. They weren't little kids I needed to shelter. They were old enough to handle the truth. Well... maybe some of it.

So I told them I'd been helping the police with the drug case, and we'd solved it tonight. "It all came together at the concert, so that's why I was there." I didn't go into detail or anything, but gave them enough information so they'd know what had happened and that the drug dealers had been caught.

"Wow, mom. That's really cool," Savannah said. "So how did you get that bruise on your cheek and that rip in your pants?"

Dang... should I lie now? "All in the line of duty," I said instead.

"Does that mean you fell or something?" Josh asked, his eyes dancing with mischief.

I chuckled and nodded my head. "Yeah... something like that. So what did you guys do while I was gone?" I listened to their stories, content to be surrounded by my family, soaking in their smiles and laughter and grateful to be alive.

Later, after a nice, hot bath, I snuggled in Chris' arms. It took a while, but I finally opened up about everything. How Stephanie's gun had gone off when we'd fought for it, and how, if not for Lacie, she would have shot me. How Luke thought about killing me, but decided to let the gang do it, and how it had turned out to be the same gang I'd met just a week ago.

Then how I'd held Dusty's hand while he'd died, and how his last thought had been of protecting his sister and niece. The tears flowed freely then, and Chris held me close, stroking my back and arms. I finished by telling him about Jodie and Emil getting back together... all because of Dusty... and cried some more.

Through it all, Chris held me close. The only time he really got upset was when I told him about the motorcycle. He had to swallow a few times to keep from blurting out a few choice four letter words, and I admired his restraint. Then he hoped that I'd never try that again... and hoped that Ramos had learned his lesson.

I wasn't sure what lesson that was, but I let out a breath instead of asking, and finally relaxed into sleep.

The next morning, Chris took Josh to his soccer game and let me sleep in. It was sweet of him since I'd woken up with more aches and pains than I'd gone to bed with.

I got a call from Billie Jo, asking me if we could go out to lunch. "I heard all about the drug case from Drew, so I'm hoping you'll fill me in on the details for an article at the paper. There's also something I need to ask you. So can you come?"

"Uh... sure." We decided where to meet and disconnected.

That's when I realized that I'd left my car in the parking garage of Thrasher Development. I called her back, and she said she'd be happy to pick me up and drop me off there when we were done.

Not long after that, Uncle Joey called. "Shelby, I'm glad to hear you're all right. Ramos told me what happened."

"Yeah... it was a little touch and go, but it all worked out."

"I just wanted you to know that I appreciate that you used your influence to keep Ramos out of the police report. That means a lot."

"Oh... yeah... well, I'm glad I could help."

"I have to admit that I never did like that you helped the police much, but after last night, I'm starting to see some advantages."

My breath caught. "Uh... yeah... right."

"So I hope you'll keep that in mind the next time it looks like there's a conflict of interest. It's nice to know you have an in with the police... so to speak."

"Oh... yeah, I guess I do." Oh great! So now I'd just agreed to ask the police to look the other way when it came to Uncle Joey? I wasn't sure I could do that. Of course, I could warn Uncle Joey if I needed to, but any more than that might be crossing a line that I wasn't comfortable with.

"Don't worry, Shelby," Uncle Joey said, picking up my reluctance. "I'd never ask you to do anything that could get you arrested. Family comes first. Sometimes we make sacrifices for each other, but it goes both ways. I hope you know by now that you can trust me after all we've been through together."

"Of course... I do," I said, and the realization hit me that somewhere along the line, I had come to trust him. How crazy was that?

"Good. Oh... I just got off the phone with Frank. Things are pretty good between us now, and I have you to thank for that. They'd love to meet your family, so I think we should all go to New York together sometime, maybe for Miguel's opening night. How does that sound?"

"That sounds great. We'd love to come. How's Miguel doing?"

"He's starting to settle down from all the excitement. I think the reality that he's leaving for New York is hitting him, but I'm not too worried since we have family there. Oh... one more thing. I know it's short notice, but we're having a little impromptu celebration tonight at the house for Miguel. We'd all love it if your family could come."

"Oh... sure... we'd love that," I agreed.

"Good. Come around six, and bring your swimming suits."

Billie took me to Thrasher so I could get my car before we headed to lunch. We had a great time, and I finally found out what was giving her the wedding jitters.

"I know it's silly," she began. "But I feel like I'm just planning the typical wedding. There's nothing new or different, and I'm a little disappointed."

"Yeah... but this is your wedding. It doesn't have to be different, as long as it's what you want. I think brides put too much pressure on themselves to have the perfect wedding. Why not just call it a party and have fun?"

Billie nodded, then I heard her thinking that Dimples wanted to wear his police uniform, and she wanted him in a tux. She didn't want to disappoint him if that was what he wanted, but as much as he rocked the uniform, she didn't want him wearing a hat.

"Oh... um... so... have you picked out a tux for Dimples?"

Her lips turned down. "He wants to wear his uniform." Her gaze met mine. "I love the uniform, but is there something that says he has to wear it?"

I shrugged. "I don't know, but I can find out. I'm pretty sure he doesn't have to, but it would make your wedding a little different if he did, and I'm pretty sure he doesn't have to wear the hat during the ceremony, or for all the pictures."

"Really? Hmm... okay. Check it out and let me know."

After that we talked about what went down the night before at the concert. I didn't offer too much that she didn't already know, and I wasn't going to tell her all the juicy details, but she knew I was hiding something. "So you did all of that by yourself?" she asked.

"Oh... well... mostly."

"And it was all tied in with the murdered drug dealer you and Drew found yesterday?"

I nodded, but mentioning that brought an image of me into her mind. It was the fifteen-second video she'd seen on social media, and she pressed her lips together to stop from laughing.

Before she could razz me about it, my phone rang, and I welcomed the interruption. I checked the caller ID, and surprise rushed over me. "I'd better take this," I told Billie. "Hello?"

"Hey Shelby, it's Blake Beauchaine."

"Wow, what a surprise. Uh... how are you doing? Are you back in the states?"

"Yeah. I've been given a clean bill of health which, at my age, is a real blessing. You're probably wondering why I'm calling, especially since the last time we spoke, I told you we were even."

"Uh... well, I was kind of thinking that. So what's going on?"

He let out a breath. "Well, I just thought I'd give you a heads up. I had to write a report about what went on in Paris, and... well... I mentioned that you went with me. Believe me, I hardly said anything about what you did, but it looks like it caught someone's attention. Anyway, to make a long story short... my boss might want to meet you."

He heard me gasp, so he quickly continued. "Now... you don't need to panic. I don't know exactly why he's interested, but it's probably a formality, nothing more. Maybe he wants to thank you for your service. At any rate, I just wanted you to know."

"Okay... thanks. I appreciate it."

"He'll probably just send a note in the mail or give you a call. But don't worry. You don't have to do anything you don't want to."

"That's a relief." I let out my breath. "Well, thanks for letting me know. Uh... I'm glad you're doing better." We said our goodbyes and disconnected.

"Who was that?" Billie asked. She was thinking that my face had gone pale, so it had to be something bad.

"Oh... nothing."

Billie rested her hand on my arm in concern. "Okay. But Shelby... you'll tell me if you're in trouble, right?"

"Oh... yes, of course. But I'm fine." I smiled. "Thanks."

We finished up our lunch and said our goodbyes. I walked to my car, glad that I knew what was bothering Billie so I could let Dimples know, and they could work it out. That was the good part. Too bad Blake had called and ruined everything else.

I got in my car and sat there in a daze. I didn't think Blake would have called to warn me if his boss didn't mean to get in touch with me, so I needed to prepare an answer and be ready to turn him down when he did. There was no way I was ever going to get involved with anything like Paris again.

A little calmer, I started the car to head home. My phone rang, but this time the ring tone brought a smile to my lips. It was set to the tune of *Devil Rider*, so I knew it was Ramos.

"Babe. How you doing?"

"I'm good, thanks. You?"

"Good. Hey... if you're not too far from the Tiki Bar, the boys have something for you. Can you stop by?"

"Yeah... I'm not far... oh wait... did you already know that?"

He chuckled. "Maybe."

"Okay, I'm on my way." We disconnected and, this time, I actually looked forward to going there. What could they have for me? Plus, I was grateful to have some time with Ramos and see how he was doing after last night.

I pulled up in front of the bar and went through the main entrance. The bartender sent me a scowl, and I picked up that he wasn't too happy to see me. With his attitude, he probably wasn't happy to see anyone, so I decided not to take it personally.

"Go on back. Big Kahuna's waiting for you."

I got all the way to the pool tables before I found Big Kahuna playing a game with Ramos. "There she is," Big Kahuna said, smiling. "Come on over here."

I strode to his side, and he pulled a cue stick from where it was mounted on the wall. Holding it in both hands, he offered it to me with his palms up and a quick dip of his head. "This is for you."

"Wow. Thanks," I said, looking it over. "This is great." From his thoughts I knew this was an honor, so I gave him a big smile.

"So whenever you come, you'll always have your own stick." He was thinking that I'd done him a favor by keeping him out of the police report, and maybe I could help him in the future.

I sighed... oh great. Not him too? Why couldn't Blake have done that for me?

Then I picked up that he was hoping I'd look a little closer at the handle because that was the best part.

I glanced down and found some letters etched into the wood. "Wow. It has my name on it!" I caught Big Kahuna's gaze and grinned. He smiled back, thinking that having my own stick in his bar was a real honor, and he hoped I appreciated it. "Want to play?"

I chuckled at his sly grin, and took him up on the offer.

The game didn't take long. He took it easy on me, but even then I only got a couple of balls in the pockets. I did get a diet soda with a lemon though, so it was all good.

Ramos hadn't said a word, but he'd enjoyed watching the game, and he walked me to my car when it was over. There was a calmness about him that hadn't been there before, and I wondered what was going on, especially after the heartbreak from last night.

At the car, he turned to me. "I know Lacie's not mine," he said.

"How?" I asked.

"When we went after Luke, Dusty told me that after he'd talked to me at the club, he'd called her dad and had a long talk with him. Emil told Dusty he'd wanted to come back for years, but he didn't think Jodie wanted him. After Dusty told him what was going on, Emil said he was coming no matter what Jodie wanted. Dusty also told me that Emil had always been involved in Lacie's life, and that they had a great relationship."

He caught my gaze. "To be honest, it kind of took me by surprise when he showed up. But you have to admit that was a totally different reaction from the one I had."

"Yeah... but you had no idea she existed. Besides, Dusty was threatening you... and in the end... using you. Don't forget about the pills."

Ramos let out a breath and nodded. "True. But when Luke didn't show, and the motorhome was gone, Dusty made me promise to look after Lacie and Jodie if anything happened to him. That's why I ran inside instead of staying with you."

He sighed and shook his head. "But I shouldn't have left you there. You could have died, and it would have been my fault."

"Hey... you had no idea Stephanie was still out there. She was supposed to take Lacie inside, so that's where I thought she was too."

He nodded, but still felt a lot of remorse for what had happened to me.

"Uh... is that remorse for me, or because I wrecked your bike?" That got a grin out of him. I glanced around hoping to find it, but couldn't see it anywhere. "So, where is your bike anyway?"

"Come and see."

I followed him around to the parking lot in back of the bar and spotted a different bike than the one he normally drove. It was silver and black and pretty sleek, with only a small seat for a second rider. "What kind is that?"

"It's a Ducati."

"Did you buy it?"

"No. It's on loan while mine's getting fixed." But he was thinking he might want a change. As much as he liked the classic style, this one was pretty awesome too. "Want to go for a ride?"

I laughed. "You know I can't pass that up."

He grinned and unclipped the helmets from the bike. Handing mine to me, he was thinking that his life was pretty good, but maybe it was time to make some changes. Then his thoughts turned to driving the bike, leaving me to wonder what kinds of changes he was thinking about.

We took off, and the only thing in my mind was hanging onto Ramos and enjoying the ride. We didn't go too far, but it was enough to get a feel for the bike. It was smooth and sleek, a lot like Ramos, but I liked the old one better.

We pulled up next to my car and got off the bike. "So what did you think?" he asked, leaning against the seat.

"I liked it. But I have to admit, I like your other bike better. It's a little more comfortable than this one... for me anyway, but..." I shrugged.

"Yeah. That makes sense." He liked them both, but he'd probably stay with the one he had. "Glad you came."

"Me too."

He took a deep breath and glanced at the helmet in his hand. "Uh... after last night..." He caught my gaze, then glanced back at the helmet. "I saw them together." He was thinking about Jodie, Lacie, and Emil. "The way Lacie ran to him... then Jodie... it was easy to see that she loves him."

I nodded, picking up that he was talking more about Jodie than Lacie. I waited for him to continue, knowing it was hard for him to talk about this.

"It made me realize something." This time he caught my gaze and held it. "I want a relationship with my brother. I think I'm ready to let him know I'm alive." He sighed and shook his head. "I'm tired of always going it alone, you know? Do you think that would be okay? I don't want to put him in danger or anything, but..."

"I think that's a great idea. I'm sure Javier would want you in his life too. He's such a great guy. I'm certain that if you explained your circumstances and took precautions he'd be fine." I grinned widely, then gave into temptation and threw my arms around him in a big hug.

Surprised, it took a moment for him to put his arms around me, but then he straightened and held me tight. He started thinking that if he got a hug like that every time he talked about his brother, he'd have to do it more often.

"Ha, ha." I pulled away. "When do you want to do this?"

"I don't know." Now that he'd made the decision, the small worry that Javier would be disappointed in him came to the surface, and he began to doubt that it was the right thing to do.

"Hey... of course it's right. The fact that you're alive will make up for it. He's a grown man... give him a chance. Besides, what have you got to lose?"

Ramos shook his head. He'd never meant for me to hear that thought. "Can't keep anything from you, can I?"

"Nope. But you know I'm right."

"Yeah, I guess so. You have his email address, right? Maybe you can help me figure this out."

"Sure." I could still hear some doubt in his mind, so I continued, "I know this is a big step for you, but I really think it will be worth it."

He let out a breath, thinking that facing a cold killer or a hardened criminal seemed easier than reaching out to his own brother. "All right. I'll do it. Thanks Shelby."

"You bet."

He nodded and then slipped on his helmet and got on the bike. As he drove away, I couldn't help the sense of satisfaction and happiness that came over me. This was a huge step for Ramos, but it was a good one, and all of the sadness from last night finally left my heart.

Since I was close to Bella's Bakery, I made a pit stop for some Dirty Johnnies. They're the best brownies in the world, made with layers of cookie dough, chocolate brownie, and creamy fudge frosting. Since I had neglected my family for the last few days, I wanted to bring them something special.

I pulled into my driveway and found Chris, Josh, and Savannah all playing basketball together. With a smile on my face, and all the love in my heart, I opened the box and set it on the trunk of the car, then hurried to join them.

Thank you for reading **Laced in Lies: A Shelby Nichols Adventure.** Ready for the next book in the series? **Deadly Escape: A Shelby Nichols Adventure** is now available in print, ebook and on audible. Get your copy today!

Want to know more about Ramos? **Devil in a Black Suit,** a book about Ramos and his mysterious past from his point of view is available in paperback, ebook and Audible.

If you enjoyed this book, please consider leaving a review on Amazon. It's a great way to thank an author and keep her writing!

NEWSLETTER SIGNUP For news, updates, and special offers, please sign up for my newsletter on my website at www.colleenhelme.com. To thank you for subscribing you will receive a FREE ebook.

ABOUT THE AUTHOR

USA TODAY AND WALL STREET JOURNAL
BESTSELLING AUTHOR

As the author of the Shelby Nichols Adventure Series, Colleen is often asked if Shelby Nichols is her alter-ego. "Definitely," she says. "Shelby is the epitome of everything I wish I dared to be." Known for her laugh since she was a kid, Colleen has always tried to find the humor in every situation and continues to enjoy writing about Shelby's adventures. "I love getting Shelby into trouble... I just don't always know how to get her out of it!" Besides writing, Colleen loves a good book, biking, hiking, and playing board and card games with family and friends. She loves to connect with readers and admits that fans of the series keep her writing.

Connect with Colleen at www.colleenhelme.com

Made in the USA
San Bernardino, CA
13 May 2020

71690204R00192